An Invitation To Come

An allegory

By

Jan Clark

www.xulonpress.com

However, as it is written:
"No eye has seen, no ear has heard,
no mind has conceived what
God has prepared for
those who love Him"
1 Corinthians 2:9

Acknowledgements

I want to give all thanks and glory to the Pursuer of my soul, Jesus. His influence and Presence in my life's journey has given me meaning, defined my real purpose for being here and given me hope. His love is amazing!

To Alan my husband, you have been so supportive and encouraging through this entire process. When I gave up, you still believed in me and that means the world to me. Thank you for being such a supportive husband. I love you.

To Dave, your willingness to walk alongside me through so many difficult places in my journey has been a Godsend. Your faithful trust in the Pursuer of our soul to supply the answers and guidance in His timing has transformed my life and faith. You have been an example of Jesus longsuffering watch care through many difficult times. I am so grateful for you.

I want to thank Terri, my best friend who has been beside me every step of this journey. You have encouraged me both in life and in writing this book. Thank you for the countless hours you given in help preparing this book. You are such a gift, that despite knowing all my idiosyncrasies, you love me anyway.

I also want to thank my friend, T. My friend who can see inside the hurting hearts of others and loves those tossed aside. You are precious to me and precious to Jesus.

To my friend Lynne, thank you for all you have taught me regarding the walk of faith. You are an inspiration. Thank you for your prayer and loving support all these years.

I also want to thank Leslie, Rose, Sara and Perla. You have been such supportive friends. The hours you invested in editing and preparing the book was a blessing. Your friendship and love means the world to me. Thank you for your support.

I love you all.   Jan.

Table of Contents

The Heavenly Assignment

Hearing his name called from inside the Light, Mentor stepped up to the throne. The light's brilliance illuminated with such purity; he disappeared inside of it as his Student watched on.

The Shekinah glory of God embraced Mentor as he stepped into the light. The Heavenly Father and Son overwhelmed him. He bowed.

Student watched on as Mentor became visible again. He was holding seven envelopes, all with a red seal on the back.

Student knew what these envelopes were. It would be another opportunity to watch in awe as the Lord King unveiled His glory to blinded souls. He loved these assignments.

From inside the light the Voice spoke. "Mentor and Student, deliver these seven invitations, which have been sealed by the blood of the Lamb."

The voice paused a moment as if to prepare them for what they were about to hear. "You will find them all residing in the town of Self Absorption."

Silence blanketed the air. Student was stunned. Self Absorption? That dark place? These divine messengers felt their spirits sink in heaviness at the mere mention of the town's name.

From previous assignments, they had personally witnessed the fierce darkness covering that town. Soul after soul held onto the lies brought by the dark side, the enemy of heaven. These souls believed they were in the land of great freedom. They were ignorant of their own captivity. As Mentor looked down at the envelopes, he pondered. "Who could these citizens be?"

An excitement grew at what he would witness, and he had a front row seat for this pilgrimage to come.

He knew his God. His plans were never thwarted, not even the powerful darkness over Self Absorption could defeat His purposes. Mentor praised Him, "How great Thou art."

"Eye has not seen, nor ear heard, nor have entered into the heart of man the things which God has prepared for those who love Him." 1Cor. 2:9

A Little Citizen in Self Absorption

Light glowed on the horizon but had not yet defeated the black night sky. Dew carpeted the lawns as puddles collected on the sidewalks, driveways, and trashcans.

The early morning dampness formed droplets just missing the peaceful face of the sleeping occupant inside his tight quarters. Freckles decorated the bridge of his nose and repelled the grunge blanketing his face. Dew drops caused Little Bin's eight-year-old sleeping body to stir from within the garbage container.

His magnetic blue eyes remain closed, reluctant to meet the new day. His clothes were no dirtier than any other active boy.

To Little Bin, this container was a sanctuary, a safe harbor from the storms of his home life. Inside this bin, he felt safe. Who would ever think to search for him here? Taking out the trash was his responsibility, his only chore. That is what gave him the idea in the first place.

He was taking out the trash one night, when things escalated between his mom and dad. Their voices inside the house were getting louder; crashes of breaking glass punctuated the cusswords thrown back and forth. Little Bin, on an impulse, jumped inside the container and lowered the lid to wait out the civil war going on inside his home. He was amazed at how comfortable the black plastic bags were. It was as cushiony as their couch. The brilliant idea came. He would just double bag the trash to insure loose pieces would not escape and make this his new hideout.

He did not worry about the can filling to the top each week because there was not much food trash anyway. There were more aluminum cans and glass bottles for the recycling can than anything else.

Once a week, Little Bin climbed out of the bin because of the early morning trash pick up. This is how he got the name "Little Bin."

One morning he overslept. He woke up falling into the monstrous green bed of a sanitation truck. His high pitched scream alerted the workers something was terribly wrong. The Sanitation Department quickly settled out of court and Little Bin received a substantial settlement. He told his parents he was looking for his homework that he accidentally threw away. They believed him. They remained unaware that he had not slept in his own bed for over a year.

Experience taught him to see tornados coming. When clouds of resentment and bitterness gathered and billowed out between his mom and dad, he stood on the balls of his feet. When the winds of insults strengthened in ferocity, he hunkered down and formulated the best pathway to his sanctuary canister.

When flying objects accompanied the drunken slurs tossed at one another, Little Bin dodged the unfriendly fire using his duck and cover maneuvers. His stealth and labile moves prevented him injury thus far, at least the kind you could see.

Little Bin no longer tried to change the circumstances at home. Neither one of his parents noticed him anymore. He blamed the town for his parent's misery. They did not always fight. Things did not get bad until after they arrived in Self Absorption. Consequently, Little Bin enjoyed annoying the town people as often as possible.

As the early morning dew continued to drip on Little Bin's nose, he was slow to awaken, trying to hold onto his dream as long as possible.

He leaned against the inside of the canister, wondering if today would be any different from the countless before. His mind wandered backwards to a family car ride…a car ride of deafening silence. Little Bin watched from the back seat, as his parents stole glances at each other, both longing to reel in the lost months of cold distance between them.

It seemed like just yesterday his parents were holding each other in their arms, excited about the great news of his coming sister.

But that was before. Before the medical tests, before the doctors told them the baby would not be normal, before his father insisted his mother 'take care of it.' Before the late nights, they yelled back and forth at an unseen enemy mistaking each other as the source of their pain. Before his father said, "We do not have the resources to raise a special needs child." Before his mother, listless in grief, gave in and 'took care of the problem.'

Little Bin was not sure what it all meant, for he was only six. What he did know was before this, whenever something went wrong, his parents would paint it, sell it, trash it, or give it away. He figured his parents had chosen one of those things for his sister, the sister he would never meet.

Little Bin sensed his mother resented his father for pressuring her. He could see it in her eyes every time she looked at him. His father saw it too. His dad did not know how to make it better, so he tried to paint it over with drinking. He waited in denial for the paint job to dry so things could get back to normal. But alas, it never did.

Little Bin became restless as he leaned against the canister. If only they had not come upon that billboard, that stupid billboard, on that life-ruining day. His parents were like two fish on a hook, reeled in for the catch.

They desperately needed a change. *Any* change would be better than their present situation. There it was. It looked so appealing, with its beautiful picture of green grassy hills, well watered land, and pure blue skies. The sign read:

"Come to Self Absorption where all your dreams come true"

The picture caused his parents to forget their pain and launch themselves into hope. This would be the place, where all their dreams would come true. It was the first thing they agreed on in months. They nibbled at the bait of this bill-board lie, hook line and sinker and illusion reeled them in.

Little Bin shook off this memory and the chill of the morning fully awakened him. He finally surrendered to waking and opened his eyes. He stretched his arms and loosened up for his day. It was always such a cold reality to awaken, another day requiring him to duck and cover. But, within his vibrant spirit, it was also another day to embark upon his own personal mission, to revive the walking dead in this town. If he could not resuscitate them, then he would settle for just making them mad.

Their self- made blindness angered Little Bin. His secret hope was that if he could awaken even one town member to the reality of this dark and plastic town, maybe his parents still had a chance. The leprosy of comfort numbed the town members' hearts. Illusion buried all vibrant signs of life.

The Town of Self Absorption

To man's understanding, Self Absorption was a thriving metropolis. It had risen to be one of the most promising up-and-coming cities. When the maps promoted Self Absorption to bold print and a star in the center, they celebrated with a parade. People loved the notoriety, for it contributed to each citizen's own sense of importance.

However, despite all the growing popularity, there was a dark deception hidden deep below the surface, which had begun to infiltrate the hearts of the townspeople. Delusion built retaining walls against truth, barring its entrance a long time ago. Truth however was steadfast and kept knocking.

Mentor and Student instantly appeared on Self Absorption's main drag. They decided to walk down Main Street to update themselves on the current climate of the town.

After walking a while, Student began to do what set him apart from average students; he asked his Mentor questions. "Mentor, do people even notice the darkness that surrounds them?"

Mentor was pleased with his young friend's discerning heart, and he understood his bewilderment. "Student, you need to understand how pride blinds. This has been the plight of humanity ever since the fall of man.

Sin blinds. The dark side hides in the shadows of compromise. Unless people have Truth's purity of light to reveal the shadows, people remain blind to the fallen state of things."

"Is there any hope for them?" asked Student.

"Hope is only found in God, and today we bring hope to seven citizens. *With God all things are possible*. He placed a hole inside men's hearts. Those who belong to Him, will come to understand that the longing in their hearts can only be satisfied with Him."

The Angels Watch

The angels walked down Main Street looking like every other person making their way to work. They listened intently.

Pieces of conversations were overheard as people walked next to them. The hearts behind the discussions grieved the two messengers.

"I want..." one woman was sharing about her expectations in her no longer exciting marriage.

"It's not my fault, she should know better," one man justified why he drank the night away because his wife, practically told him to drink when she left cash out on their dresser."

"I want more," a woman proclaimed explaining why she was going to leave her husband.

"He doesn't deserve me," was the reason a woman charged $400 on her husband's credit card.

The angels' hearts sank in heaviness over all the selfishness that surrounded them.

"Mentor, they believe they are the creators of their own happiness."

Mentor wanted to comfort him but these lessons were important to learn.

Student asked in a pleading way, "Can we leave now? I am not feeling very well."

Mentor gathered him closer as if to strengthen him for the answer. "There are three places I need to show you before we go."

Student bolstered up an inner discipline to endure. "If our Lord resolved to endure the cross for these same sinners, the least I could do is remain focused despite my grieving spirit."

Mentor offered a proud smile to his protégée and nodded in affirmation. "The first of the three stops is the City Administration Building."

The City Administration Building

Though discontentment was an unwelcome visitor in their town, it had become the fastest growing problem. It somehow crept in unannounced and unseen. Though it made everyone uncomfortable, no one knew what to do about it.

The City Council had made some quiet efforts to attempt to hide the consequences from the public's eye. They arranged with a sister city one hundred miles away to host any Self Absorption citizens in need of mental health treatment.

Their struggle was apparent. They needed to try to address the subtle uprising of discontentment without making the public aware. They had an image to maintain. All their dreams were *not* coming true.

The Town Council meeting began just as Mentor and Student entered through supernatural means from the back of the room. They sat down unnoticed in the very last row. The mayor stood up to comment on the first topic of the day. Twenty-five people were sprinkled about in the audience.

The Mayor started the meeting, "It is not acceptable that our citizens feel uncomfortable living in Self Absorption."

The Commissioner of Public Works stood up immediately and parroted what the Mayor just said. "It is not okay that Self Absorptionites feel uncomfortable!"

He always did this. Everything the Mayor said, he would repeat. That is how he earned his nickname "Echo" because he only spoke the Mayor's words.

The mayor picked right back up with his thought. "As leaders of this fine city we have a responsibility to preserve our right to comfort."

A cheer came from every occupied chair in the room. (Except that of Mentor and Student.) The true sentiment of every citizen had been identified – their inalienable right to comfort!

Mentor transported thoughts to his pupil, as whispering would have been distracting. "Discontentment is a tool the Pursuer uses to alert the heart of men. Discontentment shakes things inside and causes one to thirst for truth. Political correctness disdains truth because Truth does not compromise."

"I understand." Student reported to Mentor.

The meeting held some votes over a few issues about additional traffic lights on Vicious Circle Drive and set the official date for the City's "We are All Okay" parade. Then the meeting adjourned.

Mentor exited and went quickly down the stairwell. Student, unsure where Mentor was heading, stayed close behind him.

"Come with me. I want to show you something out front." Mentor said.

The dependant sheep stayed close to his shepherd's heels.

As Mentor walked down the stairs, he explained further. "The town council came up with a plan they thought could appear as a solution. Their brainchild backfired, and now they are stuck with the consequences of their bad decision."

"Do you mean this is another case of the Pursuer working all things together for good?"

"Yes Student it is, it certainly is. The dark side may be allowed its schemes, but their plans work for the Pursuer's purposes."

Mentor reached the bottom of the stairs and walked through the stairwell door, opening up into a lobby area with glass window walls and marble floors. It was the main entranceway leading to the offices of the city government. In the center of the foyer was a desk, which had a sign on it, 'Information'. A receptionist wearing a headset sat behind it fielding the incoming calls.

Her bright red nails caught Student's eye as he walked by. They curved over so far under they looked arthritic. He wondered how she could work with such long nails.

Approaching the front door, they paused in front of the tall marble counter with a glass sign reading, 'Security.'

A bored, middle aged man wearing a scowl was leaning back against a high steel chair. The well worn crease across his forehead matched his finely creased pants. He was probably a lot younger than he looked.

Bulletproof windows encased the lobby, from floor to ceiling. Mentor turned, letting Student catch up and then resumed his quick, paced stride, and walked right through the front glass doors without any hesitation. It was the Angelic messenger's prerogative. After they walked a few feet down the walkway, Mentor stopped and turned around.

As Student followed, he found himself facing the front entrance of the City Administration Building. Mentor pointed just to the left of the entrance, where a broom hung from a hook. Next to the broom was a bronze plaque.

In front of the plaque, a young woman holding a second broom was sweeping furiously under a big industrial size rug. Student noticed the rug was engraved. He stepped closer to read it. "Sweep your discontentment under here, then, enter with a happy heart"

Student did not understand what he was seeing. He did not even know what question to ask. He just looked at Mentor and waited for him to offer the missing pieces.

"This is their solution…"

"Brooms? Mentor, I don't understand."

"The brooms were an effort to apply social pressure to keep anyone from admitting they were struggling with discontentment. They thought this would publicly humiliate anyone who wanted to acknowledge they struggled with this. They thought this was perfect, they could pretend to have a solution while deterring those from admitting to be in such a condition.

"See the plaque next to the broom on the wall? It is the bronzed face of Self Absorption's first Mayor, Indy Nial."

"Was he a good mayor?" asked Student.

"Depends on which side you would ask. He died while still in office. There were rumors as to his traffic accident being alcohol related but they never investigated. The council voted to 'sweep the truth under the rug' in the interest of the town's image and for the comfort of everyone involved. It is sweet irony that these brooms hang right beside his memorial plaque."

Student watched in amazement as the long line of people waited for their turn to sweep. They all waited with blank stares on their faces.

"It doesn't look like it deterred many people." Student gazed at the long line waiting to sweep; it wrapped around the corner.

"Yes, it surely backfired. Yes, many citizens responded to this opportunity thinking it was a viable hope, to sweep away their discontent." Mentor went on to explain. "Initially people were excited about this new opportunity and they responded in droves. The line grew longer every day."

"You mean they actually put hope in being able to sweep their discontentment away?"

"Yes, but their hope quickly died and from the ash pile of broken dreams, Sweepers were born."

"What is a Sweeper?" asked Student.

"A Sweeper is one of these," Mentor pointed to the line of people. "The definition of a Sweeper is simply, one who sweeps. In their attempt to rid themselves of their discontentment, they became prisoners to sweeping. The harder they sweep, the more discontent is stirred up inside. They have become a sub-culture all their own. This precious gal is one of them."

Mentor pointed to Pleaser. Broom in hand, she was furiously sweeping. Oblivious to others around her, she was in the 'sweeper's zone.' The sweeper's zone is the place of intense focus where everything fades from consciousness except for sweeping. Pleaser clung desperately to the false hope she could sweep her way into contentment.

Mentor tapped Student's shoulder and whispered, "She is one we will be visiting tonight."

"Oh she is?" Student became excited.

"She is His, but does not yet know it."

"What should we do about him?" Student pointed to the dark side warrior who was whispering into Pleaser's ear. They did not hear his words to her but they could see the impact he had upon her sweeping.

As she listened to him, her sweeping intensified. Sweat was rolling down her face; she did not even stop to wipe it off. She took hold of his evil words so they became her own thoughts.

The warrior's name was Defeatist. He whispered lies in her ear as rapidly as she swept.

"You must show determination in order to succeed" He whispered. "You must believe this will work in order for it to work. You know this is your last hope. If this does not work, there is only one option left. Quit life all together, so unless you want to quit, you better sweep harder, sweep harder and faster," Defeatist whispered.

"Mentor shouldn't we take him out?"

Mentor looked into Student's eyes. "We are to do nothing right now. Our Father has allowed this for the moment to bring about His good purpose. It is not yet our time to intervene. Be encouraged, this evil warrior is ignorant of his usefulness to the Pursuer's plans. Our Lord is using him to prepare her to receive Himself. Come now Student, there is one other place I must show you."

In a twinkling of an eye, they disappeared, leaving Pleaser with broom in hand furiously sweeping under the industrial rug.

Pleaser

Pleaser, a rookie sweeper, held tightly to the broom as if a veteran. Her tight grip reflected how desperately she clung to the hope that perhaps today she might find freedom.

Yet with each day, her discontentment grew, causing her to sweep more furiously.

Her determination to fix her defective personality fueled her motivation to sweep.

People must be right about her. She always saw disappointment on their faces. She had always been the source of people's disappointment.

Her recent loss in the City Council re-election reinforced that this was true. She was the first Council member ever to lose a re-election in over a hundred years.

This was the final straw. After her lost election was when she first picked up the broom. She analyzed through every choice she made as she swept. Of course, Defeatist was right there with her making sure all her life's unanswered questions taunted her. As they did, she swept harder. "Who am I? What do I stand for? Why would people want to vote for me anyway?"

Pleaser was completely unaware of the demon, Defeatist, who was whispering in her ear. His daily work assignment was to harass the sweepers. His job was simple; to condemn and to accuse.

Pleaser was one of his favorites because she was so gullible. She was Playdoh in his hands. He felt powerful as she received his words line after line without question. He couldn't help but squeal in delight as she tormented over his suggestions.

"Putty in my hands you are." He laughed at how easy it was to make his thoughts hers.

"I try so hard to be what others want me to be, yet they always end up disappointed." The thought created a reaction. Pleaser swept with even greater fury.

Defeatist leaned over and whispered again, "You are unlovable. Your mom was so disappointed it killed her."

Despondency arrested Pleaser's heart. She tried to talk herself into being satisfied. The old fear of being crazy visited her despondency. The evidence that she really was crazy seemed to build with each passing day. She was unsure of everything.

Yet something deep within her screamed, "Keep fighting." She struggled to find good things she had done to counter her fear of being a complete loser. Yet even with her substantial list of accomplishments, it did not erase her discontent. Her itemized lists of successes found her contentment still wanting.

Her greatest sense of pride was assisting in the acquisition of the town's giant 3-D mirror, displayed in the center of the park just off Main Street. This mirror, with its special filter, had become the very heart of the town.

The Town's Mirror

Mentor and Student angelically 'appeared' at the entrance of the grassy park on Vicious Circle Drive. In the center of town, a circular road wrapped all the way around a public park.

The street had the reputation for being a very dangerous place to drive. People made many reckless maneuvers to exit the turnabout early, which resulted in serious traffic accidents. This street held the record for traffic accidents for the entire county. That was why it was officially renamed Vicious Circle Drive.

There in the center was a relatively small grassy park, with a looming overly grand sized mirror. Student stepped back to behold this mirror in full view. Immense in size, it stood over twenty-five feet tall, displayed on a marble foundation with one stair leading up to it. The town had given this mirror the very center of its heart, and exalted it high above everything else.

The arthritic branches of the infamous town tree hung slightly over the mirror. The tree's roots were already so deep in the ground before the inception of the town that engineers decided to build the town around it rather than remove it.

Though the tree's fruit looked enticing, reports were that it harbored a very bitter taste. Being the oldest tree in the state, it had been affectionately nicknamed the 'Tree of Knowledge'. This stemmed from a joke Mayor Indy Nial made, "If this is the oldest tree, it must be the wisest."

Mentor pointed to the mirror and began to explain to Student the dark presence it brought to this town. "This mirror was reported to be one of a kind. (Though, the art dealer who sold it to them said it to all his buyers.) There was a special film applied to this mirror. It is this special film that sets this mirror apart from others."

"What kind of film is it?" asked Student.

"It is called illusion. This film of illusion prevents any unsightly images to reflect back from its glass. It comes with a lifetime guarantee."

Student closed his eyes in grief, recognizing the spiritual cost to this illusion. They would never see truth. "This lifetime guarantee holds such grave eternal consequences to every soul who stands before this mirror."

"Yes Student, if people knew the costs to clinging to illusion it would change things immediately. Each person chooses if they want to receive truth or reject it."

Mentor pointed to the swarms of people lining up to seek the mirror's reflection. "As you see, crowds gather at all hours to gaze into the mirror. People are mesmerized with images of themselves. They are slaves seeking approval and the mirror freely lies to them so they can have it. Deception comes at a great cost. Truth is rejected so illusion can be maintained. Citizens like the mirror's mirage because it keeps them comfortable."

"Mentor, I don't understand man at all." Student sighed.

"To accept truth, man must face the emptiness within them. This brings great discomfort. The scheme of the enemy often takes place gradually. No one notices the slow erosion of a soul. When the town Council officially sanctioned this mirror as part of the town, people liked it because it allowed them to feel good about themselves, and in Self Absorption, that is what matters most."

Student grievously watched as one blind soul after another reverently walked up to the mirror. Each one carried an unseen burden of great weight. Student spoke His Lord's words, wanting the deafened ears to hear and know. *"Come to Me all who are weary and heavy laden and I will give you rest."*

He wanted to shake them free, but knew he would not influence a heart unwilling to hear. He decided instead to praise the longsuffering heart of the Heavenly Lord of Hosts who, in steadfast and faithful love, pursued after a people blind to His beauty and righteousness.

Grieved, he watched each soul carry their heavy, dark secrets up to the mirror. He watched them peer into the mirror's reflection and believe its lie. He watched them turn from the mirror and walk away smiling with the same weighted burden still upon their shoulders.

"What are the consequences to this madness?" Student grew angry at the blatant disregard for truth.

"Be encouraged Student, by the grace of God, complications surface. Take this man here." Mentor pointed out a tall, lean, good-looking businessman in his mid-thirties. "Sometimes people come to the mirror really in need of truth. This man has food caught between his teeth from lunch. He is on his way back to the office but stopped to see if he had food in his teeth.

"This would seem to be no big deal. What could go wrong with a harmless piece of hamburger in your teeth?" Mentor went on to explain. "What he does not see is the big remnant of hamburger stuck between his teeth; and the mirror will not reveal it either.

The film of illusion will only portray him to have his pearly whites; it will not show piece of meat. He will walk away believing he is fine. The plot will thicken for him this afternoon. He has a career making or breaking presentation today. It is a critical meeting where he will compete against other firms for a highly prized contract. He needs this deal to keep his present position in the company. His sales have been down for the past few months. Do you think this piece of meat in his teeth will distract his clients?"

"I would think so," answered Student

"Yes it will. In fact, it will be so distracting they will not even hear his sales pitch. He will not earn the contract and will be placed on probation without pay by the end of the week."

"Or take Dr. Know it all there." Mentor pointed to a short, squat middle-aged man who walked quickly while looking down at the ground all the way up to the mirror.

"He is the High School Principal."

"Does he know that his toupee is half way off the back of his head?" Student inquired.

"No Student and that is my point." They both watched as Dr. Know It All walked up nervously to the mirror and peered in. He broke into a big smile as the reflection showed that 'he was just fine.'

"Another dangerous part of this film of illusion is people become deaf to their own internal alarms. They hit the snooze button on their own self awareness, preferring to be told by the mirror what is true."

"What about other people? They have to notice his toupee slipping off the back of his head? Why don't they tell him?" asked Student.

"The cost is too high for them to tell him. It would mean they were going against what the mirror showed. It would create a ripple of doubt and suspicion in the mirror. Controversy might threaten their accepted place in the town.

If the choice came down to picking between a citizen and the mirror, it is the mirror that would stay."

"Controversy?" Student was confused. "What could be controversial about telling a man his wig is falling off his head?"

"Student, try to walk in their shoes for a moment. What do they risk by telling someone that what they just saw in the mirror was not accurate? This would start a domino effect of doubt. The credibility of the mirror would come into question.

People here in Self Absorption have made their choice. They do not want truth; they want the illusion that all is fine. That is how they are controlled. Remember, discomfort is persona-non-gratis in Self Absorption. In the name of comfort, unmet expectations are shoved away, despite the personal cost.

In fact, this poor doctor is unaware of the great discomfort he triggers for everyone else. When people see him in town, anxiety rises in their hearts. He forces people to ask those hard questions.

"I wonder if there is anything I am not seeing." People avoid him as much as they can. The school board met privately and decided not to renew his contract next year for this reason."

As Mentor was explaining this, Dr. Know it All walked right by Little Bin. Little Bin was on his way to the Tree of Knowledge. In his frankness and complete lack of reverence for authority, he seized the opportunity.

"Hi Dr. Droopy Hair. How are you today?"

Dr. Know It All was shaken by his mocking disrespect. Little Bin's reputation preceded him. Everyone knew he lacked restraint especially in the area of political correctness. He continued on, without inhibition, to point out the fallen condition of his toupee.

"Looks like your hair follicles are in an avalanche Doc."

In horror, Dr. Know It All clutched the back of his head to discover Little Bin was right.

"How in the world?"

Dr. Know It All hunched over as if to crawl into an invisible hole and scurried off toward his home. His hand remained on his hair the entire time. He wondered how many people had seen this and never said a thing.

"What must they think? Oh this is all so humiliating."

Like every good citizen in Self Absorption, Dr. Know It All took this embarrassment over to Indy Nial's rug and swept. After breaking into a huge sweat, he re-checked his toupee's placement. He headed back toward the town mirror once again to find peace of mind.

Student wanted to go over to that little boy and give him a high five. They watched as Little Bin climbed up the trunk of the Tree of Knowledge. He maneuvered himself to a branch and swung upside down hanging from the back of his knees. This is where he did his best brainstorming. What would be his next good prank or mischievous deed?

"Student, this little ball of energy is one of our special invitees."

Student smiled and shook his head. "Good, he is a breath of fresh air in my book."

"So Student, do you now understand this town's sickness? To effectively minister to people, it is critical we understand where they come from."

"Mentor, I cannot wait to see how the Father's glory will turn all these things together for good. Can we go now?"

"Yes we can leave Vicious Circle Drive now. This evening we get to invite others to leave the vicious circles of their lives too. Tonight earmarks the beginning of a great transformation for seven of our new friends."

Unaware to all the onlookers, Mentor and Student disappeared.

The Dark Side Territory

The citizens waiting in line to approach the mirror were unaware of the squatting dark side force resting on the branches above them. Demons mocked, taunted, and deceived. They sat on the branches and screamed out taunting remarks to the ignorant drones below as they looked into the mirror. The Tree of Knowledge was the demons base camp while they flew out to whisper a lie or taunt a soul with flattery. They wanted to keep these citizens blinded in their captivity. Truth be told, these citizens were nothing but marionettes on Satan's string.

Pleaser Wonders

"I feel like a puppet on a string. The question is who is pulling my strings?" Pleaser decided to quit for the day. She dutifully handed her broom to the next person in line. She recognized their looks of great anticipation.

She wondered why no one ever saw the emptiness in her expression as she finished for the day. She always ended feeling restless within. Discouraged, she headed home. Sweeping had become part of the problem, not the solution.

"How did things come to this?" She thought back to when her parents used to host all sorts of community activities. They were well-respected leaders in the town. With outgoing personalities, their social graces shined brightly in their elite inner social circle.

Insecurities never surfaced outside their home. Her mom was always the most elegant woman at a party. Conversations would stop when she entered a room.

The parties they hosted were always heralded as 'the best of the year.' She handled social events with grace and dignity. She treated everyone with respect, from the most prominent guest to the kitchen staff.

Pleaser loved to watch the festivities from the banister rail just off her bedroom. She would curl up in a ball to be as small as possible to watch the fullness of life go on below. She loved watching her mom in action.

She recalled how her mother disarmed Mr. Impatience who was known to get out of hand at parties. As the night event progressed, he would begin a barrage of insults to someone whom he found irritating.

One particular night, her mom walked up to him as he was ranting. She smiled warmly to him, tilted her head to his ear and whispered. It must have been funny because he burst out laughing. He ended up giving her a hug, and there was no further incident from him the rest of the night. She just had a gracious way with people. It was a gift. It was not something she could be taught.

It baffled Pleaser how her mom so willingly extended grace to others, yet she could not extend it to herself. The day after a successful party, Pleaser would find her mom curled up in a ball filled with despair. At times, she was unable to perform even simple tasks.

Her dad asked her to pick up his suit from the cleaners in the morning before he left for work. When he got home that night and asked for his suit she burst into tears. She had forgotten to pick it up. This type of error would make her so distraught, she would retreat to bed for days. She berated herself over the simplest of mistakes, for weeks at a time.

Pleaser knew intimately the worthless labels her mom identified with because today, Pleaser held to the same ones herself.

It was all so difficult to understand as a little girl. Pleaser concluded that her mom was unhappy because she had let her down somehow. She dedicated her childhood days toward trying to make her mom happy again. It seemed however, the harder Pleaser tried, the sadder her mom became.

When Pleaser was twelve years old, her mom committed suicide.

The aching pain feels as raw today as the day it happened. She came home from school, ran up stairs clutching a test paper, hoping this would bring a smile to her mom's face. It was the algebra test she studied for all week; she received a perfect score.

She leaped three steps at a time to get to her bedroom more quickly. She bolted through the door, to find her father stooped over her mom's lifeless body, sobbing. A doctor stood next to the bed and pulled a sheet over her face.

Pleaser never did get to see her mom's face that day. She never saw her face again. When she pictures her mom it returns attached with terrible guilt. She had let her down. Guilt stalked Pleaser. It whispered at night, "It is my fault." "I should have done something to save her."

That day, Pleaser emotionally froze in time. She never fully left that bedroom, even after all these years.

Paralyzed in time, Pleaser bound with fear, felt strangled by every decision. She learned to follow other people's opinions. She could not burden the responsibility for destroying another person's life. Decisions were left to others more capable.

Making people happy was her penance.

Making other's pleased brought a moment of reprieve from the ache deep in her heart. The voices spoke to make her in the dark, night hours, how she just was not enough to her mom happy.

Pleaser felt as though she was whittling away, more with each passing day. "Something has to change. I need to change." Pleaser screamed silently under her breath. "I need help."

One person came to her mind, as a possible ray of hope. Maybe Counselor could help. Counselor had a good reputation among sweepers. A few retired sweepers recommended her. She really helped them walk away from the broom.

"Maybe Counselor is someone I can trust." One thing she knew for sure, she was running out of time in her search for hope. Her greatest fear was that hope was not real.

She rubbed her calloused hands as she walked home. It was time to feed her dog, Impressions.

Counselor

The familiar knot in her shoulder returned as it typically did at the end of the day. All the emotional pressures weighed heavy upon her soul. She got up from her chair where she had been sitting for the last three hours listening to heart wrenching accounts of how humanity can wound, injure and shatter one another. Walking around her office, she moved her head side to side trying to knead out the kink in her neck.

Counselor cared deeply for her clients. Their burden often became her burden, which by the end of the day, left her feeling old and tired.

More recently, however, she felt a growing unrest. A quiet desperation echoed within her to find answers to the same questions her clients were asking. At times, she had to restrain herself from screaming out in confession that she was just as lost as the ones who came to see her.

There was a superficial glaze, which sealed over everything unpolished, attempting to imitate what was genuine. She couldn't stomach its falseness any longer. She wanted truth for answers, but truth was not welcome in Self Absorption. Although a native of the town, she no longer felt she belonged here; she felt like an alien.

Her heart sighed as she returned to her chair.

It was taking a great deal of energy for her to offer encouragement to her clients. She respected their courage and their strength to keep on fighting, their perseverance to keep fanning the flame, to not surrender to insanity. Self Absorption embraced insanity and called it happiness. Counselor would frequently joke with her neighbors, "My clients are the sanest ones in this town."

She did not know how close to the truth that was. The simplest of statements were life vests thrown to drowning souls in tempest of discontent.

Counselor spent a great deal of time affirming her clients. "You make sense," she would say to them all the time. For them it was a life rope to hold.

When she spoke these words, they were not counseling platitudes either, Counselor meant it. Her clients made more sense to her than those who saw no problems with their life.

She had always been able to see the misery clearly. She never trusted the lying image from that town mirror. This town fraudulently feigned light and peace while darkness and chaos stood out of view, armed and ready at every corner.

"How do I lead people out from their muck and mire, when I have no good option to offer them?"

She longed to find an answer.

Recalling a statement made to a colleague at a recent meeting, "At least her clients are honest enough to admit they are stuck. They are more honest than me." Counselor sighed.

"Good thing I am done for the day. I am worn out." Counselor put her files in her brief case, grabbed her coat and locked her office door. She walked everywhere, though she had a car, she rarely drove. Walking allowed her to think. With each day, her gait became a little slower, as unseen burdens weighed down her heart.

She headed home with her head down and her eyes fixed upon her next step. Her familiar slump forward when she walked earned her the nickname of the 'old woman', from those in her neighborhood. Counselor was forty-four years old but she felt like ninety.

Her mind began to wander. The same thought kept returning. "The answers to my questions cannot be found in this town."

She walked by the Tree of Knowledge. So much time has passed since she used to climb that tree in a childlike innocence. Childlike innocence died off a long time ago.

Long before the mirror lived below the trees, she loved to climb it's branches. They stretched out so far through her child's eyes it looked like the tree was waking up and stretching out in a big yawn.

Oh how she loved life then. She could climb higher than any other kid in school. She used to sit on the highest branch and look out at the horizon and dream. Dream about her future, wondering what it would be like.

Princes would ride up to her on their horses, hovering just below the tree branch where she sat. She would leap onto his saddle, wrap her arms around her prince and ride off into the sunset. Her prince would give up his whole kingdom just so he could have her hand in marriage.

A sad reminiscence rose up within her; she extinguished it with a regretful laugh and a shake of her head. "And if you tried to climb that tree now you would break your neck."

Those days seemed foreign now, as if they belonged to someone else. Her childhood started, as one should. She felt loved and safe. She lived inside her family's protective bubble. She did not realize then how fragile bubbles could be. It took so little to pop them.

She had dedicated her whole life to helping others deal with their bubbles that popped. She learned early on, things were not as they appeared.

Gazing back up at the tree, she thought it was symbolic that the tree limbs blocked the sunlight below. She hated the tree but more so the mirror. As she stood before it her disdain could not be denied.

Since the mirrors' arrival, the tree developed an even darker presence. A presence she could not explain but felt. Counselor yearned to leave this town, but her concern for her clients bound her to stay. She could not abandon them to this town's oppression.

She had experienced first hand the evil behind the mirror. This mirror lies, robs and steals. It stole from her the most precious person in her life, her father.

When the mirror first arrived in the town, people exalted it as if it was some kind of guru to their soul. Everyone accepted the Council's approval as to its credibility to reveal the truth. They accepted without their own investigation. Her own father began to go to the mirror every day.

He was such a great dad. He worked hard as the family provider, but prized every moment he could be with his family. When dad came home from work, he would sneak into the kitchen where mom was cooking dinner. Counselor would be the first to notice him because mom was facing the stove. He would wink at her and put his finger to his lips, telling her to be quiet. His eyes would stay on Counselor the whole way across the kitchen. She watched his smile light up his whole face, growing bigger with every step closer to his beloved wife. She was sure sometimes she saw his eyes dancing.

"Your eyes are dancing again dad." Counselor used to joke with him. They danced in anticipation of being close to his wife. He would gently wrap his arms around her from behind and just hold her, swaying gently side to side and then she would lift her head back onto his chest and reach over and touch his cheek. He would draw his cheek to hers and ask the same question every day.

"How is the most beautiful girl in the world today?" Mom melted into him and said his name. "Tony."

No one could say his name better than mom; she exhaled as she spoke it. All life's difficulties fled in utter embarrassment with the love expressed in that kitchen. They would take a walk together before dinner so they could share their hearts and their day.

He had such a magical way of making mom feel and look so beautiful even after thirteen years of marriage.

That was life inside the bubble, before it burst. After the mirrors arrival, dad went to it for reassurance instead of mom. There were many troubles for him at work, which increased his worries. Things got so heavy that he was too tired to sneak into the kitchen and hug mom; he was too weary to dance and embrace her. He didn't have time to go for walks with her anymore.

He spent his time waiting in the long line for a look in the mirror. He needed to in order to go home feeling assured everything was fine. However, nothing he saw from the mirror stuck. The images it gave seemed to last less and less each time. This just created a need for him to return more often, trying to keep hold of the idea that everything was fine. Yet it so easily left him.

He was ill at ease all the time, filled with doubts about his abilities, which he used to trust in. He felt threatened by co-workers, who at one time were friends. He spent his lunch hour in line at the mirror so he could return to work confident to finish out his day.

When the line was long, he came back from lunch late and sometimes missed afternoon meetings. This meant he needed to return to the mirror again before going home because he wanted to feel okay. His insecurity enslaved him to the delusions of the mirror and delusions always faded.

Counselor felt an anxiety rise up within as she walked down this memory lane.

If he'd only asked her, she would have told him the truth; he was *not* fine. He was a great dad before the mirror, but the mirror sucked his soul from him. She didn't even know who he was anymore.

Then one day, what little part remained of the old dad snapped. He didn't doubt in the mirror anymore. He believed whatever the mirror showed him. That was when everything went from bad to worse.

From a quiet, humble man, he slowly transformed into an opinionated, arrogant one. His walk became a strut and he lectured colleagues instead of enjoyed lunch with them. He became convinced that people should feel lucky to know him.

He stopped flirting with his wife altogether. His compliments and loving eyes became absent. Mom felt invisible and ugly because his eyes never wandered her direction anymore. He sat in his lounge chair expecting her to come to him.

He became irritated when she didn't, because he was so important to so many people. He felt she did not appreciate all his hard work to support the family. She missed who he used to be. They no longer had fun together. Mom stopped saying his name all together.

Over time, Counselor learned to expect the stranger living in her dad's clothes. She remembered walking into her mom's bedroom and seeing her blot away tears. Mom tried to hide it but Counselor knew.

She could not bear to see her dad hurt her mom. She focused on her mom's sadness rather than her own. It seemed easier, because she missed him too. Time passed and distance grew great between her and her dad.

A few years back, as she walked home from work, Counselor passed by her father's car. She knew it was his car, because of the bobble-head baseball figurine, which stood in the back window.

She thought it was odd he parked his car in the alley. At first, she did a double take because she could not believe what she was seeing. Counselor's father was in the arms of another woman inside the car, the bobble headed baseball player was her witness.

After many sleepless nights, Counselor decided to confront him, but the very morning she decided to, he called her, and stated very nonchalantly that he was leaving her mom. "I have met someone. She makes me feel young again."

Counselor understood his wanting to feel young again. She missed his playful fun spirit too. He used to impulsively get up from the couch and walk over to her mom and bow, then lift her mom up and start dancing with her. He hummed songs from television commercials. He always did such great impersonations, especially of family relatives. We would laugh so hard we lost our appetites and just skipped dinner.

The illusions televised from that mirror hardened her dad's heart. Then, when entitlement grew and pride wanting more room, evicted playfulness. After a time, his joyful spirit died completely.

Tears streaked down Counselor's cheek as she closed this memory's door. Her dad sold the best parts of himself to get glimpses of illusion. The mirror murdered the dad she adored.

For a while, Counselor held out hope for reconciliation. Mom would have taken him back in a second. If only he would have just asked for forgiveness. Her mom waited, but her dad never came.

He never admitted to his mistakes anymore. It was too easy to go to the mirror and feel fine. That was easier than the truth. It would have been too painful to face what he threw away. Her dad broke their hearts.

As Counselor sauntered home, these thoughts caused her to walk more slumped than usual. A question kept tossing around inside her heart. "Who can turn light on in the depths of such darkness? Does someone have control of Truth's light switch?"

All this pondering wore her out. She arrived home and shut her front door, she slammed shut this memory's door. Nothing good ever came from opening it. She stripped off her clothes, attempting to strip off her day. She took a bath and retired early with a book.

Reading was her escape, her plane ticket out of Self Absorption, without abandoning her clients. She launched into the pages, leaving behind all painful memories. Frequently during this red eye flight into the pages, she fell asleep before landing. Her eyes grew heavy and her dreams took over. The book lay open across her chest and her reading glasses lay crookedly across her nose.

The One who does control the light switch had His eyes upon her. He knew the depth of Counselor's pain. It pleased Him that her heart sought truth not illusion. He smiled as He watched her sleep. Every tear she ever shed He captured and placed in a bottle. She was precious to Him and very soon He would make His unfailing love known to her.

Fatalist

Fatalist was the security guard for the City Administration building. He stood behind his counter in the foyer. He resented the box seat view of the Sweepers. Their persevering will was an enigma to him, because their pursuit was so pointless. He mocked them aloud when his disgust got the best of him.

"Ignorant crop." It angered him to watch them hope in something so pathetic. He was baffled why people had not yet arrived at his insight and understanding. His revelation was simple; hope was pointless. The best thing he ever did was stop believing in dreams. Sweeping only became necessary when people held onto expectations. Weak people always expected things, and that is why they were always disappointed. With his way, he was never disappointed.

Fatalist came to Self Absorption when he was only thirteen. He and his family lived under a ruthless government regime. A soldier shot his father right in front of him one day when his father went to help a man.

This soldier had beaten the man unconscious and left him to die on the street. The soldier became enraged when Fatalist's dad went to this man's aid. He would make him an example to the people not to challenge or betray the government officials ever.

The soldier calmly raised his gun, aimed and fatally shot Fatalist's dad right through the heart. The citizens fearfully submitted to everything he asked after witnessing the senseless murder.

"Giving aid to someone who has been disciplined is viewed as treason," the soldier notified the crowd. Then he simply turned and walked away.

Fatalist ran over and held his father, sobbing as he died in his arms. His dad was a man of great compassion; he didn't hesitate to go to the aid of the man and because of that, he paid for it with his life.

Fatalist's mom was devastated. It left her to care for four children in a land where women were property, not people. Helpless and unable to provide for her children, she made a desperate decision.

She could either let the government seize them, where they would become wards of the state and indoctrinated into the children's army and taught the party view, or entrust her children to caring friends who had better means to provide for them.

Her three youngest were adorable. Their big blue eyes and sweet spirits instantly wooed the hearts of their potential caretakers, but Fatalist was the oldest.

43

The first thirteen years of life ravaged his childhood. War shattered his innocence. He saw too much too early and his countenance displayed it. Weariness imprisoned every face in the province. Despair scaled people's eyes like cataracts, blinding them to hope.

In complete desperation, his mom surrendered to a heart-wrenching plan, which seemed best for her boy. She packed his knapsack with fruit and bread and walked him to the boat dock.

She did not tell Fatalist of her plan. She did not want him to know until he had to. He knew anyway, she did not need to tell him.

He pretended it did not bother him to watch the ship leave the dock. The ship's destination was the 'Land of the Free.' He watched his mom grow smaller as she waved from the dock blowing him kisses goodbye. Long after he could no longer see her, he remained there staring at the dock; her goodbye locked in his mind.

His emotions got the best of him. His knees buckled beneath him and he leaned over the side rail and vomited. He was glad his mom could not see this. He lectured himself. "Do not ever do that again."

Fatalist convinced himself on that foggy morning that emotions meant weakness. He reminded himself of how emotions caused the murder of his father. Turning from the ship's rail, he walked away squeezing his hands into a fist.

"Stay strong," was his new motto, "and don't need anybody."

So he did. Just like his calloused hands barricaded his chewed fingernails inside his fist, so it was with his calloused heart that secured a perimeter against all fear and emotions from entering in.

The only ticket his mother could afford included a servitude clause. Until the ship embarked to its destination, Fatalist belonged to the head cook. A kitchen slave, he worked sixteen hours a day preparing meals for all the passengers on the ship. He was a hard worker and it was difficult work. He earned the reputation of being a 'good little servant.' He never let anyone close enough to know him as a person.

Four months later, the ship arrived on the shore of the Land of the Free. His eyes fell upon sign after sign, each offering wonderful choices. The amount of opportunities there overwhelmed him.

Each billboard proclaimed a promise for happiness, contentment and success. How did one decide? "Which great opportunity should I pick?" One particular billboard, read, "Make yourself at home in our town of Self Absorption where everyone is accepted."

The words were a pillow to his weary heart. "Could this be true, everyone accepted?" Cynical reason gave way to hope. "Maybe this place will be different. Maybe hope does live there."

A flutter of excitement arose within him. "After all, this is the Land of the Free."

Twenty-two years passed since Fatalist first followed the promise on that billboard. Now thirty-five years old and never married, he knew for sure dreams don't come true. No matter where you are, they always ended up dead; murdered by someone who didn't believe in your dream.

The most devastating assassin in the town was the blasted town mirror. He felt free to talk about it but few people listened, for Fatalist was always boisterous about his opinions.

"Mirror seekers are weak, pathetic souls groping after lying images which anesthetize their minds. They are morons, all of them."

A real thorn to Fatalist's side was where his workstation was located, right outside his window, was the station set up for the Sweepers. He had a front row seat to watch countless people attempt to sweep their misery under a rug. Sweepers triggered the restlessness within him. It forced him to see the futility of his own fruitless life.

The unnerving part for Fatalist was that people in Self Absorption most of the time would not even acknowledge their own misery. They worked overtime to ensure their minds would not go there.

His cynical attitude got him into a lot of trouble. He received on almost a monthly basis, a reprimand for speaking disrespectfully to someone. Fatalist was stingy with respect. He did not give it freely to anyone. Respect was something you must earn.

At one time, the administration seriously discussed firing him, but they concluded he knew too much about people and that it would be best not to ruffle his feathers.

Because he needed the paycheck, Fatalist conceded to play the employee game. On the surface, he appeared submitted, but his heart never really surrendered to anyone.

His day included many monotonous rounds. He always welcomed the interruptions of high action and drama, when there would be an outburst or an 'incident' that required his intervention or arrest.

In the boring portions of his day, he couldn't help himself and would hurl silent insults to the marionettes with brooms outside. When he would get really tired, his mind would drift to his mom. He wondered how she was and what she looked like. He would close his eyes to try to remember the smell of her perfume. He missed her so much. It was hard to think about her, the ache was almost unbearable.

The chained door to his memories never stayed locked. He thought about her all the time. What happened to his brothers and sisters? What were they like? What were they doing? Were they happy? The unavailable answers to these questions motivated him to re-chain the door.

His life got off on the wrong foot and was never able to recover. He was a chronic victim of bad luck, at least that was his way of looking at it.

Fatalist believed that surrendering to bad luck led to depression, so he decided to stay angry. This way he could keep up with life's responsibilities. He did not have expectations of anything good, because hoping in that was a dangerous thing. Hope killed his father. Hope forced his mom to send him away.

Worker

"Why do I always get stuck with the night shift?" Worker asked the owl on the tree limb above her. She hated cleaning up area number five, which was the entire grass area in front of the town mirror. "I should get the most frequented place in town award."

The most populated place always meant the most cluttered with trash. "You and I both know they assign me this area because I do the best job and I never complain to their faces," Worker continued to explain her plight to the owl. She shared her circumstances to anyone who would listen. For Worker, the only available ears to listen on this shift were the on-looking animal species assigned to her territory. "Too bad people during the day never ask your opinion. You would tell them, right wise Mr. Owl?"

Worker was a parks and recreation employee.

"I am not a park ranger; I am just a glorified trash picker-upper. I hate my job. Correction: I hate my life."

As one of the most industrious employees in the department, she was given the hardest assignments. They kept her on clean-up duty longer than the usual rotation because she was good at cleaning up. Worker was an employer's fiscal dream.

47

The spray of discarded trash spewed all over the grass. It was a word picture for Worker's heart. It depicted the faultiness of the human condition, wherever people stood, they dumped their trash without regard for anyone else.

"Me, me, me, me, me..." Worker chanted as she picked up piece by piece the discards of the day. She was so tired of people. She recited tonight's lecture series on the 'inhumanity of humanity' to Mr. Owl, her only enrolled student.

"You see, human beings only think about themselves. This trash is evidence of this theory." Listening to her own words caused a cold chill to run up her back.

"They? Girlfriend, at what point did you leave the human race?"

"What do you think Mr. Owl: could I be adopted into the owl family?" Worker giggled and shook her head in disgust.

"Girlfriend, you need to get out of this town."

Since living in Self Absorption, Worker had grown more disillusioned. She did not hold Self Absorption completely responsible; it started way before she arrived here.

She grew up in a big city some distance away. They lived in a nice big home, with lots of acreage. Her parents remained married today and she never remembered them arguing with each other. Her life seemed ordinary, yet there was a restlessness within.

She could never pinpoint the source of her restlessness. Everything on the surface seemed perfect. She gave up trying to understand it and instead found it was best to ignore it. So she got busy to distract herself from the undetectable noise deep inside. Worker poured herself completely into everything she did. As long as she kept busy, she could pretend to have peace of mind.

Once she graduated from high school, she was filled with expectations and excitement. She could embark on dreams of greatness.

The day after graduation she loaded up her old beloved car, packed with all her dreams and headed out. Worker loved that car. She named it "Mini Me." Like her, it was nineteen years old too.

Its faded red paint looked more like pink nowadays. There were two missile sights on top of the engine hood. She felt protected inside that car. Mini Me looked like a tattered soldier. Together they were about to embark on a wonderful adventure.

As she drove away, she held tightly to the day she would return. The day she would come back to finally receive her parent's approval. Once she achieved fame and greatness and the world gave her its approval, her family would be certain to follow.

She was not afraid of hard work. Whenever Worker put her mind to something, she performed it with one hundred percent commitment.

"On this journey, hard work and good fortune are certain to collide." She announced to Squeak. Squeak was her small stuffed bird hanging just above her dashboard from the mirror. As her parents' driveway grew smaller in the rear-view mirror, her hopes for her future grew larger.

As fate can go, on the way to the university, Mini Me broke down. Its engine died just outside the town of Self Absorption.

Mini me was very sick. The mechanic mumbled it needed a new head gasket. "Miss, you would be better off just buying a new car." The grave reality of this situation brought a lump to her throat.

"I don't have the money for a new car, I am a college student, and actually I am not even officially a college student, because I have not even arrived at college yet. How can this be happening? This isn't the way to start out in the fulfillment of my dreams."

Worker called home that afternoon after being on the road only two days. This phone call ushered in the reality that there would be major changes to her plans.

"Hi Mom, Mini Me broke down on the way to school. I was wondering if you could wire me some money to fix it. I promise I will pay you back."

"Oh honey, that just isn't possible. Before you left, we contracted with landscapers and some interior designers to renovate your old room. We are also adding a veranda and a new hot tub to the back yard. All of our cash has been committed to that. You are on your own now dear, I am sure you will find a way."

A fog of unbelief rolled in. How could this be happening? "Mom I have only been gone for two days. You sure didn't waste any time!"

"Sorry honey but your father and I are looking forward to this new chapter in our life too."

She hung up the phone feeling very angry and alone. As her anger stewed, she held onto the phone long after she hung up. She was afraid to let go, but knew she couldn't keep holding it forever. With the butterfly convention convening in her stomach, she let go of the phone and turned toward a new plan.

"Okay then, just deal with it. You will get a job to pay for the head gasket and then start college next semester. This would be a slight delay, but not a cancellation." She coached herself through.

That was eight years ago. She watched herself outside her body picking up trash. The money for the head gasket came and went. There was always some crisis, which required her immediate attention. Leaving Self Absorption was always just an arm reach away, but she never grabbed hold of it. Her dreams for greatness gathered dust. It really wasn't greatness she sought anyway, it was acceptance.

A reoccurring image haunted Worker in both her daydreams and sleep. It was always the same picture. She walked through town with a phone receiver stuck on her hand. She entered the bank and when the teller would hand her cash she couldn't take it because the phone receiver was attached to her hand. She would wake up in terror, all sweaty.

She had come to accept that going to college was unattainable now, or maybe she was just too afraid to try after all this time, knowing all the things that go wrong when you try.

She stopped fighting against the thought that she would never amount to anything. She was tired. There was more evidence to prove that it was more true than false. What Worker did not realize was she was listening to an enemy. This enemy prowled around reinforcing thoughts of failure and despair. It was an enemy she did not know, an enemy she could not see.

She continued with her lecture to Mr. Owl. "Mr. Owl, when the seas of life host rough waters, and capsize your dreams, your soul can get very seasick. You just gotta stay ahead of the dark clouds of despair. Staying busy is the key. You gotta keep moving especially when you feel the storm nipping at your heels, because otherwise it will overtake you."

Worker felt the storm's chase in an ominous black cloud of oppression. Upon arrival, it would swallow her completely and disappear from everyone's radar. This sense of impending doom brought great unrest.

Lonely and tired, Worker was too prideful to admit it. She feared people would see just how desperate she wanted to be loved. She stayed busy so no one could see. Convinced if anyone found out, it would ruin any chance she had to find love, for no one would want to love someone that desperate.

Under the dim light of the moon, she was picking up the discarded trash pieces of the day. She gave each item a pep talk, as it lay abandoned and purposeless on the grass: "You served your purpose well today little hot dog wrapper." Worker continued. "When someone needed you, you were faithful. He held you up to his mouth, counting on your protection from the stains catsup and mustard can cause, and you were successful, your mission completed. You are a fearless warrior."

"I am so sorry that after his last bite, he threw you down like meaningless garbage. I want you to know Little Wrapper; you are an MVP in my book."

Worker realized she was empathizing with a hot dog wrapper and became disquieted. Though she realized how crazy she sounded, she identified closely with that hot dog wrapper. "Mr. Owl, I have to get out of this town soon, before I lose it completely. I hope it isn't too late already."

Worker was completely unaware that the One who loved her with an everlasting love was listening. He had fashioned a love story just for her and the journey's tale was just hours away.

Tuck

At the moment when very late at night eclipses into early morning, a young girl wrapped in overalls and a moonlit long sleeve shirt, made her way down the empty sidewalk. The night air was crisp, the stars brilliant and the owls were quiet. It was the time when the air is warmer just before the predawn chill. Silence deafened the streets. No one was stirring. No one but Tuck.

Tuck was a frequent traveler this time of night. The moonlight shined on her short brown hair and always faithfully escorted her to Guardian's house, her best friend in the whole world. She was wearing her faded blue overalls equipped with the well-worn pocket reserved for Dreams. Dreams was her faithful traveling companion everywhere. He was a gift from Guardian; Dreams was a stuffed guard dog.

Guardian wanted someone to look after Tuck when he could not be there. His eyes could not be in every place despite how deeply his heart wanted to be. He wished he could protect Tuck from ever being hurt again.

As Tuck walked, she searched the ground hoping to find special treasures, some priceless item abandoned by another. She stored her discoveries in the bib of her overalls. Once she returned home, she transferred them into her special cigar box decorated with magazine pictures, securely hidden under her mattress.

Tonight had been a typical one, nightmare after nightmare once she fell asleep. Tuck was always haunted by bad dreams. Nightly she wrestled against undefeatable monsters of the dark. That is what happens when you are in charge of your own safety before you are eight years old.

All the "what if" troubles that she feared could happen haunted her when she slept. When you are eight, everyone is bigger than you. Tuck didn't just feel small in stature, she felt small in value. She tried to stay awake as long as she could, in dread of what awaited her when she fell asleep. Whispers of the worst-case scenarios accompanied every thought, and her dreams gave play- by- plays to whatever came to her mind.

As she walked, the moonlight exposed dark silhouettes lurking in the shadows. Tuck closed her eyes and made a wish that all the darkness would just go away. The only peace found would come when she arrived at Guardian's house. His house was a fortress, she felt safe inside.

A heavy sigh came over her heart as she flashed back on last year's Christmas party at the country club. She had felt so misunderstood. Adults came up to her all night long to offer her encouragement. They could see her sad, blue eyes, and would comment, "Childhood is the best time of your life darling. You should smile more, dear." Tuck gave them a token smile but only to send them away so she could breathe again. If the cliché was true, her future looked very grim. Already in her short eight and half years, Tuck found herself wondering if she would make it through another year.

"Guardian!" Her mind refocused. She would be safe under his cover.

Guardian

Guardian was eight years older than Tuck. Tuck was the little sister he never had. From the first time Tuck saw Guardian at recess in the schoolyard, she knew he was a gift straight from heaven. For Tuck, recess was the most dangerous time of the day.

Classroom gladiators competed for reign and the playground was their arena. Kids competed for the title "King of the Playground". Whoever became King held the power over all the other kids.

If the yard duty workers ever knew the true extent as to what was going on, they never would have allowed it. They didn't know, because adults were always so clueless.

For the gladiators with aspirations, Tuck was their perfect patsy. She was the shortest in class. They always wrangled the kids from the playground lining them up shortest to tallest. Every year she stood at the front of the line.

Nurses explained once to her teacher that she had a medical condition described as a "failure to thrive." It was strange how such a small, tiny body carried such giant size fears. Her fears imprisoned her making her a loner.

To the ambitious kid seeking the throne, Tuck was easy prey. They only needed to threaten her once before she would hand over her lunch to them. They would stick out their hand to her and without a word, she would place her lunch in their hands.

The recess time she first met Guardian, started out like any other... The gladiator for that morning, Michael Insecure, had just thrown her to the ground. She learned long ago, removing herself mentally from these incidents was the best way to endure them. She would leave herself and watch the whole incident as if a second party witness. Kids always encircled these events, gathering around as they formed a spontaneous arena. Michael dragged Tuck around the blacktop, holding her right arm in both his hands. Her wrist burned and she feared her hand might come completely off. She focused on a faraway place to make the pain go away.

Then, out of nowhere, Guardian stepped forward from the crowd. He was so much taller than every one else. He looked like King Kong. He stepped up to Michael from behind. Michael never saw him coming. He grabbed him and threw him to the ground. Guardian took hold of Michael's right arm with both of his and started to drag him across the pavement just as he had done with Tuck.

Guardian kept repeating, "So tough guy how does this feel?" The recess workers stood shocked. No one moved to stop him. They were glad Guardian stepped in to intervene, because they never would. They hid behind rationalizing that they were teaching the kids how to deal with conflict.

Tuck watched as this knight in brand new black Converse tennis shoes came forth to defend her honor. It was over as quickly as it started. The gladiator was reduced to tears and screamed for mercy. Guardian pressed for a moment but then stopped fearing if he continued he would earn himself a suspension.

He left Michael Insecure lying on the asphalt crying and walked over and extended his hand to Tuck. "Let me give you hand. Are you okay?"

Their friendship began that day. He remained her hero ever since. Whenever someone asked Guardian where he was from, Tuck always answered for him. "Heaven, he is from heaven."

Guardian knew what it was like to start out with rough beginnings. He never spoke about his own beginnings, because his pain found their own hiding places. He found being a crusader was a productive way to avoid his own pain. When he came to the rescue for underdogs in life, he felt vindicated and valued.

His junior high school student aid position at the elementary school had been a fruitful environment for him to play this role. His long-term hope was to become a teacher; to help kids, especially the ones no one else gave a chance.

The adults supervising recess were moved by Guardian's compassion. They overlooked the lines he crossed and never reported him to the principal. They knew reporting him would unveil their lack of response so they chose to sweep the whole thing under the rug. They extended him the grace they themselves needed.

Guardian had heard rumors about this girl's parents. Apparently, her mother and father kept handing her off for others to raise her. Nannies were hired for her full time care.

Miss Julie was the one who stayed the longest. Tuck loved Miss Julie because she knew Miss Julie loved her. She cared for her full time right from the beginning. She did the bottle feedings as a baby, diaper changes, and baths. She read stories and tucked her in before she went to sleep. She was the one Tuck ran to when she would have a bad dream. Tuck felt safe in her arms. Miss Julie was the perfect 'mom.'

Miss Julie was a nurturer by nature; and took to caring for Tuck with ease. After a short amount of time, Tuck's parents gave her full reign in making decisions for Tuck's care. She was under strict instructions not to bother Tuck's parents with trivial concerns. They only needed to be informed in case of an emergency. Miss Julie was actively pursuing citizenship for the Land of the Free. She took night classes that helped her learn the history needed to pass the test.

Tuck was quick to call her 'Mom,' but Miss Julie alerted Tuck that it would be best if she didn't do it in the company of her biological mother and father. Miss Julie was very vigilant about protecting Tuck from all the worldly influences her parents brought home.

Her parents' passion was to be accepted into the elite society circle. It was their longing for this dream that kept them from getting it. They gave up everything to pursue this. Their desperateness made them undesirable. They were allowed on the fringe, because they were useful and threw great parties. They were blinded to the fact they were never going to receive a welcome invitation into this circle of influence.

A rumor began to circulate that Miss Julie was really Tuck's biological mother. Attached to this rumor was that Tuck's dad was indeed the father. When Tuck's mom heard this whispered at a party they were hosting, she became enraged and demanded that her husband send 'that woman' away.

To avoid social humiliation and innuendo, he complied to his wife's wishes. He called immigration and notified them Miss Julie was no longer in their employ.

The next day a big green van screeched into the driveway and took her away. Tuck never saw Miss Julie again. At age six, Tuck lost the only mother she had ever known. Though her mom tried to explain to her that Miss Julie had decided to return to her homeland, Tuck knew it was a lie, because Miss Julie would have said goodbye.

From then on, Tuck distrusted what adults said. She did not believe they told the truth. She was always worried about what else might jump out and steal away her safety. To be ready, Tuck became fearful of everything.

After Miss Julie, there were many different caretakers but none of them lasted longer than six months at a time. Their exits didn't matter to Tuck, because she never let them enter her heart in the first place. That place belonged to one person forever. It belonged to Miss Julie. That was until Guardian showed up.

Guardian never minded that Tuck would seek respite at his house in the middle of the night. He was glad to provide Tuck a safety net, a place of refuge. He was in high school now and was becoming a man real soon. It was a man's job to protect the weak and vulnerable. It also helped keep away his own dragons sleeping just below the surface of his heart.

Guardian placed a stick in his window so Tuck could open it easily and climb right in. In his closet, he prepared a shelter for her, which was ready for any impromptu visit. There, she had her own little base camp complete with a sleeping bag rolled out, a fluffed pillow and an extra little blanket laid out for her stuffed dog, Dreams.

Sometimes, in a half state of sleep, Guardian heard her arrive. Tuck would crawl into her sleeping bag and if he awakened, they talked - she from the closet and Guardian from his bed. Other times she was so quiet when she entered he slept right through.

Whatever the scenario, when Guardian was nearby, she always slept more peacefully. Guardian could not see or hear the battles she endured, but he knew when he looked into her eyes it was a horrible war. It felt safe to Tuck to know someone saw her; that she was seen.

Tuck's parents never raised concerns about her staying over at his house. She knew the reason. They did not care. Guardian still insisted Tuck get their permission, so she did. They were happy for anyone offering to watch Tuck. They welcomed it without question. Typically, a concerned parent would have objections about a high school boy watching an elementary school girl, but they weren't concerned in the slightest.

Fortunately, Guardian had only honorable intentions, so Tuck's safety was not in question. Guardian himself thought it strange that her parents gave her permission, but he was glad they did.

The only time they showed interest in Tuck's where-abouts was when they picked her up from school, which was a rare occurrence. They wanted her exact location and time so they wouldn't have to park to find her. They were always "on their way" to some important engagement. There were many important people to spend time with, but Tuck was not one of them.

She adapted to it; she just grew up without them. Guardian had earned a special mentoring place in Tuck's heart. A place only Miss Julie had held before.

Tuck understood Guardian. He could be gruff on the outside; many people interpreted it as rudeness, but Tuck understood. His 'guard dog bark' was really his compassion. Tuck saw deeper than the gruff exterior, she saw right to his sensitive heart.

He was a boy who understood heartbreak personally and found his refuge in trying to prevent harm from coming to others. Guardian needed to be a protector and Tuck was happy to oblige.

He never talked about himself, but that didn't bother her. She was no big fan of words herself. More often than not, they were just tools for people to lie to each other. She trusted Guardian, trusted him on the inside.

During the daylight hours, he tried to protect her from whatever dangers came her way, but at night, he was useless. Each night he prayed for someone to come and teach him how he could help. "How do you help someone fight against monsters that aren't physically there?" He still waits for wisdom to come as hopeless as it seemed.

This night, Tuck lifted up Guardian's window and quietly made her way inside. He was sound asleep. She made a little noise hoping he might wake up. She loved their late night talks, but she did not want to wake him intentionally. He was sleeping deeply tonight; his breathing was louder than usual. She would let him be.

She crawled inside the sleeping bag nestled inside the closet, her storm shelter. She scooted down to the bottom of the bag and tried to match the same deep breaths she heard from across the room. Her breath sprayed warmth inside the bag. Before her feet defrosted, she was asleep. Two rhythmic breaths, harmonized in sleep.

Little did they know, Tuck was just the first visitor this room would host tonight.

Invitations Delivered

Letter #1 - Little Bin's Invitation Delivered

The angelic messengers arrived at the first recipient's home. They entered through the side door of the garage. Silently approaching a trashcan, Mentor pulled from his robe pocket a scarlet cord and attached it to an envelope with the name 'Little Bin' written in red on the outside of the envelope.

The back of the envelope was sealed closed by the blood of the Lamb. Mentor started to loop it loosely through the lid's handle, when Student asked, "Shouldn't we just leave it in his bedroom?"

"Our Lord's grace meets people where they are, <u>not</u> where they are suppose to be." Student nodded, wondering to himself if he would ever know as much as his mentor.

"Imagine what it will be like for this young lad when he discovers that the Lord Himself knows exactly where he is, even where he sleeps."

"Praise the Lord from whom all blessings flow." Mentor praised.

"Praise the Lord indeed." Student followed.

Letter #2 - Fatalist's Invitation Delivered

The angels arrived outside of residence number two. They stepped into the second story apartment through an unopened window. The sparsely decorated apartment had bachelor pad written all over it. There were poster-sized maps displayed like pictures throughout every room.

"Mentor, this guy has maps on the wall where you usually see family photos."

Mentor pointed to the glass globe, which held the place of prominence on the coffee table. The globe lit up on the inside. Fatalist loved to sit on his couch and look at his globe. It helped his family feel closer, not so far away.

As they approached the bedroom, a deep breathing roar greeted them. Their wings fluttered from the easterly wind coming from the figure laying lifeless on the bed. They both started to giggle, but regained composure. They deduced that his neighbors must wear earplugs to ward off the jet engine noise of his snore. Student placed the letter on top of Fatalist's alarm clock. This was practical; he would see it first thing.

As they turned to leave, a beam of moonlight pierced through the partially opened curtain in the living room. The moon ray shone brightly onto the globe on the coffee table. The angels recognized this as divine instruction. Student went back into the bedroom and retrieved the envelope from the nightstand. The light beam held an exact position for placement. They smiled in awe as they realized where their Lord wanted the invitation placed.

Written in indelible ink on the globe was the word, "HOME," on top of the land of his birthplace. This was the perfect place for Fatalist to find his invitation. They praised the Lord.

Mentor looked at Student. "This man will soon discover a home he does not yet know he has. A home the Pursuer of Souls prepared for him. He has felt like an alien since he was thirteen years old.

He is an alien of this world by design, but before the foundations of the world, he was set apart for a heavenly home. He will soon learn being an alien in this world means he is a citizen of heaven."

They exited quickly for there was plenty of work yet to do that evening.

Letter #3 - Counselor's Invitation Delivered

Counselor's reading glasses straddled her sleeping face. The rims laid diagonally across her cheeks, offering vision to her upper lip. With her every breath, the eyeglasses fogged up and then dissipated as quickly as it came.

The most noticeable thing to Student was how orderly everything appeared. Everything had a place. Her living room looked more like a library. She owned many books. One entire wall floor to ceiling was a bookshelf filled to the brim. Every possible space was taken. The books stood shortest to tallest across each shelf. Nothing looked cluttered. Order ruled this home.

When they entered the bedroom, Student was touched as he watched her sleep. "She looks weary even when she is sleeping." Mentor nodded in agreement. He was pleased that his protégé exhibited compassion.

"Yes Student, the spiritual battle these humans fight is exhausting. Though she wants truth to be her foundation, she has not yet met Truth Himself, so she battles all on her own. That is why we are here tonight Student. This invitation will introduce her to whom the battle really belongs; the Pursuer of her Soul."

They placed the envelope on her lamp at her bedside table. The Lord weaves every detail together. He is the Creator of every stitch.

Letter #4 - Worker's Invitation Delivered

As they entered through the outside wall of her bedroom, Worker was tossing and turning as she slept. Their entrance into her room seemed to calm her disquieted soul.

She was dreaming about the hot dog wrapper discarded on the park's grass earlier that evening. In her dream, she viewed everything from the perspective of the hot dog wrapper. A hand held her up in its palm. Mustard squirted in her eye and it stung. The hand lifted her toward the mouth, which looked gigantic in size.

In slow motion, she came closer and closer toward the coffee stained teeth. She got close enough to reach out and touch the taste buds on the tongue. As the mouth opened wide preparing to ingest her, she screamed in her sleep and violently turned over on to her other side.

"Where shall we place it?" Student asked holding up the envelope in his hand. "Oh I know, the bathroom mirror, yes that is perfect. The Pursuer of Souls will invite her to come meet His faithful love right when she looks into the mirror to start her day.

"Come as you are, is something this wounded heart needs to learn."

Mentor smiled proudly at his protégé. "Well done Student, well done." Student beamed realizing he had made

Mentor proud. "Their Pursuer met them in the places of greatest need."

The hot dog dream began to replay again. Mentor gently pressed his hand on top her forehead and whispered, "Peace to you, dear one. You will never be discarded by the Pursuer of Souls."

Hearing these words in her mind, her countenance changed. A slight smile creased across her face and a peace settled upon her. When Mentor and Student exited, that peace remained.

Letter #5 - Pleaser's Invitation delivered.

It was difficult to locate Pleaser when they first entered her room. At first glance, they thought she was in bed, but then a giant Labrador retriever rolled over from under the sheets and startled them both. That was when it was revealed that the lump under the covers was not Pleaser.

"Where is she?" Student asked.

They scanned the room but could find no trace of her anywhere. Student backed up to try to gain wider view of the room and discovered her on the floor half way tucked under the bed. She was sound asleep.

The blanket hanging over from the bed was drooped across her, and there was a pillow scrunched between her knees. Her head was propped up by clothes, which she had piled up as a makeshift pillow.

Pleaser and Impressions battled during the night for the prime piece of real estate: the bed. She could not bring herself to demand the bed, even if he was just a dog. She did not want to make Impressions mad. When he got mad, he ran away. Sleeping on the floor was her solution. The path of least resistance had always been the choice for Pleaser.

The angels nodded to each other in disbelief and with some pity. They contemplated where to place her invitation.

They looked around and then Mentor announced it. "I know just the place." Mentor reached into his white robed pocket and pulled out a thin piece of string and he pressed it against the envelope and hung it from the doorframe of her bedroom. It hung about eye level. She would be sure to find it.

"Our job is finished here. We have one more stop to deliver these last two letters."

Letters #6 & 7 Guardian and Tuck's Invitations Delivered

The angels entered through the locked front door and walked up the stairs into Guardian's room. They first made sure they were both fast asleep. The rhythmic inhales confirmed they were sleeping nicely. Mentor took both letters, laid Guardian's envelope on his chest as he slept. Guardian never moved when he slept, he slept like a rock. Mentor then laid Tuck's letter on top of Guardian's night table.

Mentor whispered into Guardian's ear, "Give Tuck's envelope to her directly. Do not open her letter or read it yourself. It belongs to Tuck."

Mentor stood back up and looked over at Student and smiled. "Our night's mission is completed." In a twinkling of an eye, they disappeared from Guardian's room and returned to heaven.

Surrounded again by the unrestrained Majestic Glory of the Lord delighted their hearts. They always returned from these missions with a richer appreciation for the holiness of heaven.

"It is good to be home." Student smiled.

"Amen," said Mentor. "Amen."

Invitations Received

Worker Awakens To Receive Her Invitation

A baritone voice screamed into the silent morning air, "This is Radio Station K-Labor 100.2. Good morning, brothers and sisters united in the endless pursuit of labor! Rise and shine; the sun is almost up; you must not be late. Arise to meet this day and all the labor that awaits you."

Worker sat straight up in bed, wide-awake. She turned the alarm off quickly, to silence the booming voice, harshly summoning her to the day.

As her senses came into focus, she had a strange sensation that someone had been in her room. With military precision, she scanned the room. Was there an intruder lingering in a corner? Her visual search gave an 'all clear.' A thought came to her mind. "You will never be discarded by the Pursuer of Souls."

"Pursuer of Souls?" she growled. She picked up her bear, Freckles, from her pillow, and started to converse with him. "Well Freckles, if someone was pursuing me, they failed to mention it to me.

"Are you my Pursuer, little guy? No but you are my faithful friend aren't you?"

She put him back on her pillow and stumbled out of bed. With one movement of her arm, she flung her comforter up and her bed was made. She did not worry about the bulge from the sheets still bunched underneath. What she cannot see, cannot hurt her. She could hear her ankles click all the way to the bathroom sink.

She always cringed when she looked into the bathroom mirror. It revealed a tired, sad, disheveled face. She tried to avoid looking into it as long as possible. She lowered her head and splashed water on her face. She continued her conversation with Freckles.

"Freckles, I ask you who in their right mind would pursue someone who looked like this.

"What is this?" Curiosity overrode her fear as an envelope hung from her bathroom mirror. She studied the lettering detail on the outside of the envelope. It was impressive.

There was something very royal about the envelope. "Freckles did you see who put this here?" Freckles looked back with the same fixed expression.

She finally took the envelope off the mirror and opened it by tearing it away from the red seal. Inside was an invitation. It was written with gold letters:

My Precious hard Worker;

I have heard your heart and seen your despair. I have a new assignment fashioned just for you. Do not worry about the details; I want you to cast all your cares upon Me. Come to Me at Lake Still Water. You must leave today. I have prepared a table for you. Come by walking. I will lead and guide you along the way. You will soon learn how deeply you are loved. You are valuable to Me. I will never discard you. Come just as you are. I will see you soon.

Eternally,
I AM, the Pursuer of your Soul.

Worker did not know what to make of this invitation. Dream collided with reality.

"I cannot possibly go today. I have to go to work." She glanced over at Freckles and saw disgust on his face.

"You are right, what am I insane? I was just telling Mr. Owl last night that I needed to get out of this town soon. This might be my only opportunity before it is too late.

"Who is this Pursuer of Souls? How did this get on my mirror? Is he some kind of stalker of something? I could be walking into the hands of a serial killer or something."

Her heart was pumping fast. Though afraid, she felt alive. Alive for the first time in a very long time. "Oh sometimes you just have to throw caution to the wind. I am so ready for a change. Let's face it girl, if you stay in this town much longer you will end up in a home where they keep people who carry on conversations with hot dog wrappers.

"Hey, and the good news is that this time, I am supposed to walk so at least my car won't break down." She chuckled out loud. She enjoyed a good irony.

"What do you suppose it means that he has 'prepared a table for me'?" Looking over at Freckles, she looked for his approval.

"Well it's not like I have any competing offers. What will it hurt? Last night I was empathizing with pieces of trash. I am losing my grip. Ok I will go. I have a window of opportunity right now, I am not going to let a another opportunity pass me by. This invitation is too irresistible to turn down."

Worker began to pack a small backpack. She stood in front of her closet and labored over the proper outfit to wear to meet the Pursuer of Souls. She was really wrestling over the plethora of choices, when a small still voice whispered to her heart. *"Just come as you are."*

Worker felt anxious coming just as she was; being herself never impressed anyone before. She was worried the Pursuer of her Soul, might change His mind. She enjoyed the possibility though. It had been a long time since she hoped for something good. For the first time in years, she caught herself singing in the shower!

Little Bin Finds His Invitation

Little Bin awakened by the dew alarm clock dripping irregularly on his nose. He was always slow to wake up, but once he crawled out from his safe harbor, he was fully charged with energy.

Little Bin sat inside and opened both eyes. Pretending to be a cannonball, he burst from the trash bin with great force. In his launch with perfect precision, he swung his feet over the side of the can and landed in a perfect dismount!

To his surprise, he spotted a red cord, dangling from the lid of his can. It was fortunate the cord held the envelope securely to the lid because his cannon fire would have launched the invitation into the neighbor's yard.

Little Bin was very excited about the red cord. It reminded him of the medals they gave athletes when they won races. He put the cord around his neck using the envelope as the first place medal he received for winning the 100-yard dash.

He raised his arms over his head and imitated a crowd noise. He circled around the garage receiving accolades from millions of his fantasy fans.

The next moment, he was in Greece, inside Olympic stadium receiving the admiration of the whole world. He felt on top of the world as he circled around one more time; he savored every moment.

He didn't notice his skateboard on the garage floor and slipped on it. He fell back into a bunch of suitcases recklessly thrown to the side of the garage. The suitcases had not moved from that spot since his parents first unpacked.

They had not taken a family vacation since arriving in Self Absorption. Reality returned abruptly; Greece was gone and so were all his fans. A heavy sigh came over him as he returned to the garage. Little Bin got up to start his day, leaving the invitation around his neck. It was cool. He would leave it around his neck for all to see. He headed out the side door of the garage towards town, with his medal still unopened.

His most favorite prank was marking a mustache on the Town mirror. As he drew a mustache onto the mirror atop the specialized film, it was still seen.

The men in charge of park facilities would find it in a few hours, but meanwhile he loved to watch people's reactions as they looked into the mirror and saw themselves with a mustache. Some would even touch their face to make sure they really did not have one. This always made Little Bin laugh hard.

It was early enough so no one would catch him in the act. Most folks were just waking up.

Pleaser Receives Her Invitation

Every morning Pleaser awoke in a panic, fearing she might have slept through the alarm. She often woke up disoriented. She would forget she had moved to the floor in the middle of the night and would whack her head against the bottom of her bed frame. This morning was no exception.

"Ouch" seemed to be the first words she spoke each morning. She laid back against the floor, rubbing out the throb from her head.

This morning she lacked energy. She was so tired of herself. She just lay on her back, lifted her knees up, and began counting the pockmarks on the ceiling.

"I hate my life. If someone were watching me at this moment, there would only be one word they could use to describe me; Loser."

After a good self debasing comment, Pleaser was motivated to move to a sitting position and leaned up against the bed. "If people only knew..."

Pleaser never finished that sentence. If people would find out, it might be relief. She was so afraid of people knowing yet she thought about it every minute of everyday. It was her fault. She was responsible for her mom's death.

Impressions began to stretch out in the bed. He yawned loudly and Pleaser saw the paws stretch overhead as he began to mobilize himself.

Pleaser and Impressions had been roommates for twelve years. It was not the typical master and dog relationship. Her neighbors joked about being unclear who the master was and who the dog was. Pleaser always laughed with them, but did not really find it funny because she knew it was true.

Impressions ran away often. Pleaser was always so happy that he returned she never reprimanded him but rather lavished him with many dog treats. She would apologize to him for days, taking full blame for the reasons he ran away.

Everything was always Pleaser's fault. She made a vow never to make people angry again. So consequently, even Impressions could be in charge in their relationship. He was easily enticed to adventures outside the home, especially when he knew that upon his return, his life would get even better.

This just added to Pleaser's sense of worthlessness. She couldn't even satisfy a dog in her way of looking at things. She worked harder than anyone to be pleasing; she always managed to fail miserably. The harder she tried, the more she failed.

With a spirit of heaviness, she pulled herself up off the floor and started to shuffle into the kitchen for a cup of tea. There hanging from the doorway, was an envelope with gold lettering and a red seal on the back. "This was not here last night." She looked around to see if there were any other changes in her dwelling. "How did this get here?"

"Some guard dog you are Impressions." She looked over at the bed where Impressions had sprawled out on his back, with his legs up in the air.

This envelope intrigued her. Why was it hanging from the doorway? She immediately flashed on the doorway into her mom's bedroom that day she walked in. If only she had stopped and not gone in. She had a hard time stepping through doorways sometimes. There was a fear of what she might find on the other side.

"Is it some kind of cruel joke?" She read her name on the envelope twelve times to reassure herself that she was really the intended person.

The suspense was killing her, so she cautiously opened up the envelope and read the letter inside:

Dear child whom I love;

To the one who works so hard to find love, I AM calling you to receive Mine.

Your pursuit of love and value has been in all the wrong places. Do not seek after ones who cannot satisfy you. I AM a fountain that never runs dry. I will completely fill your parched and thirsty cup. I know your dreams and your unspoken cries. I know your thoughts in the dark nights of your soul. I have been watching over you and it is time we meet. Come to Lake Still Water. Leave today. You are to walk. I will teach you all that you need to learn. So come. Come now. Come quickly.

Eternally,
I AM, the Pursuer of your Soul.

This letter sounded wonderful but it felt so scary. "What a wonderful thought. Someone actually watches over me?"

She looked all around half expecting to find a camera device of someone watching her. A cold chill ran down her neck as she thought about this Pursuer. What if this Pursuer knew the truth about her? How could He love her knowing who she really was? He must hate her.

"But, if He hated me, why would He invite me?" She reread it a couple of times. It seemed to have been written by someone who knew her. Every word in the letter touched deep into her heart, where words could not normally reach. She was parched and dry. Was this too good to be true?

"Could there really be someone pursuing after me? He chose to hang it from the bedroom doorway. Was this some kind of accident? Accident or not, I am going."

She was tired of feeling worthless. It was worth the risk. "Yes. I will come. I am coming. Wait for me." She spoke to air as if she knew the One who sent it was watching her. She quickly packed and ran out the door. She was running so she wouldn't change her mind. She got to the end of the driveway and abruptly stopped. She dropped her pack to the ground.

"I cannot go, what about Impressions? What will he think?" She walked back inside, wrestling with how she was going to need to convince him to go. He never listened to anything she asked him to do. She wanted to go on this trip more than anything. An inner strength surged from inside her.

"I am going to go whether Impressions likes it or not." She grabbed Impressions dog dish and water bowl and whistled for him. He did not notice her placing his bowl and water dish on the front porch. He thought today was going to be like every other day. Impressions had not known about the Pursuer of Souls. When He entered the scene, things changed.

Impressions heard the call to "Come" but chose to go in the opposite direction.

Pleaser didn't hesitate. She took the big bag of dog food and carried it over to her neighbor's porch. Her neighbor had already left for work, so she left a note on the food at the front door.

The note on the bag read; "Hi. Would you please feed Impressions for me? I am leaving on a trip and I do not know when I will be back. Impressions will not miss me. He spends more time away than at home anyway. I appreciate it. Thanks Pleaser."

Pleaser picked up her backpack in the driveway and began to walk down the street. Fearful her new enthusiasm would disappear any minute, she broke into a run. She kept telling herself, "Whatever you do, don't look back." Pleaser did not look back nor did she stop running until she exited the town of Self Absorption.

As she left Self Absorption behind, she reflected about pleasing people. For most people it was a sign of popularity but for her, it was a heavy weight of bondage. People's opinions had incarcerated her long enough. Today was liberation day.

"This captive is free." She screamed in jubilation but then looked around hopeful no one saw her. "What might they think?"

Impressions had not noticed Pleaser left. He was in hot pursuit of a rabbit. His mind wandered to the special treat that would be waiting for him when he returned home. Maybe if he came home later than usual, she would try to win his favor with some ice cream. Rocky Road was his favorite.

Fatalist Receives His Invitation.

Each morning Fatalist awakened and while still half – asleep, bumper balled his way to the kitchen, bouncing off the furniture in his room to redirect him toward the kitchen door. He poured from his auto-brewed pitcher a fresh cup of coffee into his big mug.

Coffee was one of the few pleasures he enjoyed. The smell of fresh brewed coffee reminded him of the breakfasts his mom used to make.

Back in the day, his mom would have coffee ready for his father when he first woke up. She would greet him with it in the bathroom as he shaved.

He remembered with fondness how his father used to sip it so noisily, it woke up the rest of the family. Their family didn't need an alarm clock. The volume of his sips expressed his great enjoyment of the taste. He would chap his lips together and give a big "ahhh." It always made his mom giggle.

No one made his mom giggle like his dad. But he never saw her laugh again after his death. She might as well have been shot that day too. Everything precious to Fatalist was lost that day as well. He and his mom both died with his dad that day.

While he was still inhaling his first cup, Fatalist walked back into the bedroom to change and get ready for his day. Once dressed, he plopped himself onto the couch and picked up the current biography he was reading.

He enjoyed reading true accounts of people's lives. He never chose to read about famous people. He enjoyed the stories about the insignificant people who did extraordinary things, the stories that recorded the unsung heroes.

This was Fatalist's secret way to hold on to hope. A thin strand though it was, it was hope nonetheless. He would daydream how he too might have an opportunity to do an extraordinary thing.

As he turned the page, out of the corner of his eye he noticed an envelope dangling from the globe. "How did this get here?"

Fear seized him. He heard about all those conspiracy theories. He believed they were true. Could this envelope be some conspiracy plot against him? He attempted to pull it from the globe, but the stickiness of the tape had a strong grip.

He moved closer to the envelope and stood up to gain leverage. This is when he noticed it was stuck where he had written the word "HOME" on his geographic birthplace.

This could not be an accident. This was intentional.

Did someone from his native country find him and now was leaving threatening letters? Maybe they kidnapped his family and they wanted money. Initially he was too afraid to open it. He just laid it across his lap and stared at it.

He weighed out all the pros and cons to opening the letter but the 'not knowing' gnawed at him. He could not stand it any longer and tore it open. It read:

Dear precious son;

I have watched your suffering and loneliness in this life. My heart breaks with you. You are right, there is more to this life than what your eyes can see. Do not deny your heart. Learn to listen to its cry. I have been using your heart's ache to draw you to Me. Come meet me at Lake Still Water.

I know you feel like an alien in this town but I will show you where your "home" really is - where you really, truly belong. You are to leave today and come on foot. In your first pilgrimage when you were thirteen, you came alone. This time I will bring others to your side. I will answer your questions. I will give meaning to your doubts; you will learn what holds true value and substance. So come now and come quickly.

I AM, the Pursuer of your Soul

Fatalist was speechless. The words to this letter lit up dark places in his heart. This invitation's words reached in deep enough to penetrate his feelings. Feelings he had locked away for a very long time.

This Pursuer not only spoke of the deadness inside his soul, but also managed to reignite a life. There were no words to explain it, but something indefinable was going on inside his heart.

It bewildered him how this strange letter caused him to feel excited more than scared. Even the possibility that there was someone who might understand him was comforting. He had been on his own for so long. "How could He know?"

This letter turned on a faucet of fresh water landing upon his calloused and crusty heart. He felt life percolating inside of him. "I think I am feeling excited."

This took him back to the dock when he first arrived on the shores of the Land of the Free. His eyes looked upon each sign that day with a great hope. He learned quickly that hope they boasted was just a gimmick, a false fabrication.

This invitation seemed different. This was personal. He never trusted promises. Promises always left people derailed on the side of a road. He couldn't remember a time he hoped in anything but himself. This time he couldn't help it. Hope was released and roaming about inside of him.

"I need to get a hold of myself and approach this rationally." He tried to re-sequester the hope inside, before it could do its damage.

He coached himself, "Okay this is strange. I am going to go. Get a grip. You don't do this kind of thing. Look I am tired of this silly job anyway. I need to invest in something or I will die – I may live to an old age but I am dead inside already. I cannot stay in this town – it is stealing my soul.

What is the harm in checking it out? I am merely investigating, I am not going to be excited or believe any of this. I am just checking it out."

His security guard uniform was already on.

"I am not going to wear this for this journey, that is for sure. Oh what a shame, I loved this uniform so much." Fatalist, cynically mocking it, rolled it into a tight ball and threw it into his hamper.

He redressed in civilian clothes putting on his most comfortable pair of tennis shoes. He was ready for his journey. His feet already started to throb as he contemplated the long walk to Lake Still Water.

He called work to tell them he would be out indefinitely, he took one final peruse of his home and then remembered his wallet. He pulled out his wallet from his back pocket. He opened it up and fingered through it until he pulled out a tattered old black and white picture.

He held up the last and only picture he had of his family to the light. It was taken when he was eleven years old and his youngest sister had just been born.

"I just wanted to make sure you were making this journey with me."

He touched their faces as if to touch them. A heavy sigh joined in as he returned them to his wallet. He patted it after slipping back into his pocket as if wishing them a good journey as well.

As he locked the door to his apartment, somewhere within he knew he would never return. A new chapter in his life was beginning. He slung the backpack over his shoulder, stepped out into the sunlight, and began walking. He never once looked back.

Guardian and Tuck Receive their Invitations.

Guardian woke up quickly. He liked being the first one up, ready for whatever might happen. He thought he remembered Tuck come in last night, but he was sleeping too deeply to check.

Tuck was still sound asleep. He could tell by the curled-up lump at the bottom of the sleeping bag. Guardian sat up in bed to get his bearings when an envelope did a front flip and landed on his lap. "What is this?"

Guardian's first thought was that Tuck left him another card. Tuck was always writing him cards telling him how much she appreciated him. She was so free to express her gratitude. Guardian cherished every one of them, even more than he let on. This envelope however, was not from Tuck. "What the heck is this?"

He opened the envelope and read the letter inside:

Dear my faithful warrior;

I am so pleased to see your compassion and your willingness to lay your life down for your friend, there is no greater gift one can give another. I want you to meet the One who has laid His life down for you. I love you with an everlasting love. As you learn about Me, you will find the equipping you seek to help others, including Tuck. Leave today for Lake Still Water.

I have so much to show you. Travel on foot. You will meet others along the way. They will need your strength and you will need their willingness to wait and their ability to rest. Use discernment because some of those who converse with you along the way are pretenders. Leave today without delay.

I AM, the Pursuer of your Soul

Guardian got up and started to look in Tuck's general area for her letter. He looked everywhere in the closet and around where Tuck was sleeping but to no avail. He was burdened.

"I am not going if Tuck isn't invited." He looked up to announce it to the air.

"This will break her heart. Why wouldn't He invite her too, she has been through so much." He turned to sit back on his bed and then saw Tuck's letter on his own nightstand. Guardian sat on the bed and reflected on the fullness of all that was transpiring.

"I cannot wait one more minute. Tuck wake up." He gently shook the bottom of the sleeping bag to awaken her. He tried to calculate the right spot to shake her. As he studied the most peaceful method to awaken her, a little voice boomed from within the sleeping bag.

"Guardian is that you? I am awake." Guardian felt relieved. He hated to wake Tuck up. She was always startled.

"Come out of there Tuck, I have something very important to give you."

Tuck was excited. She raced toward the bag's opening trying to imagine what the great present was. Guardian's best present ever was her stuffed guard dog, Dreams.

Dreams comforted her every night when the nightmares came. She cuddled him so tightly sometimes she thought he had changed her nightmare back into a normal dream.

As Tuck dug furiously to get out of the bag, she was unaware she was going in the wrong direction. She moved further away from the entrance to the bag as the slinky silky lining inside worked against her. She stopped to pant, and Guardian coached her towards the bag's opening all while trying to hold back a chuckle.

"Tuck you are going the wrong way. Stop and listen to my voice, follow my voice. That's it, good, now you have it, keep coming. Ah, there you are, good morning!"

Tuck's head poked out of the sleeping bag. She looked like a gopher peaking out from its hole. Her hair filled with static electricity, was very comical in sight, and her electric smile was warming to his heart. She greeted him with a good morning too.

"So what do you have for me?" She said expectantly.

Guardian handed her the letter.

"Is this from you?" Tuck asked.

"No" said Guardian.

Hearing that it wasn't, she handed the letter back to Guardian. She treated it as if it were laced with poison. "Then I don't want it."

"I am not really sure who it is from Tuck, but it is good. I got one too."

Tuck re-took the letter and slowly started to open it.

"We have been invited to go on an adventure and I think we should go." Guardian wanted her to keep an open mind.

Tuck handed the invitation to Guardian. "Well read it for me; what does it say?" Guardian pushed the letter back into Tuck's lap. "Tuck, you need to read this letter, it is addressed to you."

Tuck reluctantly took it and read the letter inside:

My precious, precious child;

> *You have been hiding far too long in darkness. I have watched you as you hide and run from fears that seem too big to face. I want you to know you are not alone; I AM with you even right now. I AM your strong tower that you can run to and be safe. I want you to know the real safety of resting in My arms. Come meet me at Lake Still Water.*
>
> *You and Guardian can come together. I AM watching out for you. Leave today. Come quickly. I will see you soon.*

Love,
I AM, the Pursuer of your Soul

Guardian could not read what Tuck was thinking. He had always been good at knowing what she thought. "Well?" Guardian asked.

Tuck looked up at Guardian and she had tears in her eyes, "Oh Guardian are you sure this is okay? What if this is a trick to kidnap us or kill us or something?"

Guardian thought for a minute before he responded. "Tuck, go ahead and read your letter again. Does it sound like someone who wants to hurt us?"

Tuck read her letter again. She shook her head no.

"I think we should go. I promise you I will not let anyone hurt you. I want to go, but if you say no, I won't go," Guardian responded.

Tuck was very fearful. This was a big step. She had trusted people before who seemed nice and bad things always ended up happening. But she could not say no to Guardian and he wanted to go. "Guardian, if you want to go, then I will go too, but on one condition. I am going to bring Dreams with us."

"Good idea, Tuck."

Tuck hugged Guardian tightly, and he hugged her back reaffirming to her everything was going to be okay.

Guardian was excited. He worried about Tuck a great deal. Her battles were with things he could not see or understand and though he knew he was in way over his head, he could never give up on her. For the first time this Pursuer of their Soul might have the answers to help Tuck. For this reason alone, it was worth the journey.

Tuck rolled up her sleeping bag, stopping midway to stuff Dreams and her pillow inside. When she finished rolling it up and tying it in a knot, she announced she was ready. "I am ready when you are."

Guardian rolled up his blanket and pillow too. He sensed this would be a life-changing journey. He grabbed his walking stick, which always doubled as a weapon if needed. After toast and eggs filled their stomachs, they embarked together toward Lake Still Water.

Counselor Receives Her Invitation.

As Counselor rolled over to steal just a few more minutes, the reading glasses that seven hours earlier were resting on the edge of her nose were now pinching her skin under her arm. It was a rude wake up call. "Ouch!"

A frown frequently lead Counselor into the new day. She could not remember the last time she smiled. She retrieved her glasses dangling from a small piece of skin under her arm before they broke.

"These glasses sure have amazing endurance; an endurance I wish I possessed."

Morning after morning she found them under some sleeping body part and yet always managed to stay in tact. With glasses in hand, she placed her feet to the floor and lowered her head into her one hand holding nothing. It was customary in her wake up routine to psych herself up in order to get out of bed.

Out of the corner of her eye, she noticed an envelope attached to the lampshade on the nightstand.

"This is odd, this was not here when I went to bed."

A cold fear gripped her neck. The idea that while she was sleeping, someone was next to her head without her knowing was very unnerving. Who was this from? What was this about? The invitation attached to her light, reminded her of the question she asked before she went to sleep;

"Who can turn light on in this darkness? Is there someone who has control of the light switch?" Reaching for the envelope, she felt an expectancy rise up from within as she opened it:

Dear compassionate one;

The heavy burdens you carry in your heart have been for a purpose. You seek Truth with all your heart and you will find Him. The answers to the hope you seek, cannot be found in Self Absorption; you must leave. Come to Me at Lake Still Water where I will teach you the ways you should go.

I long for a time of fellowship with you. There will be painful discoveries Truth will bring across your path. Do not turn from Truth, but look directly at it. Lift your eyes when it seems overwhelming and ask for help.

I will give you the strength to carry on. Bring this wisdom to the companions you will meet along the way. Be encouraged for I have overcome the world. I AM the light of the world. Come quickly and come now. Do not delay. I wait for you there.

Love,
I AM, the Pursuer of your Soul

Counselor could not stop staring at the words on the page. "Wow."

The words spoke to the places inside her heart she never listened to. It was as if the Writer of these words knew her very soul. She felt known by Him.

"Maybe God is real? Might He even be personal? Could He really want to pay attention to just one person?" This was exciting.

Maybe the questions her clients asked could be found. Could their answers be found at Lake Still Water? One thing she knew for sure, truth was not in Self Absorption.

If she stayed in this town any longer, she would never be able to supply her clients with what they needed. She needed to find it for herself first, before she could offer anything to them.

She must take this quest. A new confidence sprouted inside her soul. Without noticing, a smile replaced her frown.

She wrote a letter to her administration informing them she was taking a sabbatical. The purpose for her sabbatical was as follows: "To search for truth; answers elusive in Self Absorption."

She wrote each client a personal letter telling them she was going to search for the answers to their questions because she needed to know the answers too. She promised she would be back to share with them what she learned.

She packed a traveling bag with the bare-essentials. With one hand on her travel bag and the other clutching her invitation, Counselor headed out in her search for truth.

Little Bin Finally Reads His Invitation

Little Bin loved to climb the Tree of Knowledge, despite its dark creepiness. This tree was no different from any other part of this town as far as he was concerned; everything in Self Absorption gave him the creeps. Its rough branches always left new cuts and bruises on his legs. The greatest part of climbing for Little Bin was being high enough to see beyond it. He would gladly pay the price of a few scratches to affirm to his heart that Self Absorption was not the only place in the world.

Up in this tree, he felt bigger than life. Self Absorption always made him feel so small. He could see people coming from blocks away, and no one could sneak up on him when he was up in the tree.

Little Bin had grown accustomed to making emergency exit plans everywhere he went. He wasn't even aware he did it. 'Jump and run' was the escape plan if needed from the tree. 'Duck and cover,' though it was his favorite, didn't work well from the treetops.

He focused on his mission and started to calculate his graffiti strike. He loved to draw the mustache on the mirror at the height of most of the men in the town.

This morning was not his first 'graffiti mission' by any means, but the mustache draw was one of his favorites. He climbed up to one of the lower branches overhanging the mirror. It allowed him quick and easy access in drawing the mustache.

He loved to watch how irritated people became. The more dramatic the response, the more fun they made it. The rawer the emotional reaction, the more affirming it became.

The full moon always brought more visitors to the mirror. As soon as one person would leave, another would be making their way up to gaze in. This made it harder for him to have the time to draw the mustache in between worshippers.

To manage his rising impatience, Little Bin dangled his feet from the tree and decided to swing like a bat. Straddling the branch with the back of his knees, he lowered himself upside down. He loved feeling all the blood rush to his head.

The forgotten and unopened envelope he had draped around his neck like a medal plopped in front of his nose. He tried to read it but it was so close his eyes, they crossed.

"L..i t.. t.. l..e B.i.n… Little Bin! Hey that's me!"

He forgot to keep his legs bent and slipped from the branch, and fell headfirst onto the ground. At the last possible moment, he tucked into his infamous curl and roll and spared himself from a most brutal fall.

"Ouch, that hurt." He rubbed his head.

He sat up and without missing a beat, ripped open the envelope. The branches above him were so thick it blocked the light, which could have assisted in reading of his letter.

From Heaven itself, one single beam of light came and rested upon his invitation. Recognizing this light was a gift, he looked up into the stars, not really sure who it was but said "Thank-you." Little Bin then read his letter:

My dear spirited child;

Oh how you bring a smile to My face and a tear to My eye. I love to watch your exuberance for life and your adventurous spirit. I cry with you as you have cried. I have saved your every tear in a jar. I want you to come to Lake Still Water.

My love never betrays. Come know my steadfast and faithful love. I will provide all your needs. The promises I make, I keep. I did not write on a billboard but I hung upon a cross hundreds of years before you were born. I love you.

So come just as you are and I will teach you all you need to know. You will meet others along the way. Beware of wolves in sheep's clothing. When you don't know what to do, ask Me and I will give you the wisdom you need. Come now. Come quickly.

Love,
I AM, The Pursuer of your Soul.

"Wow! I have been invited to a secret mission and this one is for real."

Forgetting all about the mirror mustache draw, Little Bin turned towards his home and broke into a full sprint. Somewhere along the way, he dropped his marker but did not even consider picking it up. He no longer needed his marker as he had a new mission now. The best part about this mission was that it took place outside of Self Absorption.

When he reached his house, he opened the side door of his garage very gingerly. The door had a loud squeak and he did not want to wake his parents; their hangovers always made them very irritable in the morning.

Inside the garage, Little Bin scanned for provisions he would need for his journey. His eyes landed upon the skateboard tossed on its side in the corner.

"Perfect!"

He removed the scarlet cord from around his neck and carefully detached the letter. Folding it up, he stuck it deep inside his back pocket. He wrapped the cord around the trash can lid and then placed the trashcan on top of the skateboard.

He tested his makeshift invention by pulling the scarlet cord in different directions around the garage. The trashcan rested solidly upon the skateboard, and made it a suitable carrier for him to bring with him on his trip.

To Little Bin's great delight, it steered gracefully around the garage without incident. Confident of his new transportation, he headed outside.

As he piloted his ship down the driveway, his excitement launched for this new journey, a real adventure.

His ingenuity pleased him. He was now equipped and prepared for his mission. He hoped to gain as much distance from this miserable town as possible before he even asked for directions. He would wait until he was well clear of Self Absorption. As he journeyed, he wondered about when his mom and dad would finally roll out of bed.

"I bet they don't realize I am missing until it gets dark tonight."

In all their pain, they had forgotten they had a son. He worked hard to remind them. He disappeared from their hearts when his sister died, the sister he never met. He didn't blame them. He saw the pain they carried. It was just the way it was, that's all.

"They are on their way!"

From Heaven, eyes watched in excitement.

"They are off. They are all on their way! Are preparations set for the enemy agent?" The Pursuer of Souls asked.

"Yes, he will intercept them tomorrow," affirmed a lieutenant in the army of Hosts.

From within Heaven's walls, all voices stopped to declare, "O Sovereign Father You are the holder of all things. You will perfect all, which concerns them. Praise Your Holy Name." All interested eyes looked down, anticipating the rocky yet miraculous roads awaiting each one of the travelers. Heaven broke out into praise, "Worthy is the Lamb."

Fatalist Meets Pleaser

Fatalist was hoping that his quick paced walk would bring confidence to his doubting heart. Though not obvious, confidence for Fatalist was a foreign experience. He never felt comfortable wherever he found himself.

He pulled out the invitation to re-read it, hoping to get affirmation that his decision to leave everything behind and pursue this invitation was the right thing to do. He clutched tightly to the envelope with his right hand, while doubt gripped him tightly with his left. "Have I lost my mind? What am I chasing after?"

He knew in the depth of his soul that the scariest scenario would be if he met the Pursuer of Souls. It would force him to embrace hope again. Hope had been his enemy for so long he could not imagine becoming an ally with it. The idea of standing on the same side of hope brought a nervous laughter to the surface. He would quickly wash away his nerves with his cynical sense of humor. His cynicism was the faithful net that caught him when he started to fall.

Fatalist did a pretty good Darth Vader impression. He breathed deeply and loudly as if wearing Darth Vader's mask. "You have crossed over to the dark side Fatalist, to the dark side of madness." He smirked in pleasure at his own humorous ways. People called it a dry sense of humor, but it always brought a smile to his face.

His thoughts were intruded upon by a female voice.

"Excuse me sir, I couldn't help but notice that envelope in your hand."

The voice returned him quickly to the present where he noticed a skittish looking woman pointing to the envelope folded in his hand. Fatalist, in auto response, hid the envelope behind his back to protect it from her trying to snatch it. "This is a private letter."

"Oh please sir I did not intend to read your letter, but wanted to say it looks just like mine." She held up the same envelope with the gold engraved letters written on it with her name on the front. "I was wondering if by chance you too were going to Lake Still Water."

"So, you got an invitation too? I did not realize this was a mass mailing." Fatalist felt less special learning this.

"So are you going?" Pleaser asked.

"Do you always ask so many questions to perfect strangers?" Fatalist, with eyes pierced forward, quickened his walking pace.

"Oh please forgive me for being so rude, my name is Pleaser." She reached out her hand to greet him but he did not extend his back.

Fatalist started to feel remorseful about his rudeness. In an effort to turn a corner, he offered a partial wave, a hello, but still withheld his name.

Every few steps, Pleaser had to run to keep with his pace. "So what is your name sir?"

"Fatalist, my name is Fatalist." He kept staring straight ahead daring not to give her any eye contact. He tried not to notice how she was scurrying to stay in step with him because he did not want to slow down.

"It is very nice to meet you Fatalist." She extended her hand again while jogging to keep up. This man was difficult. Pleaser was usually pretty good at finding people's good side. She was, however, beginning to wonder if Fatalist had one.

"You are persistent, I will give you that." His rudeness had reached a dead end. He stopped, turned and shook her hand.

She was encouraged by this breakthrough. A smile spread across her face. Her joy irritated him.

"Would you mind terribly if I walked along with you? We are going to the same destination. There is safety in numbers."

"It's a free country." Fatalist retorted.

Pleaser took that to mean yes. "This is pretty wild huh, this invitation to Lake Still Water thing? So where are you from Fatalist? "

Fatalist was guarded. He did not enjoy being chatty. He surmised the best way to keep her quiet was to answer her right away because when he ignored her, she just talked more. "I am from the town of Self-Absorption."

"Oh what do you know, so am I!"

"Imagine that!" Fatalist was not surprised that someone so annoying was from Self Absorption. It never excited him to find out anyone lived in that town. He had lost respect for everyone who lived there a long time ago, especially himself.

"To think that we have lived in the same town all this time and did not meet until now."

"Imagine that." Fatalist said again sarcastically. "I like to stay to myself." Fatalist mumbled back at her.

"You know you do look kind of familiar to me." Pleaser tried to place where she had seen him before. She began talking aloud to herself. Her incessant talking annoyed Fatalist greatly.

"I know where I have seen you before, in the lobby of the City Administration building; I did not recognize you without your uniform."

"Yeah, I used to be the security guard there."

"Oh, when did you stop working there?" Pleaser asked.

"This morning. So do you work in the building?" Fatalist asked.

"Oh no, I am afraid I am one of those out front whom you probably see sweeping."

"You are a Sweeper?" Fatalist stopped abruptly in shock. He could not believe he was in the company of a Sweeper. He stepped back as if afraid he might get the leprosy.

Pleaser looked to the ground in shame, non-verbally agreeing with his disgust. "Yes, it is not something I am proud of. Choosing to come on this trip was an easy choice. You know, I wasn't always a loser. I held a city council position in Self Absorption for two years."

"So how did you become a sweeper? I never understood you people."

"Well let me assure you, I did not wake up one day with the decision to become a slave to the broom. It evolved. I was so disillusioned with the politics of politics. I believed to serve people properly I could never disappoint them. It was an impossible task to please everyone but I felt bound to try. On paper, I looked qualified, but I definitely did not have what it took.

"I was such a hypocrite. Here I was an elected city council woman for Self Absorption, secretly filled with great discontent. I tried hard to deny it, but I could not peel the discontent away from my heart. The harder I tried to rid myself of the disquietness, the more my discontent grew.

"In a desperate moment, I tried sweeping. I took hold of the broom like so many people. I tried to sweep my discontent under the rug of Indy Nial. I held onto to the foolish notion that sweeping could free me from the misery. I expected to have a more productive life, but there were always new reasons to sweep. The next thing I knew, I couldn't concentrate on anything else. I was trapped in an effort to free myself, which is pretty ironic."

As Fatalist listened, he could completely relate. His judgmental disdain dissipated in fact, he liked her. He respected her honesty. "Well it's nice to meet you. Until now, I never understood you people but what you shared makes sense to me." Fatalist extended his hand to her for the second time.

"Thank you." Pleaser said excitedly. She was surprised by his acceptance. She was grateful to have companionship on the journey. She never felt comfortable being alone. "I can tell you are a man who likes peace and quiet so what if I was quiet for awhile?" Pleaser had discernment about what people wanted.

"Thank-you, I would appreciate that very much." Fatalist looked over, grateful for her offer and smiled.

Though his offer of acceptance toward her was bewildering, she accepted it without debate. She would try hard to ensure he never regretted his decision. Regret was what murdered her mother. For a long time, they walked in silence.

Tuck and Guardian Use Discernment

Tuck's feet were tired. She and Guardian had been walking for hours. She refused to tell Guardian she was tired because she didn't want him to treat her like a baby.

Guardian noticed by Tuck's gait that she was weary. He also knew she would walk for hours more and never say anything if he didn't intervene. "Tuck we should pace ourselves. This is going to be a long trip. Would it be okay if we stopped at this park? We can put our feet in the pond, eat a snack and rest for a few minutes."

"I think that is the best idea I have heard all day."

They both laughed. Laughter often celebrated their friendship. Could there be a better friendship anywhere?

"Hey can we make it into a picnic? But we won't invite the ants." Tuck asked.

"Sure Tuck, a picnic it is."

As they entered the park, they saw the pond just a few yards away. As Tuck's eyes connected to the water, a burst of energy surged within her. She took off in a full sprint straight for the pond. While running, she tore off her shoes and socks, dropping them wherever loosed.

"Cold water - sore feet - Hooray!"

Close behind, Guardian kept his stride plucking up the abandoned clothing Tuck left in her wake. Guardian delighted in seeing Tuck with a smile.

It was a rare moment when she was happy and carefree.

She plopped her feet into the pond. Rejoicing, she lifted both hands over her head and bellowed out a cheer. "Oooh hooo!" She cried, shaking her hands upward in a joyous but cold celebration.

The freezing water gripped her bones. She curled into a tummy tuck to keep the cold from spreading. She sat onto the bank, lifted her knees to her chin in an effort to spare her frozen fish stick feet out of the freezing water. "Oh my gosh! That is so COOOOLD!"

Guardian caught up and dropped all the shoes and socks he collected along the way, reached into the water with one swift motion and splashed her.

"Tuck, put your feet back in that water or I am going to splash you big time. "One…" Guardian looked at her before saying two. "Two, aaaannnnd three!"

Tuck returned her feet to the water just as Guardian said three. She giggled at how close it came to him saying three.

"Girl that was close." Guardian bent over to catch his breath. Tuck sneaked behind him and gave him a little kick, launching him into the pond. "Be careful Guardian, you might fall in."

Tuck squealed in excitement Guardian stood up quickly with his arms out to the side, purposely preventing any body part from touch another. His body rigid as goose bumps rose to attention. He held his breath in an effort to keep what little heat remained, inside his body.

"Ohhhhh, you are really going to get it now." Guardian moved stiffly to shore. The whole time Tuck watched with a smirking smile, while his lips quivered uncontrollably from the cold.

Tuck took comfort by his smile reassuring her he was not mad, just pretending. As she turned to flee from Guardian's revenge, she ran right into a short little man who had been watching them play.

His long hooked nose and beady eyes added to Tuck's cold chill. He squinted so intensely Tuck could not detect what color his eyes were. Distrust slammed the brakes on her playful spirit.

"Oh Gosh, you scared me." Tuck said stepping backwards to make safer distance.

Tuck felt so uncomfortable, she behind Guardian as he made his way out of the water.

"You two look like you were having fun," said the strange figure. He was unaffected by Tuck's fear response.

Guardian felt Tuck's grip on his shirt. She was tugging so tightly she pinched his skin. Peering around Guardian's leg, she waited for Guardian to take the lead.

"Hi, sorry for the collision, we did not see you there."

"Do not worry fine sir. It takes much more than a little girl to hurt me."

Tuck watched little flowers spray from his mouth as he spoke. Flowery words parachuted downward, but when they landed, they died upon impact. His flowery words had no life. Tuck knew this man was not good.

"Where are you folks headed?"

"We are going to Lake Still Water."

Tuck pinched Guardian expressing her displeasure in divulging too much information.

"Oh, I know the place well. It is hot spot for foolish and desperate souls."

"Oh, do you know people from Lake Still Water?" Guardian asked.

The question amused the strange figure. He laughed at his own private joke. "No, not really, I personally am not impressed with the place; there is so much hype about it but trust me, it will disappoint. There is nothing to do there. I have been to many corners of the world and I have seen many things. I can be a great resource for anywhere you would want to travel."

"I am sorry; I did not get your name, mine is Guardian and this here is Tuck."

"Well it is a pleasure to meet you both." The stranger avoided giving his name.

Tuck pulled dramatically on Guardians shirt. She had a growing concern about this man. Guardian understood the shirt pull code. He concurred. There was something very wrong about this fellow.

"If you would be interested, I have a map to Lake Still Water. I can make it available to you for a steal of a price." He laughed at the irony of his word choices.

"No thank you, we will be fine with the directions we have been given."

"Well I just hope you two are not disappointed when you get there. In my opinion, it is highly over rated."

The odd fellow lingered hoping for a question or idle gab, but Guardian was only interested in ending the conversation. The little man appeared disappointed that there was no more dialogue. With nothing left to say, he bid farewell.

"Well maybe I will have the fortune of meeting up with you again." His exit was as abrupt as his entrance. Tuck and Guardian looked up and he was gone.

"Guardian that guy gave me the creeps. Did you notice he never gave his name?"

"Yes he was very evasive. Tuck, I think you were right about being cautious with that guy."

A sentence from his invitation came to Guardian's mind, and he pulled out his letter to look for the exact place. *"Use discernment with those who have not been invited."*

"Did you notice he did not want us to go to Lake Still Water?"

"Yep, he did not have anything good to say about it. I am glad he is gone."

"I am glad he is gone too little one."

As Guardian realigned his shirt from where Tuck was tugged on him he said, "Hey, thanks for communicating with me so clearly." He looked over at Tuck with a playful look of disapproval. She broke out into a big smile. Guardian rustled up her hair.

"So how are your feet feeling?" Guardian asked.

"Much better thank you. I can feel them again."

"How about you? Are you dry yet?" Tuck asked breaking out into a giggle, reliving her kick that launched him into the pond.

"I think we should get some distance from that guy so get your rejuvenated feet in gear. We need to go. I can continue to dry as we walk."

With socks and shoes back on, they headed off in the direction of Lake Still Water.

Little Bin Finds a Companion

Little Bin's carrier system was working nicely. The only challenge came when big tree roots lifted up from the sidewalks. Rolling the skateboard over uneven sidewalk caused the trashcan to teeter but it had managed to stay afloat thus far.

Little Bin, moved cautiously in these spots, taking it slow. He took his piloting responsibilities very seriously.

"I am so excited. I am on a real deal adventure. Who knows what I might face; lions, tigers or bears!" His imagination led him to danger. "Oh my."

"I need directions, Dr. Watson. You, doctor, are in charge of directions okay?" Little Bin often fantasized he was Sherlock Holmes, the greatest detective in the world. His invisible friend was Dr. Watson.

"Watson, we are on a case of mystery and intrigue. Keep your reasoning skills sharp. Are you up for the task Watson? Good man Watson, good man."

"Someone is following us Dr. Watson." Little Bin noticed out of the corner of his eye someone in the distance was gaining ground.

"Let's turn off to the side of the road and wait for them to pass by. Brilliant Holmes, brilliant!"

"Thank-you Watson."

Little Bin pulled off the sidewalk and lay down on the plush green lawn. The smell of the fresh cut grass brought a huge smile to his face. "I love this smell."

He lay on his back, putting his arms out to the side, and moved them up and down trying to make a grass angel. The warmth of the sun lulled him to a rare stillness but soon interrupted, when a friendly shadow greeted him.

"Hi there, are you taking a break?" Counselor looked down at this modern day Huck Finn lying before her. Everything about him bought a smile to her face. "Nice trash can," she offered, hoping he would explain why he was hauling a trashcan with him.

"Thank-you!" he said, impressed that an adult would even comment on such a thing.

"Are you traveling alone young man? Where are your parents?"

"They are back in Self Absorption. Someone named 'Suer of my Soul' invited me to a very important mission. I am on my way to Lake Still Water. You wouldn't happen to know where Lake Still Water is would ya?"

"Why yes, I am also headed there. Would you like to travel together?"

"Boy would I, what luck. Hey, did you get one of these too?" Little Bin pulled out of his back pocket a very dirty, but still readable letter. "It's from the 'Suer of your Soul'"

Counselor smiled at his adorable dialect.

"Why yes my young friend I did." She pulled out her letter and envelope as well. "My name is Counselor, what is yours?"

"Hi, I am Little Bin. It is very nice to meet you." Little Bin noticed she only had a knapsack with her and became concerned.

"Where are you planning to sleep?" He looked for a tent of some kind. "I will just play that by ear. I brought my sleeping bag. I enjoy sleeping under the stars."

"Cool."

"Do you sleep in there?" Counselor pointed to the trash can with concern.

"Sure do. It has been my secret hiding place when things are not so good. I am the invisible man in there." Little Bin began to explain to her the successful tactics of 'duck and cover.' Tears welled up in Counselor's hidden heart as she listened. This boy's enthusiasm was admirable. She envied his resilient spirit.

"It is an honor to share your company." Counselor bowed.

"Mine too Maam" Little Bin smiled standing on his toes.

Counselor folded her right arm offering Little Bin her elbow. Little Bin proudly weaved his arm through hers and pretended he was escorting the Queen of England.

Pleaser and Fatalist Meet Worker

Hours had gone by since either Pleaser or Fatalist had spoken. They were in perfect step. Pleaser was at ease with Fatalist. She could not remember a time she felt comfortable. She thought quietly, "I have not swept in almost twenty four hours! Back in Self Absorption, I made promise after promise to cut back on sweeping. Every time I failed, I rationalized it away by claiming I could quit anytime."

This freedom brought a joy that made her want to giggle.

Her thoughts were interrupted when a stranger stopped directly in front of their path.

"Hello there, how are you folks doing?"

Fatalist, startled and irritated asked this woman, "Do you always sneak up on people like that?"

Fatalist's rude greeting made Pleaser nervous. She tried to run interference.

"Hi, what, ah, he means is we just didn't notice you coming."

"Oh I am sorry I didn't mean to startle you. You two had a good rhythm going."

"So you felt like you had to ruin it? How long have you been following us anyway?" Fatalist sneered.

"Oh I think it was about two hours outside of Self Absorption when I first spotted you."

"My name is Worker what is yours?"

"Hi Worker it is nice to meet you. My name is Pleaser and this here is...?" Pleaser paused out of respect to let Fatalist introduce himself.

"I'm Fatalist." He said begrudgingly.

"Where are you heading?" Worker asked.

"Lake Still Water." Fatalist answered.

"Really, I am going there also. Did you receive an invitation from someone referring to Himself as the Pursuer of your Soul?" Worker inquired, pulling out her invitation as evidence.

"Yes." Pleaser was excited but also very preoccupied with what Fatalist was thinking. She kept looking over at him attempting to read his facial expression. He was a hard one to read because he always looked angry. "You know it would be most cost effective if we would all travel together. What do you say?" Worker suggested without intimidation.

Pleaser deferred to Fatalist, not wanting to ruffle his feathers. She stared at him waiting for his answer. He remained unresponsive. He resented this new person. Pleaser and he had a good thing going, especially with the silence. Now this new woman wanted to ruin everything.

"Do we have a choice?" Fatalist retorted.

"Whoa, did someone wake up on the wrong side of the bed?" Worker barked back.

"Uh, ah what he meant to say was, uh..." Pleaser juggled to rephrase his rude response.

"Joining up with you must be fate. All three of us have an invitation to go to the same place. It only makes sense to team up." Pleaser maneuvered her way through the pleasing minefield.

"Oh is that what I meant?" Fatalist did not appreciate Pleaser being his translator. Then he turned to the new gal and said, "If you are going to walk with me you better get used to me. This is who I am and I offer no apologies."

"Actually Fatalist I find you refreshing. You say what you mean without pretense. I can respect that." Worker affirmed Fatalist and then looked over at Pleaser and noticed all color had left her face. "Oh dear are you okay? You look pale." Pleaser's anxiety typically stole color from her face.

"Oh I am fine. I just don't like it when people don't get along," explained Pleaser.

"Oh don't worry; he and I are going to get along just fine." Worker replied.

Leaning in for more effect, Worker whispered loud enough so Fatalist could hear. "He doesn't intimidate me."

Fatalist's stride increased, as did his irritation. He mumbled under his breath, "I don't care if I get her approval. She talks way too much for my liking anyway."

Worker, un-intimidated, started right into a conversation with Fatalist. "What do you think about this Pursuer of our Souls?"

"What do I think? I don't know anything about Him.

I haven't met Him yet. We are going to meet Him if *someone* would stop talking. Then you can answer the question yourself."

Worker looked over at Pleaser, "Is he always this touchy?"

Fatalist recognized his attitude was unusually abrupt reeled himself back in. He started by slowing down his fast paced stride.

Worker looked at Pleaser and studied her intently. "Gee, have we met? You look familiar."

Pleaser felt her heart sink. Blood rushed to her cheeks. "Well, I live in Self Absorption. Maybe you saw me there?"

"Maybe that is it."

She knew Worker was searching her memory banks for the specific time and place. She always hated waiting for people to make the connection. It felt like waiting for someone to push her off a cliff. She dreaded that moment when they remembered where they have seen her. She tried to delay their connection as long as possible. When they remembered, she felt like death all over again, her mom's death.

"What did your letter from the Pursuer say?" Pleaser attempted to change the subject.

"You know it was the strangest thing. I woke up and found the envelope on my mirror. Someone placed it there during the night." Worker reviewed in her own mind how it all happened. Her greatest concern was in not understanding all that had taken place. Worker asked them both, "Are you as shocked as I am that you came?"

"Oh yes. This makes no logical sense. I have left my whole life behind to accept an invitation from someone I don't even know. What is even more preposterous is what He promises! Is anything he wrote possible to deliver?" Pleaser concurred.

"For me, it was the words He wrote in the invitation, it was like He knew me or something. He brought up things I had not even admitted to myself." Worker added.

They walked by an olive tree and Pleaser noticed a sign hanging from its lowest branch: *"With God all things are possible."*

She looked at Worker. "Hey, look there, read that sign." Worker giggled and then commented, "Was that tree listening to our conversation?"

Pleaser nodded in agreement. "That is weird."

Fatalist followed them up with the Twilight Zone theme song. "Deedee ...dee dee..... dee dee ...dee dee..." They all broke out laughing.

Fatalist decided to contribute. "Well I have nothing to return to. If this doesn't pan out, I am not going back." Fatalist shook his head in disgust. Then he began to share one of the many worst-case scenarios always mulling over in his mind.

"The joke will be on us when we find out that this was just one big market research experiment. You see they probably sent out thousands of these invitations and only three losers responded."

Worker jumped in to add to the embarrassing scenario. "Yeah and when we get there, someone will sticks a microphone in our face and ask for an interview which they will air all across the country."

"Oh man, they might as well just tattoo our foreheads with the word 'loser.'" Pleaser concluded.

They looked at each other for a moment, and then broke into laughter. A friendship had begun.

Fatalist found himself intrigued by Worker, "You are pretty imaginative. You must have horrible nightmares."

Worker laughed under her breath and admitted, "Oh you have no idea."

Fatalist smiled in appreciation and then looked at Pleaser with a repentant face. "Okay, maybe she isn't as bad as I thought. She is starting to grow on me."

"Hey how far are we from Lake Still Water?" asked Worker trying to redirect his compliment to something more comfortable.

"By my estimation we could be there by late tomorrow afternoon, if…" Fatalist paused.

"If?" Worker inquired.

"*If* we keep a fast pace." Fatalist emphasized.

"No worries Fatalist, I am not afraid of a fast pace walk."

Fatalist was impressed she could take it as well as dish it out.

Pleaser envied Worker's perfect comebacks. She didn't hesitate or stammer even for a moment. Pleaser had never been able to respond quickly. Fear paralyzed her. Pleaser flashed back at the sign they passed. "*All things are possible with God.*" She liked the sound of it, but did not believe it.

She was always the exception to any miracle. She was too far-gone.

What Pleaser did not know was she was about to experience just how possible things are with the Pursuer of her Soul. He was the fashioner of circumstances. *"Tomorrow."* He whispered to her soul. *"Tomorrow."*

Tuck and Guardian Gain Distance
From the Odd Fellow

Guardian's wet chill had been dried by the sun. "I am sure glad that man didn't follow us." Tuck said.

"Me too kiddo, me too." Guardian agreed.

The flowery worded man did inspire a game they camp up with as they traveled. They called it 'Animal Charades.' One picked an animal to act out, and then made a sound of a different animal, creating a new combination animal. Guardian had thought of a great one. He got down on all fours and pretended to trot, then added "bzzzzzzzzzz."

Tuck waved her hand high and started to jump up and down. "Oh I know, I know it is a horsefly." Tuck fell backwards laughing, and rolled around like a ball.

Guardian loved to see her laugh. Most of the time, Tuck curled in a ball from complete fear and despair. This scene delighted his heart, and he was so glad they had come.

He flashed back to the time Tuck was late to their meeting place at the fountain in the center of town.

After waiting a long while, Guardian grew concerned. He hoped it was because Tuck's parents picked her up though that was rarely the case. He headed over to her house to make sure she had gotten home safely.

When he arrived, he saw Tuck on the porch floor just below the living room window, curled up in a ball. Her eyes were closed. She had tear-stained cheeks. She didn't notice Guardian walk up. He stooped down to comfort her and caught part of her parents conversation from inside the house.

They were talking about a trip. A trip of a lifetime. It was to be the "who's who" cruise. Powerful and influential people would be there. Tuck could not go. She would ruin everything. They didn't want to be strapped down with a kid when there were all these great opportunities.

Guardian did not understand why this caused Tuck's tears. She was used to her parents not spending time with her. He heard Tuck's mom continue, "Charles you know motherhood is a ball and chain to me. It hinders my freedom. I regret the day I had her. I was not cut out to be a parent. Nurturing a child does not come natural for me."

This followed with them brainstorming ideas of what they to do with Tuck while they were gone. Guardian felt her pain in his own heart. He watched her sob. He drew her to his arms and just rocked her back and forth.

He wished someone rocked him when his pain got bad. A rage against her parents stirred deep inside of him. His rage ran much deeper than Tuck's mom and dad. It scared him it made him want to run but he stayed because Tuck needed him. He would not abandon her, as she had been so many times before.

Guardian returned to the present and was relieved that that life was behind them now. An unexplainable heaviness had lifted once they left that town. He was thankful that the arms of Self Absorption's could not stretch this far. "Tuck, I think we should start looking for a place to camp for the night."

Tuck felt burdened by the word 'night.' Nighttime carried her nightmares. A somberness in mood took hold. Her head hung low. Guardian sensed her dread. He snuck up behind her and messed up her hair.

She knew he was trying to make her feel better and she loved him for it, but it didn't help. She gave him a big smile, even though she didn't believe in it. It was a gift for the best kind of friend a person could have in the whole world.

Counselor and Little Bin Find a Place to Camp

Counselor was being treated like royalty. Little Bin convinced her that she was the Queen of England and he was her faithful servant. Little Bin had nestled deep into her heart, a heart usually efficient in locking others out.

There was something about his innocence and joyful spirit. He showed so much resilience. He brought to life her playfulness, which had lain dormant for a very long time. She enjoyed his playful adventures equally. She could not have asked for better company.

"Well my young escort, where do you think the Royal court should camp tonight?"

Little Bin enjoyed how she participated with him in everything. She was not like most adults who would just supervise him. He thoughtfully pressed his fingers to his lips, trying to answer the queen's question with wisdom and dignity.

A huge revelation came upon him. The whole world was available to them. They were not stuck with just Self Absorption's rules anymore. Anything was possible here in this place.

"There are so many choices to choose from!" Little Bin stood on his toes as if the idea had lifted him up off his feet.

Counselor tenderly inquired about one specific spot. "My young prince, what about the spot over there?" She pointed to a corner in a grassy field just off the pathway. Rocks and trees encircled a plush area of grass making it a nice encampment. It looked like a private oasis.

"Do you want to check it out and see if it would be suitable for a prince and his queen?"

Little Bin was delighted with the assignment. Where did this lady come from? He never met an adult who was so much fun.

"You bet!" In the excitement, he fell out of character and spoke without his English accent. He quickly regained his composure and in full English dialect responded. "I mean it would be my pleasure my lady."

He bowed valiantly to his queen and then tore off in a full run to inspect their potential palace. About ten yards out, his spirit was overtaken by freedom. The open field and sense of safety, he could not help himself. He did a cartwheel and then another and another.

"Oooh Hooo!" he screamed doing his own rendition of the Tarzan yell at the top of his lungs. He had to wait for the spinning in his head to stop before he could regain his bearings.

Entering into the private oasis, he thought things looked good. He had to wait for all the spinning to stop before he was sure. Once his balance returned he turned back in a full sprint to give the good news to his queen.

This was just the first day of his journey and he had already made a new friend. Counselor was the first adult friend he ever had. Adults never liked Little Bin much. They liked to lecture him and tell him how he was going to be in prison one day. It was okay with him, he didn't like adults much either. What Little Bin considered were his finest qualities, adults disdained, but this lady was different, he could tell right off.

He shouted the good report before he returned. She couldn't understand a word he said but discerned by his enthusiasm that it was a great place. She waved to him in affirmation and started to move out toward, him pulling his sanctuary by the scarlet cord, behind her.

"Oh I will take that my lady." Little Bin took the cord from her hand.

"Thank you kind sir." Counselor smiled back and curtsied.

Little Bin became concerned again that his queen did not have a place to sleep. Noticing the change in his countenance, Counselor asked, "What's wrong Little Bin?" She got down on her knees so she could see into his eyes as he shared.

Little Bin handed her his scarlet cord. "I want you to sleep in here tonight my queen. You should have the best place to sleep."

Counselor was without words. "Little Bin you are the nicest person I have ever met." She knew his offer was self-less and sincere.

"My prince, yours is a most generous offer but my size would make that impossible."

"But it is going to get cold out here tonight. How are you going to keep warm?"

Counselor reached over and touched the side of Little Bin's cheek, "I will keep warm just thinking about the generosity of your offer! I think we can find some wood and make a fire too."

"Ok. but if you get cold, wake me up, and you can sleep inside."

"Thank you my friend. Let's set up our camp now shall we?" Counselor pulled out her sleeping bag and unfolded it out onto the ground. She began removing the small little stones that were underneath to ensure a comfortable night sleep. Then she started to look for some wood for a fire.

Little Bin pulled his home between the gathering of rocks. "This looks like the perfect place." He dropped his string and ran off to explore.

The Threesome Settle down for the Night

Now Fatalist, Pleaser and Worker, as a group had traveling rhythm. Though they were walking in silence, it was comfortable. Each one entertained thoughts, anticipating their journey's end. The memories of Self Absorption faded while discarded dreams were re-explored.

Worker wondered about going back to school. She wanted to study archeology. Old relics seemed romantic to her, the connection to our past. She had felt disconnected for so long. She appreciated stories about real people who struggled to find their way. She loved working with her hands, and enjoyed being outside.

"I wonder why my dreams always pertain to work. At least I am dreaming again." This was a healthy sign. She was finally moving in the right direction for a change.

As Fatalist walked, the faces of his family ran through his mind. He tried to imagine what they looked like now. He wondered if his mom was even still alive. He was curious about his brothers and sisters, and worried that the country had hardened them as it had hardened him.

There were so many unanswered questions. This trip triggered so many feelings about those he cared for the most, and he didn't understand why.

Pleaser's lower back was really screaming out for rest. It was one of the consequences of being a sweeper. She didn't want to be a burden to her companions so she suffered in silence.

There were moments she had to freeze to catch her breath from the sharp stabbing pains that shot down her left side. "Does anyone have an aspirin?" This was a subtle way to alert them of her deterioration.

Fatalist responded, "No, but I see a drug store ahead. We can stop and get some. I think it is time we settle in for the night." Fatalist's feet hurt. He noticed there was a cheap motel two doors down from the drug store and there was a diner in between. "Hey are you two up for staying here for the night? There is a diner right next to this motel. We could eat dinner there."

Pleaser was thrilled with the idea. The word 'cheap' excited Worker but the word 'stop' excited Pleaser. "Sounds good to me what about you Fatalist?"

"Looks like my price range." Fatalist joked.

"If you want, Worker, we could share a room and save even more money." Pleaser loved opportunities to help people.

"Deal," they smiled and playfully shook hands.

Pleaser thought a real friendship might develop between them but following that thought was a huge case of anxiety, so she quickly released the idea.

"Does anyone else feel like you can breathe better being away from Self Absorption?" Fatalist asked.

"You mean how the air here doesn't have an unseen weight, pushing down on you?" Worker asked.

"Yes I felt that way too." Pleaser jumped in with agreement.

"Let's eat first. I am starving." Fatalist changed the subject.

As they approached the entrance to the diner, Pleaser told them she would meet them inside and went next door to get some aspirin. She hoped the aspirin would bring relief so she wouldn't have to pretend she wasn't in pain. She was so tired of pretending.

Guardian do you believe in Magic?

Inside his sleeping bag, leaning back upon his arms, Guardian took in the breathtaking night sky. Tuck held Dreams was arranging Dreams for bedtime, making sure his head was outside the sleeping bag so he could enjoy the stars too. "Aren't they beautiful Guardian? Even Dreams is impressed."

Dreams was well loved and the proof was in the decaying strands on his back. Thin some places and lumpy in others, all were places where Tuck gave him hugs and squeezes. One of his eyes was missing, which prevented him from seeing the crusted drool stuck on his face.

Tuck slept with him every night. For Dreams, these tattered and crusty places were badges of honor. What could be better than loved when you are crusty?

Tuck talked with Guardian until she fell asleep. Guardian answered her every question and there were many, one right after the other. She kept asking questions so she could keep hearing his voice.

His voice brought her comfort. He made her feel safe. She knew she would be fighting the monsters in her nightmares soon, so she tried to delay it as long as possible. Sleeping was the place Guardian could not protect her. She faced everything there alone.

"A penny for your thoughts Tuck." Guardian kept her engaged in conversation.

"I was just thinking... well... do you believe in magic Guardian?"

"What kind of magic do you mean Tuck?"

"The kind of magic where something wonderful happens and no one can explain how it happened?" Tuck explained.

"Well when you describe it that way, I guess I do." Guardian continued, "take the stars above us; they are so amazing. When I look at them, it makes me think anything is possible."

"Anything?" Tuck inquired with hesitant hope.

Guardian sat up inside his sleeping bag and looked at her very seriously. "Tuck I want you to know something. Whoever this Pursuer of Souls is, I believe He is going to help you and not just in the daytime but in your night times too. I don't know why, but I believe that with all my heart."

"Well I know better than to argue with my best friend in the whole world. I hope you are right." Tuck scooted deeper into her sleeping bag and took a firm hold on Dreams. "I love you Guardian and Dreams loves you too!"

"I love you too little one. Now get some sleep. Sweet dreams morning will be here quick enough." Guardian remained sitting for a while to oversee her falling asleep.

She closed her eyes and repeated Guardian's words. "Morning will be here quick enough." It was a comforting thought. It was the last thought she had before slipping into sleep.

Heaven Prepares

Morning came quickly. The Army of Heaven was in a flurry of activity. Swords were drawn. Intense battles will occur today, fighting in defense of these citizens. The angels lifted up their voices to praise His Holy Name. *"How great Thou art, You who reigns forevermore."*

Each officer was prepared and knew their role. The Army of Heaven was set. There was never confusion and strife on Heaven's side. All preparations were made everyone was in place.

The Threesome Awaken To Start a New Day

Pleaser awoke disoriented from her sleep. She actually remained in the bed the whole night. Impressions wasn't there to bully her to the floor. She was not able to set limits on his behavior.

His aggressiveness intimidated her so she took the path of least resistance and surrendered to the floor. It was nice waking up in the bed. "I could get used to this." Her back felt a lot better.

She looked around at the sparse and very poorly decorated room and reoriented herself to the journey. Her roommate's bed covers had been thrown back, and she was no where to be found.

Pleaser heard the keycard open the door and Worker walked in carrying two cups of coffee and two muffins all balancing on one napkin. She had a newspaper under her arm and was chewing gum.

"Wow you sure are a bundle of activity early this morning. What time is it anyway?" Worker tried to look at her watch but realized she better put something down first.

She leaned over the table and let the newspaper fall from her arm grasp. She lowered the napkin with the muffins and then walked a coffee over to her roommate. "Cream? Sugar?"

"Wow I am impressed. Cream please." Pleaser took the coffee gratefully.

Worker reached into her sweat pant pocket and pulled out a mini tub that said non dairy creamer. "Here ya go."

"Thank you very much." Pleaser said.

"So how did you sleep Did your aspirin work?" Worker asked.

"I slept like a rock, thank you. I enjoyed having the bed all to myself." Pleaser realized she should probably explain before she got the wrong idea. "I live with a dog who takes up the whole bed, so I end up sleeping on the floor. So last night, I slept like a queen."

Fatalist knocked and then spoke through the door. "Good morning. Does anyone need coffee? I am going down to the diner to get some."

Worker opened the door and smiled, while holding her own cup in her hand. "No thanks just got some, but go get a cup for yourself and then come back up. We should be ready to go by then."

Fatalist agreed and headed toward the diner. Pleaser, hearing the plan, made a mad dash to the shower. She could not be seen in her undone condition. What would Fatalist think? As she turned on the shower, she began wondering what this day would hold. "I wonder what He looks like." She mused, thinking about the Pursuer of Souls.

Pleaser took a quick, no nonsense shower, fearing they might leave without her. She frequently feared being left behind so she found herself rushing through everything and never enjoyed herself. She could not relax because she was always worried about the next thing.

Once dressed, Pleaser came out of the bathroom brushing her hair, nibbling at the muffin. Worker gathered her stuff together and threw it in her backpack.

"The sooner we get on the road, the sooner we can get there and find out if this was all a sham. I don't know about you guys, but I am getting nervous. The closer we get, the more fearful I am that we will find out this is a false claim."

Worker hoped Pleaser's pace would speed up. When Worker felt anxious, her pace quickened, and she moved faster through things. When Pleaser was anxious, she slowed down and became more deliberate about everything, fearful of making a mistake. This combination was moving toward certain strife.

Dreams is Abducted

The ground dampened by the dew harvested a special mud bath for Dreams when he landed outside the sleeping bag during one of Tuck's wrestling matches during the night.

From a nearby tree branch, a loitering dark side warrior with his nameless dog looked on. The dog was unkempt in appearance. His hair was scraggly and long. His teeth were visibly rotten.

He was very grateful for the few scraps his newly adopted master gave him. For the smallest of price, he would be loyal. For the first time since he was a puppy, someone fed him. He would gladly do whatever he was told if there were more scraps in the deal.

A big smile leapt across his master's face as he saw Dreams. "Perfect. Our job has just been made easier." He referred to their target laying out in the open, vulnerable to the morning drizzle. The warrior swung down from the tree branch looked at his four-legged slave and pointed to Dreams lying in the mud. "Fetch," commanded the warrior.

The dog walked over, picked up Dreams between his rotting teeth and dropped him at his master's feet. The master picked Dreams up heralded a dark, evil laugh then disappeared with Dreams still in hand. The dog left behind still waiting for the biscuit promised.

It was a swift abduction, all while his friend slept unaware.

From Heaven it was announced "And so it begins…"

Little Bin Goes Fishing

Counselor awoke as the sun just started to rise. She leaned toward the warmth of the early sun and it touched her face. The closed lid on her young friend's hotel helped delay the arrival of his morning a bit longer.

She pulled herself from the sleeping bag and began stretching out the creaking parts of her body. She grabbed her toothbrush and collapsing travel cup and walked toward the stream to brush her teeth.

Using the water's reflection, she tried to re-assimilate her hair. She cupped her hand with water and splashed it onto her face. It felt good to be shocked. The cold water woke her up.

Counselor sat down on a rock and soaked in the peaceful morning. There were two birds playing tag within the trees, flitting from branch to branch. "I wonder if there have been these sweet sights around me every morning and I never noticed."

She thought back to the peaceful mornings she remembered as a child. She shook her head refusing to allow those thoughts take hold. She could not let the old days gain access to her heart. Every good memory ended in loss.

She now remembered why she never sat still long enough to savor mornings. She lifted herself from the water's edge and headed back to camp to check on her young friend.

"Well good morning Little Bin" A little figure with hair standing straight up on the left side of his head stood outside of his trash can rubbing his eyes. The rest of his hair looked like it had been flattened by tractor wheels.

"Good morning!" said Little Bin rubbing his eyes.

"There is a stream just around the bend. The water feels real good." Counselor shared.

"Okay." Little Bin was slow to wake up. Though his energy level was on high all day long, it took a bit longer for him to be revved up in the morning.

Little Bin made his way toward the rocks Counselor pointed to, with his eyes still only half open. Once his eyes saw the water from the stream, the caffeine jolt he needed kicked into gear. "Cool!"

He took off at full speed to the stream's edge. His shoelaces were still untied and so was his imagination. His thoughts leaped about to all the wonderful potentials of this place. He picked up some rocks from the shore and skipped them all the way across to the other side. He was really good at skipping rocks, better than anyone he knew.

As he looked down in front of him, he saw three fish hiding under a protruding rock. Little Bin shrieked with excitement. "Fish! Hey I found fish" He looked for Counselor to announce his discovery, but realized she was too far away to hear. He didn't want to lose eye contact with his potential breakfast. He stepped very gently onto the sheltering ledge that jutted out of the water. The fish below remained still.

Little Bin, utilizing his stealth duck and cover technique, got close enough to reach in without alarming the fish. He squatted down close to the edge, studying them. Their backs were to him just below his feet. He could see their scales as the water magnified their size. He figured he could just reach down and catch one with his hand.

As he leaned down, the slipperiness of the rock caused him to fall and he got tangled up in his untied shoelace, which pulled his body forward. The centrifugal force of his lean launched him head first into the stream. Little Bin remained focused and despite freezing water, he stayed fixed on the fish. Water quickly filled up inside of his shirt. The fish, in all the chaos swam for a getaway, with one making a fateful wrong turn, and swam right inside Little Bin's shirt.

The fins tickled him as the fish flapped against his stomach. He pulled together the ends of his shirt to block off the exits for the fish. Little Bin waddled his way to shore. The desperate fish flopped dramatically as Little Bin maneuvered to shore and fell to the ground.

On his back, he just started laughing. He scooted on his back away from the shore's e edge, to ensure the fish would not flop back into the stream.

Counselor ran toward the water when she heard all the commotion. This tranquil place was not used to the likes of Little Bin. In a matter of seconds, the most peaceful setting found itself in chaos. As Little Bin saw Counselor approaching, he pulled from inside his shirt a full size trout. The size of his catch would have made any fisherman proud.

"Breakfast! I caught us breakfast!" Little Bin held up his trophy.

Counselor was elated for him. Every part of Little Bin was wiggling. He was so excited he couldn't contain himself. The fish almost equaled him in size. Counselor smiled as she beheld the picture of this boy encased in mud, smiling so big, holding this shiny fish as proud as he could be.

His white teeth were the only thing not drenched in mud. She cheered for him loudly, while trying to swallow her laughter. He was so transparent in his joy. She envied him.

Little Bin bowed to her accolades. In doing so, he dropped the fish. It wiggled toward the water and began flipping from side to side. Little Bin screamed and dove after it. He retrieved with a diving catch just like a left fielder in baseball.

He held his catch up like an outfielder would show the umpire the ball was in his mitt. Little Bin confirmed he recovered the dropped catch. He pointed to the fish and scolded it, "Bad fish, you stay."

Counselor intervened. Sticking out from under some leaves, she found a dirty grocery bag. "Here Little Bin, put our breakfast in here." She shook it out and opened it up for Little Bin to put the fish inside.

"Oh that is great" Little Bin said, grateful for the help.

"My young friend you are a sight for sore eyes. I want you to step back into the water, but take off your shoes and socks this time. Take off your shirt and those pants too."

"But then all I will have on is my underwear!"

"I know, I promise I won't look. While you rinse off the mud, I will rinse out your clothes. Then we can head back to camp, so you can put on some clean clothes."

"Umm, I didn't bring any other clothes." Little Bin informed her.

"Well I think I may have some things you can borrow until these dry. The sun should dry them quickly." Counselor wasn't sure exactly what she had but it was something dry at least.

"No offense my queen, but I don't wear lady clothes." Little Bin said, concerned about this offer.

Little Bin walked into the water with his arms extended out to the side. Counselor walked around the other side of the boulder to give him some privacy and rinsed each article of clothing.

She quickly walked back to camp with the clothes and laid them out on the rocks by the fire. She searched through her bag, pulling out a towel and some overall shorts that would probably fit Little Bin like pants. "This will do just fine until the sun dries his clothes."

She ran back to the stream and opened up the towel, indicating it was time for him to get out of the water. He stepped into the towel and allowed her to dry him. It felt good to have someone take care of him. He had stopped needing that from his own mom. It was too hard for her to care for him because she was so sad all the time. He felt safe and cared for inside the towel.

Counselor had fallen in love with this little boy. She loved him like he was her own son.

Little Bin stepped into her overalls and started to giggle at how funny he looked in ladies clothes. She was pleased at how well the overall shorts worked out; he looked like a normal kid in oversized overalls. "Let's go get you warm by the fire. You must be freezing."

They made their way back to camp, when Little Bin stopped and screamed, "Oh wait a minute." He made a u-turn and sprinted back to the shore's edge and picked up the grocery bag.

"We almost forgot our breakfast!" In the bag was a very still fish. He had no fight left. He was dead.

The Threesome is Off

The threesome decided to head out early instead of socializing in the room. They could drink coffee and eat muffins while walking. Pleaser was relieved that the aspirin and restful night sleep in the bed was the remedy her lower back needed.

As they set out on their way, they enjoyed the fellowship talking and sipping. Worker looked for a trashcan to throw her trash away and found a container off the side of the road. Stepping out from behind the large metal container stood a very strange looking man who came up to them. At first, they didn't notice the mangy dog with him.

"Now there is a perfect match." Fatalist mumbled loud enough for Pleaser to giggle, the disheveled man traveling with his mangy dog. Drool flowed from the dog's mouth; between his teeth was a stuffed dog with a charm around its neck that read 'Dreams.'

Pleaser's heart filled with compassion for the poor captive inside the canine's mouth. She could tell that dog had been loved well, unlike his living counterpart.

"What an adorable stuffed animal." Pleaser tried to break up the uncomfortable silence.

Detour was this eerie deceiver's name. He was small in stature, but a giant in the eyes of the other dark side warriors. His unkempt appearance was his ploy. He loved judgmental opinions about him. People often judged him to be uneducated, homeless, a loser, and a bum. This gave him great advantage.

They taught him in warrior school that the pride of men leads to gross under estimations of their others. This gave an opponent the edge.

"Hi there, where are you folks headed?" Detour entered into innocent conversation.

"Uh, we are on our way to Lake Still Water." Pleaser answered nervously.

"Oh" Detour responded, indicating concern but wanting them to initiate the question as to why.

Pleaser picked up on a subtle discontent and inquired. "Is there something wrong sir?"

"Well since you asked, you folks are off course. There was a washout on the bridge a few days back and no one can cross up ahead. I will be glad to show you on my map where they have set up a detour. If you follow it, it will be a good short cut."

"Wow good thing we ran into you." Pleaser confirmed.

Detour pulled out a map from his back pocket and opened it up in front of them. The man's crooked dirty fingers followed a pre-made mark all the way down his map. Fatalist thought it was very suspicious that the line was already there.

"So do you just walk around helping unsuspecting visitors from wandering off course?" Fatalist seeking an explanation as to what he was doing in the middle of nowhere. Fatalist also recognized this could be his cynical nature acting out so he didn't press things too far.

The deceiver responded with an odd laugh. The joke amused him. Detour turned on his charm sensing Fatalist's suspicious nature.

"You guys are fortunate our paths crossed. I am glad I could save you from heartache and disappointment."

Fatalist did not trust this stranger, though he couldn't explain why, except for his unsightly appearance.

Detour followed his boss's orders. He took hold of Fatalist's map and transferred the same markings that were on his map. Then he went to his best sell tactic, it worked so well with men. It was his famous short cut routine. Man loved the short cuts and the easiest way to get some place.

These were top sellers for Detour. He figured these three would be no exception.

"You know this way I am suggesting has less hills, and it is flat walking. It will cut down a half day's travel."

This perked up Worker's ears. "Wow that is great news. I love hearing about the most efficient way to get somewhere." Worker extended her hand and was quick to thank the eerie figure. She thought it odd that instead of him also extending his hand; he waved to her and stepped back.

"Okay then, luck to you all." He backed up toward the trees.

The three agreed to head toward the suggested detour. It was their good fortune to find a short cut. Fatalist read the markings on the map and reported to his companions, "Okay we need to look for something called the 'Tunnel of Tour own Understanding.'"

Worker looked over Fatalist's shoulder and pointed to the newly marked route. "He is right you know. In looking at this map, this new way will cut out a lot of unnecessary hiking. We walk through this tunnel right there and then there is only an hour or two more after that."

Pleaser was fearful about walking through a tunnel. She didn't want anyone else to know she was afraid, so she kept quiet.

As they walked away, Detour's devilish grin expressed his pleasure. He pulled a crumpled piece of paper out from his back pocket. Three words were written on the page, "Distract and detain."

"Mission accomplished!" Detour said very pleased. He knew that once the three entered the tunnel, they would never find their way out. His evil laugh resonated where he stood, and then he abruptly disappeared.

Heaven Prepares For Battle

Two observers from Heaven watched in anticipation of the battle about to be waged.

Two observers, one affectionately nicknamed Gentle and the other Soother shared their bewilderment. "All this activity is taking place around them and they do not notice. I do not understand human beings. What does the Pursuer see in them anyway?"

Soother responded, "His heart for these humans is a mystery to us all. They are blind because deception thrives in darkness. Remember they have not yet met the Pursuer. They do not see with His light to recognize the deceptions from their unseen enemy. Their enemy is skillful at staying out of their view.

Most do not really believe he exists. That is why so many of their marriages end in divorce. The enemy exploits the unmet needs of each individual, then, he whispers lies. It is only a matter of time before their pain rises to their attention. When they do not recognize the real enemy they go to war with each other."

"When the Pursuer touches hearts, scales fall from their eyes. It is through the faith He gives them, they learn to walk by what they cannot see. He is an amazing God.

If they knew what was waiting for them ahead, they would never go forward. Though their path will prove grueling and difficult, they must walk it to find His love, a love that does not forsake. Each of their paths will lead to the Pursuer of their Souls. It will not be in the simple straight line they expecting."

The angels returned their focus to the war going around the threesome's heads. Swords were out and more support was in route.

"Defeat with despair; stir up confusion," barked the commander to the dark side warriors inside the tunnel.

The commander continued, "Use dive bombs of hope-lessness and arrows of fear, spin them into confusion. They prepared for the arrival of the unsuspecting travelers.

On the outside of the tunnel, Pride was stationed and waiting. He was responsible for igniting the pride inside of them. He would fuel their self-sufficiency and motivate them in their own understanding.

The dark side warrior named Fear was also stationed at the front entrance to the tunnel. Fear's assignment was to exploit their unspoken fears, planted long ago in their early childhood. Fear stood with a notebook that held a record of their experiences in the past. Records were kept on each person's history. This enabled the dark side to exploit these fears throughout people's lives. Fear would use a trigger word to initiate fearful responses. Trigger words, smells and familiar dynamics, were powerful ways to utilize well-entrenched lies and false beliefs rooted deep inside hearts.

When people were afraid, they did not want to wait and hasty decisions led them to trouble. Fear and Pride were stellar saboteurs. They want to steer people away from the One who really loved them.

Heaven's warriors were present to defend. When accusing arrows struck the travelers' hearts the Heavenly warriors never fretted, for every dark arrow that landed was used for good.

The Heavenly host protected as the arrogant dark side anticipated with delight their schemes and plans. The dark side warriors were sure they were going to thwart them from getting to Lake Still Water because everything was working according to plan.

One of the Heavenly warriors commented about their enemy. "Their pride blinds them from seeing that victory has already been declared. They have been defeated." His partner broke out in praise. "Glory to the lamb of God, Glory to the Lamb."

I heard the Pursuer of Souls once explain it to King David long ago:

"They encourage each other in evil plans, they talk about hiding their snares; they say, and "Who will see them?" They plot injustice and say, "We have devised a perfect plan!" Surely the mind and heart of man are cunning. But God will shoot them with arrows; suddenly they will be struck down. He will turn their own tongues against them and bring them to ruin."

"All schemes allowed by the Pursuer of Souls are for His purposes, not their own, but their arrogance keeps them from believing." the warrior added.

From the battlefield, they watched their futile celebrations. The dark side creatures were giving each other high fives, convinced they would be leading this threesome to their death and destruction. (The saboteurs were sure they would never make it to Lake Still Water. They laid their snares and it was just a matter of time before the humans became captives.) The Pursuer wasn't going to snatch these people from their clutches; after all these citizens from Self Absorption came from a town owned by the dark side.

All spiritual eyes focused on the Tunnel of Your Own Understanding entrance, each side ready to battle for their cause.

The Tunnel of Your Own Understanding had been the source of many souls getting lost and trapped. Many died within the tunnel without making it out to the other side. The bowels of this tunnel hosted countless branches of dead ends and thousands of inlets of choices. There were a million different perspectives, which paved every road. When travelers entered, he/she discovered why it earned the nicknamed the Tunnel of Insanity.

No one ever went straight through the tunnel. Sojourners seduced by all the options, made choices by reasoning in their own understanding. They trust their own insight to be their compass. This left them vulnerable to be misdirected and deceived.

The dark side warrior and their commander knew far too well the tendencies of man's thinking. They were experts at deluding images to match a person's preconceived idea. Lie infiltrators assigned early on in a person's life, made lies seem true and truth a lie. The Tunnel let the travelers own understanding lead them further into the darkness until they lost all hope. Most that entered in, never found their way out.

A Heavenly officer reported to his commanding officer, "Sir, we are deployed inside and outside of the tunnel, and the sign you requested has been set and the boat is in place."

"Praise be." said the Captain.

"Good, we are prepared. Now we wait." A holy, expectant silence fell upon the area.

The dark side was busy celebrating their anticipated victory; they did not notice the newly placed sign or the boat.

Dreams Is Missing

Tuck woke up and saw Guardian folding his sleeping bag. She felt strange waking up and feeling peaceful. She remembered only one nightmare through the night. She felt good this morning.

"Morning Guardian!" Tuck said rubbing her eyes.

"Good Morning Tuck." Guardian replied, while he rolled up the bag and tied the strings.

For the first time, he felt optimistic about getting help for Tuck. He awoke during the night when she screamed. She went right back to sleep this time though she seemed to sleep through the night. Guardian could not fall back to sleep right away so he laid there and worried about her. He tried to imagine what her enemy looked like. He had asked her before but she never remembers what they look like by morning.

Tuck crawled out of her sleeping bag and started to roll it up. She grabbed her pillow to put it inside and looked around for Dreams, but Dreams was nowhere to be found. She crawled back inside her sleeping bag calling out his name. "Dreams where are you? I can't find you, boy where did you go?" At first, she thought he was hiding in one of the crevices inside her bag but after an exhaustive search, she came up empty.

"Guardian, have you seen Dreams?"

Guardian stopped what he was doing and looked around for him. "No I haven't Tuck. He is probably inside your sleeping bag."

"No I just looked there." Tuck began to panic. When Tuck panicked, she skipped right to the worse case scenario. "He is gone Guardian. Do you think one of the dragons from my dream came out and kidnapped him? Or maybe it was that wolf guy who looked like a sheep that we saw yesterday? Guardian, Dreams is gone!" Filled with terror and tears, Tuck ran to the comforting arms she knew.

"It's ok Tuck. He's got to be around here somewhere." Guardian held her and patted her on the back. Guardian wasn't concerned, where could a stuffed dog go on his own? How far can a stuffed dog wander? He began to search more seriously, knowing once he was found, it would calm down Tuck.

The longer they searched, the more bewildering his absence became. "Well you are right about one thing Tuck, Dreams is nowhere to be found!"

"What do we do Guardian? What do we do?" Tuck looked over at Guardian with hope. He was always so good at making things work out when she was worried.

Guardian looked over and saw her hope. He hated that look in this moment because he had none to offer her. "Well I don't know where he went Tuck, but I know we have looked absolutely everywhere and we need to stick to our travel plans. Hopefully Dreams will show up along the way."

Tuck didn't know what to make of Guardian's horrible idea. They never disagreed before. But Guardian was wrong about this. You never abandon your friends.

To Guardian it seemed foolish to delay going to Lake Still Water because a stuffed animal was missing.

"No Guardian, we cannot abandon Dreams."

"Tuck we can check around for a while longer, but then we need to go and trust it will work out."

"But I can't just leave Dreams behind, what kind of friend would that make me?" Tuck was mad at Guardian for even suggesting it. She wanted a choice. "He might just be a dumb old stuffed animal to you, but besides you, he is my closest friend."

Dreams was Tuck's faithful companion in the night. He was alongside her in every battle against the dragons and monsters. He endured many tortuous squeezes, and offered himself when she needed someone to cling to. "Guardian, what are we going to do?"

Guardian tried to comfort her but Tuck did not want his comfort, she wanted Dreams.

"Nothing about leaving Dreams behind is okay. We are abandoning a friend." She lectured Guardian, pleading to his sense of morality.

She knew deep down if Guardian left, she wasn't brave enough to wait alone. She hated herself but she knew when Guardian got up to leave, she would follow. She would follow him, out of fear of being alone.

For the first time ever, she felt a barrier come between her and Guardian. They searched and searched but Dreams was nowhere to be found.

Though it was hard for Guardian to do, he told Tuck it was time to go. She grievingly submitted, but made a silent vow in her heart she would never forgive Guardian for this.

"This is wrong. This is wrong Guardian." She blamed him but she knew she was responsible. She too left her friend behind. With every step she took, she felt more certain about Dreams' demise.

Counselor and Little Bin Start their 2nd Day Journey

Counselor was pleased at how quickly Little Bin's clothes dried. The rock itself grew hot from the sun's rays, providing assistance to the drying process. Though his tennis shoes were still a little soggy, all in all, he was in pretty good shape. He changed back into his own clothes. Their fish breakfast, along with an energy bar, made for a great meal. Little Bin didn't like fish much, but he caught this one so he didn't let on that it tasted nasty. Counselor enjoyed it thoroughly, making all kind of noises and 'mmm's' when eating it. Her enjoyment made Little Bin all the prouder.

There was an urgency to get going this morning. The line Counselor read in her invitation about "*Come now, come quickly,*" made her anxious to reach their destination. She carried a fear that something could steal away her opportunity.

She never really investigated her own fears much she preferred to deal with her clients' needs. At least that was the justification she gave to avoid issues too painful. Staying away from painful things used to work a lot better in the past than it does these days.

There was normal time, daylight savings time, and Little Bin time. Little Bin's time was fast, fast in everything. Speed allowed him the frequent off road adventures and impromptu thrills along the way adding depth to his daily experiences.

Little Bin thought, "it's only morning and already it was a perfect day. I caught a fish, ate the fish and we have not even arrived at the good part yet, Lake Still Water."

"Well are you ready to head out my little fisherman?"

Little Bin smiled wide, raising his right arm up with a stick in his hand, he did his Braveheart imitation, "To Lake Still Water or Bust!" Then with a fierce roar, he burst forward into a full sprint.

His leadership charisma had Counselor following in a slow jog. After about thirty yards her breathing was the only thing she could hear. She slowed down to catch her breath. She needed to pace herself for the long walk today.

The Threesome Divide Up

The threesome had been walking about half an hour after parting from the odd fellow that traced new directions on their map. They came around a sharp corner and there in front of them stood a massive opening in the face of the mountain. The tunnel looked like a huge mouth with the road its tongue.

"Why do I feel like I am about to be eaten?" Fatalist asked, staring into the giant mouth of the tunnel.

Worker was amazed at how they cut the opening out and wondered how long it must have taken. As they walked toward the entrance, their eyes caught sight of the sign hanging above the entrance:

"The Tunnel of Your Own Understanding."

Below this sign hung another sign, it was bright yellow with a thick black border and it was triangular shaped. "Caution, Poor lighting inside, enter at your own risk."

As Pleaser and Fatalist read the second sign about poor lighting, heaviness weighed on their hearts. They felt a strange sense of impending doom. "This doesn't seem right." Fatalist said. Pleaser nodded in agreement.

"Yeah, this doesn't seem right." Pleaser felt her fear beating inside her chest. She hated the dark and wanted to heed the yellow sign's warning.

Worker was disgusted by these two doubting Thomases. "What do you mean this isn't right? This couldn't be more right. You heard that guy; he said this is a short cut, the shortest distance and the flattest road to get there."

"I don't think so Worker. I have a really bad feeling about this." Pleaser said, quivering as she spoke the words. She stepped behind Fatalist to offer some non-verbal support of his opinion.

Worker was really frustrated now. "Trust me on this, I am not about to get stranded in some no good town again. I am going to successful arrive at my destination for a change and I am going to be the first one there."

Fear quickly flipped to the page that listed Worker's fears. Right on the top was that she would never amount to anything. It noted she was detoured from school and never managed to return. She fears her life of opportunity is over.

He leaned in to whisper, "This is a one time chance and you are not going to blow it again are you?"

"You two can join me or you can be quitters and throw in the towel. I don't care but I am going inside." Worker blurted out emphatically.

"Hey I am no quitter!" Fatalist protested. Fatalist's dander was up now. Pride maneuvered down to whisper to

Fatalist's flesh, "You aren't going to let her show you up are you?"

Fatalist was mad. "Look here missy, I am not a quitter and you better take that back or…" Fatalist ran out of what to say next so he stopped abruptly. Pleaser instantly came between the two trying to bring calm. Conflict made her so anxious.

Fear stood right beside Pleaser and escalated her fear of conflict. He knew she believed she felt responsible for every conflict. As Fear whispered to her about it being her fault, Pleaser became more anxious by the minute. "Now, now, calm down you guys. We need each other." Pleaser pleaded to both of them.

"Correction, I don't need anyone." Fatalist retorted.

"Can't we all just get along?" Pleaser begged.

Fatalist took a couple of steps back to get his temper in check.

Worker had already made her decision. "Look, I am going in there, the only question now is, is anyone going with me?"

Fatalist stared intently at Worker, waiting for her to apologize. Worker stared right back at him for this was a power struggle and she was not going to step down.

After a long ten second silence, she decided it was best to try to make peace, so she whispered an addendum to her previous comment. "Okay, I am sorry I called you a quitter. I was trying to get you to see the best thing is to go through the tunnel."

"I think we should go to that bridge on the map and see if there is some way to cross it despite to wash out." Fatalist suggested.

Pleaser was delighted with any suggestion other than walking into the darkness. She raised her hand in approval of checking out the bridge. "We just took that strange man's word that the bridge was washed out."

Fatalist crossed his arms in defiance and looked over at Pleaser. "Well? What do *you* think?"

This was Pleaser's worst nightmare, caught in the middle of two uncompromising people. Someone was going to end up being disappointed and it going to be her fault. Both were her friends and now she was the tiebreaker. Either way she would end up guilty, guilty for disappointing one of them. "Oh I don't know what is best."

Ideally, she wanted to please both, but this was impossible. She felt trapped and helpless. She looked up, hoping for a pie in the sky miracle. Her eyes caught a hanging from a tree. It was a wooden sign and the words read; *"He always provides a way of escape."* On the bottom end of the sign was an arrow that pointed down.

The Way of escape

Pleaser went to look what the arrow pointed out. She walked to the edge and there below, at the base of some winding steps, was a rubber boat. No one was near it. It was not tied to anything; it was just drifting there in the water.

"Hey you guys, come look at this."

Pleaser had a strong sense that this boat was for them. It was not a chartered plane, but it sure was an alternate way to get to Lake Still Water. The confidence she felt for the boat helped her decide right there, this was the way she was going to go.

She didn't care if it made them mad; she knew this boat was left for them.

"We should take this boat down the river to check out the bridge ourselves. If the bridge is out, we can just take the river down to Lake Still Water."

Fatalist nodded in agreement. "I concur with that idea." Fatalist, started down the steps toward the boat. Half way down the stairs he looked up, realizing not everyone was following. "Come on, what are you waiting for?"

Pleaser followed him down but Worker stood defiantly at the top of the stairs. Her hands were on her hips as she shouted. "I can't believe you guys, this is just great."

Worker was angry. She threw her hands up in disgust as if to push them away from her. "I told you guys, I am going to take the tunnel. I will meet you two losers there." She turned back toward the tunnel entrance but wasn't satisfied leaving things like that. She returned to the stairwell and added, "And I bet you I get there first."

Pleaser felt sick. She always felt sick when someone was mad at her. This was terrible. Worker was splitting from the team. Fatalist, on the other hand wasn't struggling with the separation at all.

"Fine, you stubborn, woman!" he yelled. From the distance, Worker now out of sight, Fatalist heard her comeback.

"Well maybe so, but at least I'm not a quitter!"

Worker knew that would make Fatalist mad and that is exactly why she said it. She wanted him to pay. She may sound all confident but she was scared to enter this tunnel alone, in the dark. Her pride would not let her back down. Pride had a way of leaving people all alone.

"I'll see you two losers there." Worker, at this point, was speaking into the Tunnel. Though her words appeared to be for Pleaser and Fatalist, they were really just helping her talk her way into tunnel.

Pleaser and Fatalist could hear her talking to herself all the way into the entrance but couldn't understand what she was specifically saying.

"I'm not afraid of a little darkness. I have a brain and I can reason through problems. I have myself that is all I need."

She had no idea how wrong she would be. The swords were out and fierce fighting had begun. A loud deep voice of authority billowed across the tunnel. It was an order to both sides of the battle. "You may not touch her, but everything else is allowable."

The evil laughs echoed in the tunnel chamber delightfully anticipating their prepared torments. Worker was about to come face to face with the powerlessness of her own self sufficiency.

The dark side Commander was angry. "There is only one! Why aren't there three?"

He took his disappointment out on the warrior closest to him. Without regard to who it was, he backhanded him across the tunnel. His body hit against the far side bricks with such force, he slid lifeless down the face of the wall.

"I guess I can't ask for a promotion today," thought the beaten victim of the Commander's latest rampage. He remained lifeless looking when he reached the ground, hoping not to create any more attention. He hated when he was the convenient chew toy for his master's temper.

Mr. Chips and the Ghost Town that Never Forgets

Tuck's resentment toward Guardian increased their traveling distance. It took conscious effort for her to walk at the slower pace, she was used to journeying beside him Guardian kept checking behind him and noticed the growing distance. He knew she was angry and was trying to punish him.

He felt horrible about the whole situation. He knew however, he would make the same decision again. He cared about Dreams too, for Guardian was the one who had given Dreams to her. He understood how Dreams held a place of security for Tuck when she would not go to sleep. He knew though that she couldn't keep hoping that a stuffed animal would be her answer to the night time terrors. He was investing his hope on this Pursuer of Souls. He was the best thing for Tuck in the long- run, even if it meant that right now he had to break her heart.

Tuck stayed angry. "He hasn't even looked back to notice how far apart we are getting. Doesn't he care anymore?" She even started to doubt his loyalty. The dark side warrior kept handing her bitter biscuits.

When humans were angry they developed a special appetite for bitter biscuits. He remained alongside her and handed her one right after the other. She chewed on the offense.

"I bet he doesn't even care about you anymore; this trip has certainly revealed his true nature." The dark side warrior whispered in her ear and waited for her to take another bitter biscuit. She did so every time, and in her anger, her appetite grew.

Guardian passed by a side road that broke off from the road they were traveling. When Tuck approached it minutes later, she saw a half rotted sign hanging at a slant that read: "The Town that Never Forgets"

In marking pen, someone had written above the word 'Town,' the word 'Ghost' so it read with its addition,

'The Ghost Town that Never Forgets.'

"Hmm, how odd." Something compelled her to take this other path. She wasn't sure why, but she was so angry with Guardian maybe if he got scared when he couldn't find her, he would feel as sorry as she did.

Tuck did not know that the plan whispered in her ear was to satisfy her appetite for a bitter biscuit. So, she turned down the road towards this town that never forgets.

It felt so strange being angry with Guardian. She had never been mad at him before. Tuck followed the dirt path for a ways. There were trees lining both sides.

Peering to the side of her trail, she saw the thickness of the woods. Its depth seemed never ending and there were many dry rotted trees throughout. Many trees had fallen and were leaning onto the trunk of another. There were no leaves, loneliness permeated this scene and Tuck felt small and alone.

It curved around the hillside as she entered into a valley. A town sat in the middle surrounded by four hills on every side. A weather worn sign held up by two rotting wood posts stretched across what at one time must have been the main street. It read 'Never Forgets.'

Tuck made her way down the abandoned main street and joked to herself that it seemed people must have forgotten to come home. The joke cracked her up she even snorted when she laughed.

Tuck would have thought about the word 'forget. She tried to lose memories, but they came back in some way to haunt her.

The town silence screamed of abandonment, an eerie quiet permeated the place. It felt like death lived here now. She watched a tumbleweed roll through the street, just like she had seen in the movies.

A soft banging came from a building across the way. Tuck decided to inquire about the noise. Crossing the barren street, she stepped onto the plank sidewalk to investigate.

"Hello, is anyone there?" When she asked she did not expect to hear anyone. There was no sign of life around at all. The rhythmic banging continued but no voice followed.

Every window caked with dirt, emphasized that there was no life left.

"Hello is anyone there?" she repeated.

A faint voice, barely audible replied. "Yes, I'm in here, help me."

Trying to follow the voice, she wiped from a dirty, cobwebbed window, a crusty layer of sand and dirt. She pressed her nose against the glass where a wrinkled, scowling face gazed back at her from the inside. Tuck startled, screamed and fell backwards. The whole time she was falling, she kept her eyes on the face looking back through the window.

The face looked as startled as she was.

"Oh my goodness you scared me." Tuck soberly whispered for Guardian, under her breath. "Guardian I need you, please come quickly." She regretted now more than ever her decision to ditch him. The person who had always been there to watch her, she chose to wander away. She lay on the ground to get her wits about her. This was way over her head. Her fears spoke so loudly, she could not hear any rational thoughts.

After a few moments, she pulled herself together, realizing this crusty old face was crying out for help.

"Help me, I am trapped, please get me out of here," cried the voice once again.

Tuck's logic returned and compassion replaced her fear; someone needed her help. She knew what being trapped felt like. She had a mission! She would help him. She jumped to her feet.

"Okay Mister, it is going to be okay. How do I get inside?" The dirty window blocked a clear picture but she recognized a motion sending her around the building.

Tuck walked around the perimeter until she found a door. There was a snake around a pole, which hinted this must be a doctor's office, or at least used to be. She opened the door and stepped inside. As soon as she entered, she felt claustrophobic.

Everything seemed cramped. From the outside, it appeared much larger than it felt on the inside. A sign greeted her as she entered the foyer of the office. It read; *"Hope deferred makes the heart sick."*

Out from the next room bellowed a crotchety old voice. "I am in here."

Tuck followed the voice and entered what looked like it used to be a patient waiting room. It was homey enough looking, there was carpet on the floor, but this room had not been cared for in a very long time. Cobwebs hung from every corner of the ceiling. One spider had such an intricate web; at first glance she mistook it for a dusty chandelier.

A brick wall stood from floor to ceiling, from end to end across the room. In the middle was a lit fireplace, supplying the only light source for the room. In front of the burning fire was a worn out couch, which clearly doubled as a bed. There were blankets skewed across the back of the couch and some sheets were lying on the floor below. There was a pillow propped up at one end with a head impression still formed. A thick layer of dust painted all the furniture.

Across from the fireplace was a row of dirty windows and standing in front of one of them was the same face that greeted her from the outside. The face carried a hunched over, wrinkled body, which started to hobble towards her. The age of this man was difficult to determine but the term older than dirt seemed to describe him perfectly. As he wobbled toward her, Tuck's compassion for him grew.

"This poor, old man," she thought to herself but when the 'poor old man' spoke, he knocked all the wind out of her sensitive nature.

"Hey what took you so long you little pipsqueak?"

His criticalness caught Tuck off guard. Could this be the same person crying out for help just minutes before?

"Gee I am sorry Mister, I don't know my way around here." Tuck's nervousness kept her talking, attempting to smooth out his harsh spirit.

"Um this place seems smaller on the inside than outside, have you ever noticed that?"

He interrupted her before she could reach her next sentence. "Have I noticed? Have I noticed? Look here you puny runt, I have been trapped inside this God forsaken place for twenty-five years. Don't you think I would have noticed its smallness by now?"

Tuck again found herself intimidated by his rudeness. "Why are you yelling at me Mister? I didn't do anything."

The old man gave her a 'go away' gesture with his hands and returned to looking out the dirtied window. Tuck realized why the windows were more soiled on the inside than the outside. A dirty looking, oily type substance discharged out from this man's breath.

"Kid, I just want out of here that's all. The first human being to pass by here in a very long while, and wouldn't it be my luck that it is a snot nosed kid."

"Sir I know this sounds obvious, but why don't you just walk out the front door?"

She knew this full-grown man was smart enough to know how to exit a building, yet she didn't understand how he could remain trapped inside when none of the doors were locked. He could have broken one of the windows and climbed out that way.

"Look here you little runt, what do you take me for, some sort of fool?"

"Tuck is my name Mister, not Runt."

"All right then, don't get your drawers all in a bunch. Tuck, I am not a fool. I would have walked out the door or climbed through one of these windows a long time ago if I could. But, I can't. I have a condition that prevents me from doing that."

"What kind of condition?"

"I can't remember its full medical term, so I'll shorten it to Chips. I have Chips."

He turned around to show her his back. On top of his shoulders were two huge growths. They looked like pillow cases stuffed to the brim, except with skin over them.

"Wow, I have never seen anything like that before." It was so ugly Tuck winced as she looked at it.

"Well I don't suppose you would have kid. This condition traps people where they live. People are not free to wander; they become encased by small surroundings and are haunted by all they are missing out on."

These chips on his shoulder were distracting. She couldn't help but stare at them and every time her eyes broke free, she felt compelled to look again.

"What causes this illness?" Tuck became afraid that she might catch it being near him.

"I don't know exactly, but I believe my ex-wife had something to do with it. When I was first diagnosed, I didn't pay attention to what the doctor said. I was so mad at my ex-wife at the time; I could not concentrate on anything else.

Chips became an epidemic in the whole town. Every household had at least one person come down with a case of Chips. That is when things went from bad to worse for this town."

"I once read a medical journal that I found lying around here about Chips. It said people living in towns that never forget are more disposed to this particular condition. It had something to do with our flesh being susceptible to Chips."

"Diagnosing it early on is the key to a successful recovery. If you don't deal with it right away, it grows roots inside of you, making people resistant to most kinds of treatment.

At the early onset of the condition, a slight chip will appear above the shoulder, hardly noticeable to the human eye. Then over time, patients developed a hearing problem. It is difficult to hear what others are saying. They can only hear what they want others to say, not what they may actually be speaking."

"The next area affected is the eyesight. A plank-like obstruction covers the inside of the eye lens, inhibiting people from seeing things accurately. As a result, patients become paranoid and believe irrational things.

Many people become convinced that others were intentionally hurting them or stealing from them. As the condition progressed, the chip grew bigger and bigger. Stress has been known to escalate the growth rate."

He continued, "Our town doctor came down with Chips while treating the rest of us. He refused to call other doctors for help. He became convinced that if they came, they would steal his practice.

"As more and more people became infected, treatment was slow because the demands were so high. Everyone was blaming someone else for their condition. Some thought it was a virus… I believe it is some sort of cancer. One thing is clear, it slowly kills people."

"What happened to your doctor? Where did everyone go?" asked Tuck.

"The doctor died, right in that chair." He pointed over to the receptionist's chair in the foyer. "I found him myself. When I realized he was dead, I started to panic. I knew that this meant the end for me. There was going to be no chance of a cure or effective treatment without the doctor.

All the stress of finding him dead escalated the growth rate of my chips. When I tried to leave here, I could not fit through the door. I was unable to bend and my chips extended too high. I've been trapped in here ever since."

"So did all the people die?" Tuck whispered.

"The healthy people moved away, fearing they might get it themselves. Some left Never Forget to start fresh. I even heard a story that someone woke up in the middle of the night and their chips had fallen off and were lying on the floor.

I do not know if any of that is true, but even if it was, it does not change my situation here. I blame my ex-wife. If she hadn't been such a difficult woman, I would have been able to listen to the doctor early on and acted on his treatment plan.

"My doctor always said 'relocation never healed anyone.' He said all the time, 'When you leave, you take your Chips with you.'"

"How have you managed to live here for twenty-five years without leaving?" Tuck asked.

"Our town's emergency shelter is in this basement. I've been eating the canned food saved there in the event of a town emergency. Believe me, I am plenty sick of beans, corn, and golden peaches." Mr. Chips looked at Tuck with a serious glare. "So kid, are you going to help get me out of here or are you going to be like everyone else and leave me here?"

"Sure Mister. I will try, but how about you, will you try too?"

"What a dumb question that is! Of course I will try. Isn't obvious I want out of here?"

"Well to be honest with you sir, it isn't so obvious. If you really did want out of here, you would have already found a way out. You could have broken windows or even used the furniture to bash a hole in the wall or something. It doesn't appear to me that you want out as badly as you want to stay mad about being trapped inside."

This made Mr. Chips very angry. "You little creep, how dare you, speak to me that way!"

"Sir, don't get angry with me, I am trying to help you," Tuck cried.

"You don't know what it is like to be stuck in here for twenty- five years. It is you who doesn't understand. I am not angry about being trapped. I am angry because I have Chips!"

"Have you ever thought Mister, that maybe you have Chips because you are angry?" She shocked herself by her boldness with this total stranger.

Tuck stepped back to relieve her anxiety about what he might do next. Mr. Chips stood there speechless. Then he backed up, to gain some distance from the truth that came from this child. The words resonated in his mind.

"…You have Chips because you are angry…"

This statement challenged all his embittered dreams and his responsibility for this mess surfaced. He saw for a brief second the rotting condition of his heart. His critical spirit was why he verbally abused his wife. This was the birthplace of his Chips. When his wife left him for another man, self-pity led him to drink more heavily but he continued to blame her for every bad thing that occurred.

She was the reason he was fired; it wasn't because they found him drunk on the job. She was the reason his kids hated him; it wasn't because he criticized them so much that they chose *not* to be around him. She was the reason he got sick; it wasn't because he wouldn't listen to the doctor's warnings to address the anger in his life before it was too late.

His mouth dropped open as the weight of truth pressed upon his shoulders. Truth weighed heavily upon the Chips. Truth was Chips only cure, because Truth brought humility and offered forgiveness. He felt like collapsing, he had no strength left.

Tuck wasn't sure what to do. She wasn't even sure what she had done. She watched this old bully reduced to powder right before her eyes. She found herself breathing gently, afraid her breath might cause this fragile man to disappear in a puff.

Tears welled up in his eyes, but at the same time anger rose within him. She watched a civil war battle rage within him. She wondered which side would win.

Tuck knew about civil war battles. No one standing on the outside had arms long enough to reach in and help resolve to this war.

As the old man allowed his thoughts to continue, one side saw the truth, and the emptiness of his own life resulting from his own choices. The other side, led by pride, fueled his anger with all kinds of excuses. Like wet cement, once pride set in, his heart quickly hardened.

Tuck stood without speaking a word and watched him struggle. Mr. Chips looked at Tuck as if he himself did not know who would be the victor.

Then she saw it. A resolved countenance came. One side had clearly defeated the other. The battle was over.

"Get out... Get out of here now. Just leave me alone and don't ever come back. Do you understand me?" He started towards her. His face was emblazoned with an embittered hatred.

Tuck wasn't afraid of him physically, as he was a meager man. What did scare her was the coldness that broadcasted from his eyes.

She knew he wasn't yelling at her, he just thought he was. He was screaming at truth, the truth about his life; the truth that reflected who he really was and who he had become. He didn't like what he saw. He had chosen captivity over truth. He chose his Chips over freedom. Chained in bitterness, he chose not to forgive.

Tuck pitied him. "Oh I don't ever want to end up a prisoner like this." At that moment, she released all the resentment she was harboring against Guardian. The bitterness she had carried into this town. She saw the horrible consequence of harboring anger. She felt lighter in her own spirit as she turned to exit, leaving Mr. Chips to his own choices.

As she reached the door, she looked back at the pathetic shriveled up man. "Okay then, goodbye Mr. Chips. I am sorry for your choice."

In a final act of defiance, he took off a hole-ridden slipper and threw it at her; it landed a good ten feet away from where she stood. "It's isn't my choice to be here, I have Chips, it is my ex-wife's fault."

Before Tuck closed the door, her eyes returned to the sign, which first greeted her when she entered. *"Hope deferred makes the heart sick"*

The truth had been in front of him this whole time, but alas, he never read it with his heart. Tuck wondered as she kicked the dust off from her shoes, how such a hardened heart was still able to pump blood through veins.

Tuck walked out to the middle of Main Street to get her bearings. "Which way do I go?" Then she saw a road sign that read; "Lake Still Water" The arrow pointed towards the other end of town, a road she had not yet traveled. She had a choice. She could go back where she came to find Guardian, or proceed ahead and get to Lake Still Water on her own.

There was an independent sprit born within her. She felt confident. She took one-step toward Lake Still Water Road, to try it on for size. It seemed to fit so she kept stepping in that direction. Before long, the Ghost Town that Never Forgets disappeared from view. She felt hopeful about her certain arrival at Lake Still Water.

Counselor and Little Bin Meet a Wolf in Sheep's Clothing

Little Bin and Counselor took a break and checked their bearings. From out of nowhere appeared a strange looking creature. He looked like a sheep, but there was something indefinable about him. He was an enigma.

He gave a big broad smile and displayed the whitest teeth Little Bin had ever seen. They were magnetic. The whiteness drew their eyes in and their eyes could not break free from the white teeth's clutch.

Little Bin recognized that magnetic force; it was something very familiar to him. He saw it when people walked up and peered into the mirror of illusion back home.

He became very suspicious about this stranger. He pulled his eyes away from the teeth just as he had learned to pull away from the mirror. He felt a force trying to draw his eyes back. Though the smile was friendly looking, Little Bin sensed a trap.

Counselor found herself mesmerized by his smile. What the sheep was saying didn't really concern her, she just wanted to continue looking at his teeth. She never knew sheep had such sharp teeth.

"Hi there folks, are you one of the parties headed to Lake Still Water?"

Counselor watched with fascination as his mouth moved. She answered so he would open his mouth again. "Yes sir, we are."

"Well the One who invited you sent me to escort you the rest of the way. He wanted to make sure you didn't get lost."

"Oh how nice. We are grateful for your guidance. We know where we are though. We have no worries."

"Well it is a good thing I came when I did, because the bridge ahead is washed out. I will take you another way. It is a short cut."

Little Bin had moved himself behind Counselor, peering out from her hips at the distrustful stranger. He kept tugging on Counselor's shirt while the sheep was talking, trying to communicate his concern. He could tell she was stuck in the teeth's clutches.

Though she felt Little Bin's tugs, she could not muster up enough focus to shake free from her trance. She was a captive, to the sparkling glisten. The smile held Counselor in its deadly clutch, and he would not let her go.

Little Bin resorted to more desperate measures. He screamed out with a firm voice, "Uh Counselor can I talk with you a minute, alone?"

Little Bin glanced at the sheep's face but would not look at his teeth. He was afraid he might fall prey to its strange powers too.

"Why sure Little Bin, what is it?" Counselor put her arm around Little Bin while maintaining direct eye contact with the teeth.

"Counselor, Counselor." Little Bin moved her head toward his until their eyes met.

"There. Don't look at his teeth they have some sort of power." Little Bin whispered.

Her eyes now freed from its clutches, she was able to think.

"Counselor there is something very wrong with this sheep. We shouldn't listen to him and definitely *do not look at his teeth.*"

Counselor still was not thinking quickly on her feet.

"Did you notice he never spoke the Name of One the 'Suer of Souls.'"

"Well now that you mention it, Little Bin I believe you are right."

"He looks like a sheep but he isn't a sheep. Things are not what they appear with this guy. His teeth are dangerous. They are wolf teeth. I am telling you he is DANGEROUS."

In his desperate attempt to convince Counselor of this evil animal, Little Bin spoke too loud and the sheep heard.

"Dangerous? I am not dangerous, how could little 'ole me be dangerous? I am just a harmless sheep following his master's command," professed the evil animal.

Little Bin glanced up when a sign hanging in the tree caught his eye; "Beware of wolves in sheep clothing"

Little Bin tapped Counselor on the shoulder and pointed up to the sign. He was sly enough that the sheep didn't notice. Then an idea came to Little Bin. It was simple but it just might work.

He approached it again but this time with a smile on his face and his hand fully extended offering a handshake. "Hi my name is Little Bin, what is yours?"

The sheep was caught off guard and responded quickly and without thinking. "Oh my name is Wolf."

Right after he spoke, he realized his fatal error. Both hands moved to cover his mouth, but it was too late. His identity was compromised by his own ignorance and worst of all; it was by the hand of a little boy.

He failed to keep one of the basic fundamental principles from the <u>Warrior Handbook</u>, mentioned in Chapter 5, "The Fundamentals of Deception."

Number One, "Never reveal your identity. Mystery adds to the confusion." This little kid outsmarted him.

Little Bin pointed at him and said, "Uh huh, you aren't a sheep! You are a wolf in sheep's clothing!"

Little Bin pointed at the wolf with one hand, and reached over and took hold of his coat in the back and pulled down. The sheepskin coat fell to the ground leaving a naked wolf exposed for both to see.

At first, the wolf froze from the shock, but once his anger caught up, he growled fiercely at Little Bin's audacity.

Counselor grabbed Little Bin's hand and screamed, "Run, Little Bin, run!"

Counselor turned with urgency, holding and pulling Little Bin's hand. The wolf's fury lifted him up off the ground and upon landing again, he pursued after them.

Little Bin imagined that he had on his P.F. Flyers; the shoes that made you jump higher and run faster.

Counselor looked desperately for some place to seek shelter. She knew they wouldn't be able to out run this wolf for long. "There, over there."

She pointed to their desired destination. A tall brick tower sat in the middle of a meadow, twenty yards ahead.

This strong tower was their hope. Her adrenalin was at work. She couldn't feel her feet touch the ground.

With every step, she expected to feel a chomp on her leg or neck by the dangerous pearly whites. They reached the tower on a full sprint. The door was wide open as if inviting them inside.

The tower was not very wide, maybe eight feet in diameter, so once inside they had to stop fast. The walls of brick helped stop them. Counselor put her hands out and braced herself as she ran into the brick surface attempting to buffer the collision.

Little Bin decided to stop himself by sliding into the brick staircase as if it was second base. When Counselor hit the wall, she pushed off turning back around to close the open door.

As she reached for the door handle, out of the corner of her eye she saw the wolf launched in a mid-air strike. She quickly closed the door, pressing all her weight against it.

THUD! The solid wood door terminated the wolf's flight. Counselor heard a whimper as the wolf slid down the surface of the door.

"Yeah, he's toast!" cried Little Bin.

Counselor listened for another second to make sure there was no life left in him, before checking on Little Bin. "Are you okay?"

Little Bin wasn't scared but excited. "That was awesome. Did you see how fast we ran?" He grabbed his head with his hands trying to contain all of what just happened. "We almost got eaten by a wolf," he proclaimed with a big smile. "I told you he was trouble."

Still winded Counselor tried to gain her composure. Counselor nodded in agreement with him.

"You saved our lives Little Bin, you are a hero today!"

"Wow I have never been a hero before, for real." He came over and settled next to her. "Do you think he is still out there?"

"I don't hear anything. I know he didn't win the battle with the door. They both looked at each other and started to laugh. "I think just to be safe we should wait here for awhile."

Little Bin, still pumping with adrenaline, ran up the stairs to investigate the top of the tower. He reached the top step and it opened up into a circular shaped room. It was a mirror image of the floor plan below. There was no furniture or any indication of someone having been there. Wood shutters darkened the room, so Little Bin went over and opened them and peered outside.

He saw the wolf lying lifeless against the front door. He didn't appear to be breathing at all. The view was magnificent; a pretty green meadow sprayed with purple and yellow wildflowers. There were hills framing the background and the sun was shining on portions of the land. He noticed another sign hanging from a tree right outside the tower.

"Counselor come here I need to show you something."

Counselor slowly stepped her way up the stairs to where Little Bin was looking out. Her body was already feeling stiff from all the sprinting and her adrenaline rush had retreated. She was feeling really tired.

"Look over there - read that sign." Little Bin pointed to the sign, which read: *"I AM a strong tower you can run into and be saved."*

"These trees keep helping us out. They show up whenever we need help it seems. I am going to call them the trees of life. I think I might hug every tree I see, thanking them for their help."

Counselor laughed. "Sounds like a wonderful idea, my friend. Well are you ready to continue our travels?"

"You bet!"

They walked back down to the front door and opened it, cautiously stepping over the dead wolf wedged lifelessly against the door. Until they finally lost sight of the wolf altogether, Counselor continually looked back to confirm he was truly dead.

Worker Enters the Tunnel of Your Own Understanding

Worker stepped into the Tunnel. She gazed straight across to the other side and thought, "Piece of cake. It couldn't be more than one hundred fifty yards across."

She couldn't wait to beat Fatalist and Pleaser to Lake Still Water. She would prove to them, she was right all along.

She could hear her voice echo across the rafters of the hallowed cavern, "piieecce off caakke."

She could picture her arrival all so clearly. She would be there with her campsite already set up, sitting on her beach chair, sipping an ice tea with a straw. They would wonder how she did it. How did she arrive so quickly? She pictured them entering all dirty and tired, barely able to drag themselves into camp. The first thing they would say when they saw her was, "You were right Worker." This would be sweet validation. This has become her motivation.

The thrill of this picture quickened her pace. Enthralled in fantasy, she was oblivious to the lack of progress she had made exiting to the other side.

Every person entering the tunnel was blind to the unseen dynamics flurrying about them. To step in with their own understanding, they rendered themselves useless. They could not reckon with the unseen elements that raged around them.

Human beings were unaware of unseen things for the most part. Their physical eyesight focused on what they understood was there. Their dark side enemies were masters of illusion. They used shadow and light to create inaccurate perspectives. The second alliance to illusion was pride. Pride is the foundation of people's own understanding. What people did not understand was that pride blinded them.

Man's propensity to trust in themselves was their greatest downfall. Worker seemed to be no exception.

The light in the tunnel grew scarce. Pockets of the blackest darkness stitched next to shades of gray. Dark side forces were vigorously flapping their wings, deflecting light to project false depth perceptions.

Worker had been walking down fantasy lane and did not notice her lack of progress. When she checked back in she was bewildered. "I don't look any closer than when I started."

A cold chill went down her back but she pushed it from consciousness. "That is odd."

The on-looking warrior giggled watching Worker follow like clockwork all those that had gone before her. "Typical boss; she seems typical." They had seen this pattern over and over again.

"Now!" bellowed a deep voice from within the tunnel's rafters. Their Commander had given the order, and "Operation Frenzy" was now in play.

This was a full-scale harassment assault. They worked in pairs. One blew by or brushed against her physically, while the other whispered a taunting message. One warrior touched Worker's shirt, while his partner whispered, "Danger lurks in shadows ahead." Then another blew in Worker's face, while his partner whispered, "What could that be I am in here all alone?"

Worker's heart started beating hard, and she felt her chest press down on her lungs. Coaching herself, she gave herself a pep talk. "Keep yourself together girl, don't let your imagination run away with you." If only this pep talk worked. Her stride quickened and so did her paranoia. She attempted to focus on the small little speck of light at the end of the tunnel.

What was that?" A cold breeze blew right by her, chilling her bones. "Is anyone there?" She looked behind her hoping to pick up some sign of a person somewhere. Her panic intensified, but she began to reason things through. She chalked up the breeze to having an over-active imagination. Her confident demeanor dissolved into a puddle of insecurity.

"Some piece of cake this tunnel is, girl," she said, scolding herself for her arrogance. "It looks like I am in the middle of the tunnel, the same distance now from both exits. That's just great!

"Rumpus I am really scared." She cried out in terror.

"Rumpus? Did I just say Rumpus?" Rumpus was her childhood stuffed dog. He was her faithful listener and friend when she was growing up. She named him Rumpus because his rear end stood up in the air and his front paws were under his chin. He was the best listener she ever knew. He heard things nobody else did.

"I sure miss you boy, especially now." Whenever she was scared as a child, Rumpus was there. Even though he never talked back to her, he listened so well it helped. "Rumpus I really got myself in a mess now."

The dark side looked on and their glee increased as they observed her panic grow. They began to mock her as they watched. One demon flew over the shoulder of another demon and with dramatic style, poked fun at Worker.

He folded up his hands and placed them on the shoulders of his partner.

"Why, am I talking to a stuffed dog I no longer have? If I am not talking to stuffed animals, I am talking to owls. Whoever is there I need help."

They all burst out laughing. They loved to see confusion and panic overtake their victims. "She is talking to a stuffed

155

dog to try to keep her sanity. How crazy is that?" Cackling laughter followed.

"Hey boss, we should place a note in her file to use the voice of this dog Rumpus at another time so she thinks she is hearing voices. Then she will know just how crazy she is."

"Devious thinking Schemer, make a note in her record," said the boss.

"Got it boss – but how do you spell Rumpus?" The boss ignored Schemer and asked another warrior, "Is Sodom ready for his job?"

"Yes sir, all is set and ready," a voice reported from the darkness.

Worker was struggling to see, but she couldn't see anything. "Get it together." She felt herself beginning to unravel. She tried to slow her breathing down. When she opened her eyes, she made out a road sign right in front of her. She stepped up so close to the sign, her nose brushed up against the mildewed wood. The sign read; "Fresh Perspective Road."

"A sign! Fresh perspective that sure sounds good to me. How could this road make things any worse? A change would be good.

Rumpus, perhaps our luck is turning around for the good."

Worker turned down Fresh Perspective Road without hesitation. Sodom, the impish warrior, just finished placing the sign in front of her to catch her attention. "Gets 'em every time."

His colleagues swooped down to offer him a high five for a job well done. Sodom was famous for his signs. His first sign was his most notable, way back in the days of Lot. His first sign read, 'Well watered land,' which he placed just outside of Sodom and Gomorrah. That is where he earned his name.

This new road renewed Worker's confidence, but her restored boldness didn't last long. Each step forward along this new road, she stepped deeper into blackness. Her strong gait changed into a hesitant step.

"Why is this road called Fresh Perspective? There is nothing fresh about this road. Hello is anyone there?"

Her own voice ricocheted across the tunnel. She felt so small. Silence sealed her inside lost-ness.

From out of nowhere, a tiny man appeared right in front of her. He held a low dim flashlight up his face so she could seem him. He smiled at her but his yellow teeth gave her a chill.

The flashlight died, so he snapped his finger and a nearby lamppost turned on providing a very low light. It shone just enough to highlight his wrinkled cheeks. Other details of his face lurked in the shadows.

She noticed he was carrying a lantern, but the light from his lamp was so weak, it did not pierce the darkness at all.

"Hi there, can I help you find anything?" The eerie man asked.

He was a fast talker, and his manner reminded Worker of a used car sales man. He lifted a long arthritic finger to his nose and said, "You look like a woman who in need of options. With more options, you will make better decisions. Don't you agree?"

This time, Worker felt more hesitant to agree. She had learned that in this tunnel, nothing was as it appeared.

"Well what you say makes sense but..."

"Well really, how could more options be a bad thing?"

She shook her head in agreement, and thought, "Yes how could it be a bad thing?"

"More options would be great thank-you." Worker offered.

This impish little man lifted his hand in the air and said, "As you wish then."

At that instant hundreds of street lamps lit up as far as her eye could see. Each street lamp marked the start of a new road that she could choose to travel. The tunnel was more enormous than she imagined.

The street lamplights' were so dim they were ineffective as guiding lights. All these new options defeated her, they did not encourage. The lamplights revealed each street as an option but provided no glimpse to what she might find on them.

"Oh my, this is so overwhelming. I don't know which one to pick." She regretted her decision immediately, just as she regretted every other decision she made about the Tunnel of Your Own Understanding.

She called out for the little man to return. "Excuse me, sir? I would like to change my mind about your offer."

A devilish laugh retorted back from the darkness.

"Too late my dear, enjoy the freedom of all your choices." His laugh was like a cold spear to her spine. The laugh lingered in the darkness.

Worker initially fearful but then her fear transformed to anger. She directed the anger toward herself. How could she be so stupid? "Why didn't I go with Fatalist and Pleaser?"

"You always have to have your way don't you? You always think you know best. You have to prove to everyone that you know best. No one is going to find you in here."

The idea she just might die in here, became a harsh reality. She felt foolish and alone. Her sore feet and swollen knee were great word pictures for her weariness of heart.

Cackles of laughter caromed off the walls. There was no better entertainment for the dark side than to watch the plans of men unravel right before their eyes.

BUT...From the Commander of the Heavenly Host, Word was sent out, "Be ready, our time is soon."

Fatalist and Pleaser wonder, 'What Just Happened?'

Fatalist and Pleaser were delighted with the spaciousness of their rubber boat. They both stretched out their legs without even touching each other.

"The one good part about Worker not coming with us is we get first class seating." Fatalist said half joking, half-serious.

Pleaser smiled politely but still wrestled with the guilt about her decision, Worker had to venture into that dark tunnel alone. Fatalist put his hands behind his head, stretched out his legs as far as they could stretch, and then crossed them. "Yep this is the way to travel."

It annoyed Pleaser how unbothered Fatalist appeared about their broken team. So she tried not to think about it and fixed her eyes ahead to see where the stream waters were carrying them As the raft rode forward on the water, she hoped to leave behind the guilt. She saw a bridge off in the distance and pointed it out to Fatalist. "Does that bridge look washed out to you?"

Fatalist squinted to see, but to him, the bridge looked intact. "That bridge looks just fine to me."

Just as he said that, a tearing noise came from somewhere in the boat. "Did our boat just spring a leak?"

"I don't know but it sure sounded like it." Pleaser and Fatalist both started looking around the boat to identify where the leak might be. The water started to seep in, and then pour in. Pleaser screamed. "We are taking on water!"

Fatalist corrected Pleaser. "We are sinking! Abandon ship!" Fatalist grabbed his bag and dove toward shore, with Pleaser following close behind. When she jumped in, her bag got tangled up with the rope from the boat. It was a struggle to get untangled. She swallowed a lot of water in her effort to get free.

They both stroked their way to the water's edge, and pulled themselves onto the shore before collapsing. Pleaser coughed up water. Fatalist tried to help by pounding gently on her back.

He turned over onto his back to catch his breath, and review what just happened. Pleaser remained face down in wet clothes. She was not worried about what just happened. She was preoccupied with Fatalist seeing her in wet clothes.

"What in the world just happened Pleaser?"

"We must have struck a rock or something. I don't know it all happened so fast."

"Well that is just great." Fatalist said. "I had hoped we could float all the way to Lake Still Water."

"Well Fatalist, it seems someone has other plans for us."

"They always do." His uplifting attitude sunk with the boat. He was angry and in a real foul mood.

"Well we better start walking. That will be the fastest way for our clothes to dry." Fatalist jumped up and stormed down the trail paralleling the stream.

Pleaser was hesitant to move, but recognized there was no other option, she stood up and started to walk.

The Unseen Battle before Them

What Fatalist and Pleaser did not see was the spiritual arrow protruding from their deflated boat. It was an excellent shot, striking the seam, a rubber boat's most vulnerable place. The dark side soldiers on the bridge celebrated at the bull's-eye shot.

A rookie fired the successful arrow. He reveled in the "that-a-boy" accolades from his peers but the Heavenly host was pleased as well, because though the dark side launched their plan, no one was injured.

The deadly arrow was actually steered by a warrior from the Army of Heaven. They lost their boat, but it was because of Heaven's intervention, not the dark side's skill. The arrow striking the seam of the boat sabotaged a certain plot for destruction.

Fatalist stormed away angry and disappointed, completely unaware how this mishap spared him.

Guardian Searches for Tuck

Guardian started second-guessing his decision about Dreams. Did he make the right choice? Would Tuck ever forgive him? Would there be restoration from their first fight?

Preoccupied, he forgot to look behind him. He stopped on the road to survey how far back Tuck lingered. He waited and waited and there was no sign of her. His heart started beating fast and he began thinking the worst. Had she fallen? Gotten kidnapped? Was she calling out for him?

"Tuck, where are you? Are you okay?" Guardian ran back over the road he had covered, scanning the side of the road in case she had fallen.

"I am supposed to look after her. I will never forgive myself if anything happened to her...this is awful, just awful."

Guardian looked and looked but there was no sign of Tuck anywhere. Then he came upon a fork in the road that he had past awhile back. The weather worn sign read, *The Town That Never Forgets*. Guardian acted on a hunch and turned down the side road toward the town. He ran toward the town but needed to stop and regain his breath, he had run himself tired.

"Oh please protect her, please look out after her. Please help me find her." Guardian did not attach an official name to whom he was making this request, but he sent it up as a prayer from his heart. He hoped there was a hand that would take hold of it and answer his prayer.

He heard a soft voice speak to his heart. *"Man's ways are in full view of the Lord."* The small still voice carried comforting words. He knew this voice belonged to the Pursuer of Souls.

He fell to his knees, lifted his eyes to the sky. He had no idea what the Pursuer of his Soul looked like but pictured an old looking man with a white beard. "Please watch out for her, Pursuer of Souls. She is helpless and little and vulnerable. Help me find her."

He remained still for a moment, hoping to hear something again. When he didn't, he started to walk fast down the road toward the Town That Never Forgets.

Guardian jogged down the main street, an hour after Tuck exited. Walking in the middle of the street, he had a full view of this forsaken town. A sign hanging from a tree read; *"You will seek Me and find Me, when you search for Me with all your heart."*

Oh how Guardian wished Tuck had written that sign. At least he would know for sure that he would find her. He wondered if she was still angry with him. He had failed Tuck. Despite his best efforts to be faithful, he let her down. He disappointed her like everyone else.

The weight of his burdened heart pushed heavily upon his shoulders.

He noticed a Sheriff's office a few buildings down and decided to see if anyone was there. If this wasn't a ghost town, the sheriff's office would be the most rational place to start.

Stepping into the Sheriff's office, he was greeted by a gnarly spider web so elaborate it took Guardian five minutes to untangle himself. He looked around at the three desk tops, thick with dust. There were handcuffs laying on one desk with file folders skewed in disorder.

He thought he heard something rustling in the back where the cells were. Guardian walked across the office and opened the door. There were three separate jail cells with a narrow walkway in front of them. A little wooden bench sat in front of each cell for visitors.

There was nowhere to hide in here. He was puzzled about where the noise came from, he stepped into one the cells and looked out the barred window to see if the noise came from outside. He saw a woodpecker on a tree and figured that is what he heard.

He turned back around just in time to see the cell door shut behind him. It had an automatic locking system so as it shut, it locked.

Guardian raced to the door to try to push it open but it was too late. A cold chill shot through his spine. "Is anyone there?"

There was no one. No one he could see with the natural eye anyway.

The dark side warrior cackled just outside of the bars. He was jumping up and down with glee over the panicked look on Guardian's face. Human beings were so stupid. Putting his thumbs in his ears, he mocked Guardian, knowing he could not see him.

The warrior pulled out the papers that had his written orders, "Distract and detain." He giggled again. "This ought to detain him for a few years." He walked out of the Sheriff's office, leaving Guardian trapped inside to die. "Mission accomplished."

Guardian tried the bars by the open window. He tugged and pulled and yelled for help. He was in an inescapable mess. "Just when you think things can't get worse."

Grabbing tightly onto the bars he screamed as loud as he could, "Help!"

The reality of it all hit him. Why was he screaming? He was in a Ghost Town.

He fell backwards onto the cot, flush against the bars. Dust flew up from the blanket, causing him to cough. His hope had turned to dust. He had never felt so hopeless in his whole life.

Tuck Falls into the Pit of Despair

Tuck had enjoyed her independence for a couple of hours. She even walked confidently. She was surprised at how well she was dealing with life on her own. "Why have I been afraid all this time? I don't need to depend on someone." She proclaimed. "It isn't healthy."

No sooner did she make this proclamation, when she stepped into a camouflaged pit. Falling, Tuck felt everything move in slow motion. Gravity pulled her body to the ground so quickly that her stomach was lifted to her throat.

The bottom of the pit was thickly layered with sand, which helped buffer her landing. As she felt her feet hit the ground, she rolled onto her side to lighten the stress to her body. In an instant, everything changed and her fear returned.

She was embarrassed for even entertaining the thought she could make it on her own.

She sat for a minute trying to soak in what had just happened. She looked up toward the opening from which she fell.

She always felt so small at the bottom of pits. This wasn't the first time she had fallen into one. She had fallen into every type of pit imaginable. She was some kind of magnet to them.

In the past, she just waited for Guardian to rescue her. She knew he would come; he always did. But this time was different. Guardian did not know where she was. Fear shot through her like a rocket.

Even he had limitations. He couldn't rescue her if he didn't know where to find her. This was all her fault. She chose the side path because she wanted to hurt him. She wanted him to worry and make him feel bad for leaving Dreams behind. Now she was trapped in a pit, with no hope for help, and there was no one to blame but herself.

She talked to herself for reassurance. She sat up dejected, reviewing her day, and reliving the morning when the trouble began. She couldn't get over how Guardian chose to abandon Dreams so quickly.

A powerful anger rose within her, her cheeks turned red. The indignation inside her stood strong and immoveable.

A small still voice spoke gently to her heart.

"Is your anger just about Dreams or could you be feeling abandoned yourself?"

For Tuck's jigsaw puzzle life, this piece was a perfect fit. It really wasn't about Dreams, not like she thought. She felt what Dreams felt because she knew what it was like to be left behind.

Tuck realized she held onto a secret dream. Maybe one day her parents would change. They would wake up, one morning and fall in love with her for the first time.

To this point, they just resented her for stealing their dreams away. She saw it in their eyes each time they looked at her. Eyes couched in disappointment and their resentment grew with each passing year.

Over time, it became too uncomfortable to see her so they stopped looking. In response, Tuck raised herself. She did the best she could, but a kid only has so many resources.

She survived with the help of many imaginary friends. Whatever was too big for Tuck to handle, she just tucked it away, neatly folded and locked away in a drawer marker 'throwaways.'

Once she met Guardian, she did not need imaginary friends anymore, because she had a real friend. She felt cared for, the first time since Miss Julie went away. Guardian wore many hats; parent, friend, big brother, protector.

Through Guardian could do many things, he not read her mind. Tuck was without her rescuer.

Being trapped in a pit was miserable, it was also familiar. Misery had always been a companion to Tuck, but today she stooped to a new low. She chose misery over loyalty, she betrayed her best friend.

Looking up at the small opening above her, she reviewed how many times she arranged rescues when she needed reassurance. Guardian was always glad to respond to her need for help, so she was reassured in love.

Overtaken with shame over all her manipulations, sadness fell heavily upon her. She rolled onto her side feeling the weight of her traitorous heart. Speaking aloud in the pit she said, "Oh just swallow me up. Just eat me alive." Tuck laughed at her drama and then groaned.

"Never mind I would probably give you indigestion."

She rolled over onto her back in surrender, waiting for life to swallow her whole. She saw a tree branch extending across the opening above. A sign hung from the branch. It read; *"The truth will set you free."*

As Tuck read these words, a sour taste plagued her mouth. "Free. I don't deserve freedom. I don't even want to be free. Freedom hurts too much." In resignation, she began coaching herself, "Alone is much safer."

Tuck resigned, looked around for things help her make this a home. If she wasn't going to be rescued, she might as well make it livable.

She made a pillow out of sand and fallen palm leaves. She found an old candy wrapper and hung it up as a poster to decorate her wall. She told herself she was making the best of a bad situation. But, this was not the Truth.

Tuck was in the snare of lies spun by the enemy of her soul.

But the Pursuer of Souls Himself was stirring the restlessness within. He would not allow her to settle for this to be her home. He knew her pain and He would perfect all which concerned her heart.

Life inside the pit held nothing but time; time never passed quickly. Tuck began to smell herself, realizing she had not bathed in two days. Her nose wrinkled with disdain as her body odor permeated the stale air.

The approach of night proved time did move. This night would come without Dreams or Guardian by her side. Tuck grew disquieted, as discontentment spread like cancer within her. Anxious about the unknown, she wanted out.

The Pit Diggers

Pits can be found in every type of terrain. Pit Diggers were the name of the skilled laborers who dug them. The pit digging trade was usually a family heritage, passed on from father to son. There was very specific criteria one looked for in selecting the location for a pit. The most important detail needed was the Bitter Root Tree.

The Bitter Root Tree was instrumental in making a pit. The Bitter Root Tree has deep penetrating roots that burrowed deep into the ground, more than any other tree. As the roots branched out into the soil, they created hollow pockets enabling that holes are dug easily.

Skillful Pit Diggers let the Bitter Tree's root lead the way and they just trace their shovels along the root's course. Soil crumbles with the slightest effort against the shovel. A Bitter Root Tree was inside every pit. Once a pit was dug out, the root continued to grow around the pit's wall, fortifying the sides more securely.

Tuck Makes Herself At Home

As Tuck peered around her pit, she noticed the candy wrapper was stuck under a root intertwined against the wall.

Her eyes traced the root all the way to the top. Tuck stared at the root for the longest time. It was her ladder to freedom. "What am I waiting for?" She was bewildered. She was confused about her paralyzed state.

The more she stared at the root, the angrier she became. This didn't make any sense. She knew once she climbed up this tree root, she would find freedom, but instead, she remained still and unmoving.

Time passed, the sun began to rise, a bright sun beam filtered across the sky and shimmered into the upper part of the pit, way above Tuck's head.

In one impulsive move, she reached for and grabbed hold of the root and with a great surge of strength, she started to climb. Her face flush, her muscles tight, and her teeth clenched hard, she pulled her body upward.

With each step up, she grew stronger and more assured of her strength. Finally, she reached the top of the root and pulled herself out. In exuberance, Tuck did her Rocky Balboa imitation, lifting her arms over her head in victory, circling with great joy. She managed the impossible. She was free. "I rescued myself!"

Tuck was dusting off her dirty hands, when she caught sight of a bucket of water right next to the opening. She was very thirsty. She reached in to draw some water with the ladle attached to the bucket's handle.

She looked into the reflection on the water's surface, but at first, didn't recognize who was looking back. Tuck was horrified at the image staring back at her. The face was hers, but the features were scary.

She looked old and had a big scowl creasing her forehead. Her eyebrows were close together and her eyes, her eyes looked so angry. It was a shocking picture. She dropped the ladle and stepped back from this horrible image. "Is this me? What did this pit do to me?"

Tuck's thoughts went into a free fall. Was this image the truth? Was this what she looked like to others?

She remembered Mr. Chips and his scowling face, and realized the image in this bucket didn't look much different. Tuck shut her eyes tightly and shuddered, hoping to shed the image from her mind. In an effort to escape the image, she jumped back into the pit.

As she dropped, she pushed from her mind the terrible image. It was too disturbing to carry. She didn't want it any longer, and as she landed, it was gone.

When she reopened her eyes and tried to recall what just happened, the image was gone from her thoughts. She could not figure out how she ended up back in the pit. Unaware of her vow to forget, she had many questions and was confused about missing pieces.

"What just happened?"

Her solution was simple. She reached for the bitter root and began to climb back out. She felt a defiance rise up inside her. She was not going to be defeated.

There, waiting for her at the top, was the bucket holding this same reflection once again. Just like before she was shocked and disgusted. In an effort to flee the image, she turned and jumped back inside the pit.

As she jumped, she vowed to keep this image from her mind. Upon landing again asked the same questions. "What in the world is happening?" This cycle repeated.

Exhaustion overtook her after re-landing the sixth time. Her head collapsed in utter despair, falling inside her hands. She threw herself back against her homemade pillow and cried. "What is going on? Why do I keep finding myself inside this pit again? Why do I keep returning?"

The elusive answer escalated hopelessness. Even though she found a way up and out of the pit, what good was it if she kept falling back in? Would she remain stuck in this cycle forever? So what is the point of climbing out at all?

Idol and the Unseen Battle

Idol was the dark side warrior inside the pit with Tuck. He traveled with her wherever she went. She was his assignment. Idol steered Tuck into pits along the way. Pits were perfect for those seeking rescue and affirmation. He didn't have to do much work; her parents had done the work for him.

Early on, he whispered lies reminding her of their abandonment. He taunted her about having no value. He knew she secretly wanted her parents to come and retrieve.

Idol knew they would not come, but he exploited the hope in her heart, which convinced her to wait for them inside pits.

Idol was one of the best at his missions. He always carried the most updated map of pit locations. Pits were the most efficient way to distract and detain people like Tuck.

He whispered to her how others were certain to abandon her too. He bound her with fear and surrounded her with despair. Her reaction was no surprise; he had been doing this for thousands of years, which at times made it boring for him.

If people would respond differently to his deceptions, then it would force him to come up with new tactics. Tuck very seldom challenged Idol. She fell for the elementary distortions, just like every other human.

On this trip however, Idol was pleased to see her self-sufficiency awaken. Before this, Tuck had never exhibited an independent spirit. This had potential for her to become a greater challenge, a challenge he welcomed to remedy his boredom.

Self-sufficiency was one of the greatest viruses to man. Idol was delighted to fan the flame of her new self- sufficient spark.

He understood that those with dependant spirits were more prone to surrender to the Pursuer of Souls. They also launched into a strong faith early on in their conversion. The dependant spirit was the hardest personality for Idol, because once trust was established, it was a foundation difficult to shake.

Idol hated strong faith but worst of all, was strong faith in young people. This carried painful memories for Idol. It was a point of public humiliation, an event long ago but one that still haunted him.

Even back then, Idol had one of the finest reputations amongst his peers. Idol stood out above his colleagues. He paid close attention to every tiny detail when harassing his assignments. He wove intimate webs of deception through strands of truth, just as the father of all lies had taught him to do. He worked with the precision of a surgeon.

He was the expert at making a lie seem true. The best kinds of lies were ones that would last. He knew his assignments so well that he anticipated how they would confront things.

He knew man. He had been watching them for centuries. There always came a time where, however brief the moment, a desire for truth and freedom would rise up within them. He would use their early stages in life to sabotage the values needed to find the Pursuer of Souls.

He would inject early on in their thoughts whatever he knew would interfere, and be a roadblocks to the freedoms they would find with the Pursuer. He would lead them into every kind of disappointment, betrayal, abuses, and abandonment, he could find. In the child's limited capacity, it was easy to whisper things to a child and they believed.

Children by nature were gullible. What he whispered to a wounded child, he/she received. Idol shut hearts away early so they would distrust authority and make vows not to let anyone hurt them. All of these were barricades to discovering the Pursuer of Souls, who promises hope and freedom.

He was the military's teacher for sabotage techniques and developed many self -protective techniques to pass on to their assignments.

Self- protection, distrust, condemnation and shame were the self-destructive behaviors, he promoted. These steered people off course their entire lives.

For decades, Idol earned the prestige of being the best at using double binds. Double binds made every option look impossible.

He set it up so the door to Truth and freedom seemed the worst option of all. He capitalized on the fact that fear of man brought a snare.

Idol might whisper, "You are greedy and selfish," to someone looking to be still and rest. He might say, "They will never stay with you if they knew who you really were," to someone who is getting serious in a relationship. When someone so desperate for love was settling for someone destructive Idol would encourage, "You won't find love anywhere else, so take what he is offering - it is better than nothing."

When people are trying to decide whether to trust the Pursuer of Souls, Idol whispers, "He knows the truth of who you are." "He allowed you to be hurt before you can't trust Him."

Idol's goal was to set traps by steering people toward meaningless pursuits and hopeless goals. His system worked very effectively.

"It is so easy to manipulate men." He would share with his students.

He worked the hardest at the start of his assignment. He planted the lies and wove webs of deceit. Then he could let life take its course. He referred to lies already imbedded in their confused hearts. His system worked well and their sin nature led them into trouble every time.

Idol stepped right next to Tuck when she first saw the bitter root. He didn't need to use a lot of words, but his timing on when to speak was wickedly precise. He waited until Tuck's brow furrowed. He leaned over and whispered, "There is no one to blame but yourself for being here. You need to wait here. You cannot climb up this root. If you do, your parents will never get a chance to come and you will never feel loved again."

Tuck listened, recognizing she was looking at her way of escape, she didn't move. All through the night, Tuck listened to his suggestions about rescue. But as the sun began to rise, her desire for freedom was stronger than her desire to wait any longer.

Idol recognized the shift happening in Tuck. He knew her better than she knew herself. He switched over now to promote her self- sufficiency. "No one is going to come for you. You can climb out easily."

These words drew her eyes to the root. "You can only count on only yourself. If you don't, you will die in here." In response, Tuck took hold of the root and started to climb.

She couldn't understand where her anger was coming from. She did not see her tormentor fanning her self- sufficient flame.

As she climbed when she got a third of the way up, Idol changed his tactic to defeat. "You are going to fall and hurt yourself. You can't do anything on your own."

This stirred her self-sufficiency. Idol smiled as he watched Tuck clench her teeth. She mustered up all her strength and climbed up the root again.

Deluded by the illusion of success, she climbed out feeling victorious. Idol left the bucket of water on the side of the pit for her to find. She peered into the bucket and saw the reflection, he whispered. "Look at you; you are unlovable." "This is what people see when they look at you." "No wonder your parents left you."

Tuck exhaled in horror and jumped back inside the pit. Each time this cycle repeated, Idol's smile grew bigger. "Insanity is doing the same thing over and over, expecting different results. There is nothing new under the sun."

He could rest now for Tuck was on deception's auto play. Idol sat back feeling satisfied and watched. "It won't be long now."

He giggled to himself how outmatched people were. He laced his fingers behind his head and gloated. "No one stands a chance against me." These words did come back and bite him once. Thinking back to that particular day still causes him to quiver.

"They don't stand a chance." He shook his head side-to-side attempting to erase the memory attached to those words.

These were his last words to Goliath, a giant of a man when he faced a shepherd boy. This boy had stepped up to challenge him without wearing any armor at all. He just carried a sling and some stones. Idol remembered this as clearly the day it happened.

He whispered those same words to Goliath's ear. This giant had destroyed armies almost single-handedly, but Idol could sense that there was something unnerving him about this shepherd boy.

Goliath laughed and mocked the boy, but Idol sensed Goliath was afraid. Never before had Goliath feared an opponent. Idol knew Goliath feared the shepherd boy's faith. His faith was great.

Idol knew genuine faith when he saw it, and this boy had the strongest faith he had ever seen.

Goliath's fear wasn't visible to other men, but Idol knew the boy could smell it. He whispered those words to Goliath in an attempt to bolster his self confidence. "He doesn't stand a chance."

Ten seconds after whispering those words in his ear, David struck Goliath dead with a rock to the forehead. This defeat brought Idol much humiliation.

Idol learned from his mistakes though and became more tenacious than ever to destroy faith before it became strong. He knew if the Pursuer of Souls wanted someone, He would get them. The warriors for the dark side could only distract and detain.

Now Idol was one of the best agents the dark side had. He savored his assignments against little people. Idol's was committed to never letting a child with faith defeat him again.

Tuck Trapped in Choices

So there Tuck sat, captive to the choice of jumping back inside the pit. She was tired of climbing out. The sun went down, leaving the moon light to shine into the sandy bottom pit. Wrapping her arms around herself, she was her only source of comfort. She couldn't leave this hole, even with feeling miserable. Why are you choosing to stay inside this hole? Tuck lay on her back and reread the sign hanging above her. *"The truth will set you free."*

"What does that mean anyway?"

All alone but in the pit she liked it that way. She imagined her parents standing outside the pit looking down upon her. She pictured them sad and guilt ridden seeing how cold and lonely they had allowed her to become.

They always pretended to care but Tuck knew their hearts were committed to the world's eyes. The pit was a loud speaker trying to awaken her parent's love. If she left the pit before they woke up, Tuck would always feel abandoned.

Tuck's heart sank at her contemplation in the moonlight. She now understood why she was attracted to pits. Tuck had thrown herself into so many basins, to broadcast her need for rescue. In doing this, she was no different from her parents. They too were prisoners of man's acceptance. They never received the validation they were looking for either as they kept trying to gain favor from strangers.

Pits had started out as a bunker, but at some point had become a prison. She hoped to find their acceptance through rescue.

The ache to this reality made her sick to her stomach. The tucked away image she saw reflected in the bucket, flashed through her mind.

That reflection she saw in the water must be the truth. She had a heart of bitterness. She felt hopeless. All this truth grieved her. The last of her strength withered. She could not summon herself to sit up, so she curled into a ball and sobbed.

Her tears came with the admission of her depravity and emptiness. Her heart filled with despair. She no longer liked this pit, it was no longer appealing to her. Yet, she did not have any strength left.

A small pool of water began to collect from the dew-drops dripping from the bitter root. The dewdrops joined her tears to form a tiny pool. The moonlight revealed Tuck's face in the pool's reflection, and this time, Tuck did not turn from this image. She was ready to face the truth about her heart.

Idol noticed this change of attitude and jumped into alert mode. He was concerned. It was never good when they looked into their true reflection and did not look away.

He jumped up, stood over Tuck and emphatically started to whirl verbal attacks in her ear. "You make me sick. Your parents don't love you because you are unlovable. Do you think anyone could possibly love you? Guardian is glad you left him because now he is free."

Idol let the mental assaults fly and their direct hits caused Tuck's body to curl up tighter and sink lower into the sand. Idol never let up. Tuck was overtaken with hopelessness. He knew this was a critical moment. He wondered if it would be suicide or salvation. Idol knew this would bring death one way or another, and in the next few minutes he would find out.

There had been many times before when an assignment had been dwindled to the despairing of life, yet the King of Kings walked in without warning and subverted his plan. Idol learned not to let up, he must be relentless to the end. Idol poured out the assaults, trying to steer Tuck into a hopelessness, which would lead to death.

"You would be better off dead. The world would be better off with you dead. You should kill yourself."

If he let up, it might leave an opening for the Pursuer of her Soul to enter. Idol knew if He came, the battle was over and he would lose.

Idol continued until suddenly, when he started to speak, his voice was gone. His mind held the next set of assaulting words, but they couldn't leave the gate. No sound went forth. Idol was silenced.

Tuck entertained thoughts of killing herself. It might be the best thing for everyone. Her parents and Guardian, they all could be free of her. How could things get better when people said that childhood was the best time in a person's life?

In the midst of these thoughts, she heard a knock coming somewhere close by. Lying on the pit's sandy ground, she was trying to identify the direction of the knock. From her low view, she noticed just behind the hanging bitter roots, there was a door tucked away in a corner.

It was not noticeable at all from a standing position, but because she was in a prone position, she could see the door.

A voice spoke to her heart. *"Behold, I stand at the door and knock."* This small still voice brought comfort. The voice was soothing. She remained still to listen again. She heard another knock on the door and the voice followed again, *"If you open the door I will come in."* Somehow, Tuck knew this was the voice of the Pursuer of her Soul. Her heart initially leaped with joy, recognizing the One who had written her the invitation was here, but then the reality of who she was, crushed her hope.

"Oh Pursuer of Souls, I am so awful, You made a mistake inviting me. I have lied and cheated, betrayed my friends and I have blamed my parents for everything that has been hard in my life. I am sure now You know the truth about me, and You will want to change Your mind."

The small still voice from the other side of the door spoke to her heart again. *"It is because of My great love for you and My mercy, I made it possible for you to be made alive in all your sins through Jesus. It is by grace you have been saved."*

Tuck continued to hear knocking from the door, but the voice was silent now. Using her arms, she scooted herself across the ground to the door. She pulled herself up to a kneeling position to reach the doorknob. She turned it and opened it.

There on the other side of the door stood the Pursuer of her Soul. Tuck was in awe as she beheld His splendor and glory. She started to cry because His love overflowed onto her. She never before felt so complete, so known and so loved all at once.

She fell at His feet and reached out to touch His foot. He turned and sat down next to her limp body. His two hands picked her up and placed her gently on His lap. He just held her and rocked her.

Then after the perfect amount of time had passed, He said, *"Blessed are the poor in Spirit for theirs is the kingdom of heaven. Blessed are those who mourn for they will be comforted. Blessed are the meek for they will inherit the earth. Blessed are those who hunger and thirst for righteousness for they will be filled."*

She felt her body collapse in His arms. She leaned her head upon His shoulder and for the first time, she knew she belonged there. She never wanted to move. A rest came upon her, and she felt like an infant in her Fathers strong arms. She felt safe and secure.

He allowed time to embrace her. He preserved her in His completeness. She no longer felt haunted by her lack, for His fullness overcame her weakness. She was in His strength now.

Then He said to Tuck, *"Come and Follow Me."* He stood up, extending out His hand to her She took hold and together they walked through the doorway leading down a tunnel. He lit the way. Light beamed from His every pore. As they stepped out into the daylight, the Pursuer of her Soul turned and said, *"I have lifted you out of the slimy pit out of mud and mire. I have set your feet upon a Rock. I have given you a new song in your mouth."*

He had walked her out of the pit. She was back on top of the ground. Just a few feet away was where she had kept jumping back in.

The Pursuer of her Soul walked her over to where she originally stood at the opening of the pit. Tuck grew afraid as she stood near the edge, fearing she would jump back in again. *"Behold when you are in Me, you are a new creation; the old has gone, the new has come!"*

Keeping her eyes on the Pursuer of her Soul, she stood beside Him still gripping His hand. She thought about the bucket that stood behind her. A cold chill ran up the course of her back.

She pictured vividly the wicked, bitter face that had stared back from the water's reflection. She closed her eyes tightly.

The Pursuer of her Soul squeezed her hand, reminding her He was with her and He repeated again, *"Behold when you are in Me, you are a new creation; the old has gone, the new has come!"*

Hearing this, she opened her eyes and He gently turned her around to behold the reflection in the bucket. This time however, what once held a bitter image, now displayed her Pursuer's face smiling back at her. His Love reached out from that bucket and touched her heart. She turned to face Him and saw that same love filled face smiling at her. His eyes reached her soul.

Joy unlocked her heart. She couldn't explain why but she felt like singing. *"I give you a new song."*

"My heart sings!" She smiled back at her Deliverer of Hope.

He pointed to the Bitter Tree's root. *"Forgive as I have forgiven you."* These words entered deep within her heart, rooting this truth into her core being. She walked over to the root knowing what she must do.

She bent over and grabbed hold of the root. She attempted to pull it from the earth's soil, but it was too strong and deep for her to pull it out.

Tuck felt like a failure because even with all her strength, she could not do it. She could not pull the bitter root free. This was her Pursuer's first request and she had failed. She let Him down. Her head hung down dejectedly.

Then the voice she had grown familiar hearing, spoke to her heart. *"Tuck, in your weakness is My perfect strength."* He extended His hands out, asking her to hand the root over to Him. She noticed the scars on His palms. Knowing she had seen them he explained. *"By My wounds you are healed."*

She touched His scar and kissed it. Tuck handed the Pursuer the end of the root that she could not pull from the ground. The moment the root touched the Pursuer's hands, it was loosed, and it disintegrated.

Since the root was the fortified support for the pit walls, the pit caved in upon itself. Idol was still inside and was buried in dirt and sand. In complete silence, he disappeared out of sight. Idol was buried in defeat. No matter how skillful he was, he was powerless against the interventions of the Pursuer of her Soul.

As the Pursuer turned and walked from the pit, He called to Tuck. *"Come."*

Tuck followed behind closely. She felt so safe whenever she heard His voice.

Worker Despairs in the Tunnel of Your Own Understanding.

The last official thing Worker ate was a muffin that morning, but she was presently feasting on a full course meal of despair, with an appetizer of beating herself up. She faced her stubborn, prideful ways. She had gotten herself into this mess because of her own pride. "You just had to be right didn't you. You just had to be first to arrive."

There was no one else to blame for this predicament; she would probably end up dying inside this tunnel of darkness.

The irony of this whole thing caused her to giggle. "Here you are Worker surrounded in complete darkness, yet for the first time you can see things clearly. I hope I get a chance to tell Fatalist and Pleaser how wrong I have been."

Deep within her soul, she doubted she would ever see them again. She never felt more alone. The tunnel's blackness barricaded away any sense of time. This darkness was much more than just the absence of light; it was also the absence of hope.

A suffocating fear pressured her chest. It felt like someone was pushing a pillow against her face. Her only companions in this darkness were accusing voices replaying her past.

Worker was no longer paying attention to the paths she chose to take. They all seemed futile. Recklessness stirred within her, which sabotaged rational decision-making. It didn't matter anymore, as there was no way out anyway.

She had come to accept it. She was not going to find her way out. Acknowledging this truth dropped her to her knees and she cried out. "Oh Pursuer of Souls, if you are real and you can see me here in the darkness, please help me. I am blind, blind in every way; in sight and in mind and in heart. I am in way over my head and I need Your help."

She folded herself over onto her knees in despair and began to cry. She couldn't remember the last time she had cried. On the verge of tears many times before, she had managed to detour herself away. Crying was a meaningless exercise. This time however, she had no energy left to detour. She sobbed.

She had no plan, no goal, and no confidence. Lost, weak and hopeless, she waited for the end. Her heart craved the light, a light that might bring hope back to her soul. She looked up at the street lamps and verbalized her disdain. "These stupid street lamps are useless."

Just then, a cold wetness touched her cheek. Startled she fell backwards. She could hear a figure moving before her but it was too dark to see anything. She inhaled fear. The cold wetness touched her again but this time it was on the backside of her hand. It felt like a dog's tongue. "Who is there?"

The terror in her voice was obvious, but she hoped her loud volume would send an intimidating message to this unseen presence.

"I am sorry to have scared you, you just looked like you needed some encouragement."

As Worker heard the voice, she saw the image before her. It had four legs and fur; it was a dog. "Who are you and what do you want with me? If you are going to offer me any more deals, the answer is no!"

"Worker I am not here to make you an offer, I am His offering to you."

"His who? I don't understand." Worker was distrustful.

"Did you not just a minute ago cry out for wisdom and light? Well, the Pursuer of your Soul heard you."

"Oh. Is this the same Pursuer who sent me the invitation to Lake Still Water?"

"Yes He is the same One." The dog confirmed. Her voice was kind and gentle.

Worker began to interrogate this stranger in the dark "So have you been watching me the whole time? Why didn't you say something earlier?"

"I have been walking beside you for a while now, but I cannot be seen until you go to your knees in prayer. That is when the Pursuer equips you, to hear and see me."

"You mean when I prayed to the Pursuer and asked for wisdom, He brought me a *dog*?" Worker heard her offensive tone and apologized. "Sorry, I meant no offense."

"You asked the Lord for His wisdom and light. You acknowledged you were blind and could not see, and yes, He provided me. I am a seeing-eye dog. I am a companion to help those who are blind, travel to safety. You can choose to utilize my companionship or not." The dog started to turn away.

"Oh, please come back. I am sorry for the way I spoke to you. You are right, if I am blind who am I to have opinions about how my rescue should happen. I am so thankful you are here. I am thankful that the Pursuer of my Soul has provided you for me."

"My name is Lynne, which means 'Holy.' I have been set apart to help sojourners who cry out here in the Tunnel of Your Own Understanding. I want you to know I only speak the words the Pursuer of your Soul has given me to speak." *"The Pursuer says, 'Who walks in darkness and has no light? Let him trust in the Name of the LORD and rely upon his God.'"*

Her words calmed Worker's heart.

Lynne continued, *"Who walks in darkness and has no light?"* Worker responded quickly to the question. "I do."

"Worker, the Pursuer wants you to know, *'In MY (His) light is all other Light.'"*

Worker lifted her head and saw a ray of light streak down from the top of the tunnel. The light's rays lit up the path just in front of her feet. Nothing farther, but it allowed for one step.

Lynne continued, "The Pursuer says, *'My Word is a lamp unto your feet and a light for your path.'"*

Worker felt anxious about the small sense of direction. "This light only shines one step ahead. I can't see where I am going... How do I know this is the right way?"

Lynne assured her with a calm, soft voice. *"Trust in the Lord with all your heart lean not in your own understanding. In all your ways acknowledge Him and He will direct your path."*

Worker felt anxious. It didn't make sense. Why didn't the Pursuer just light the whole way? "Lynne, what does that mean? I don't understand. I cannot see where I am headed."

Lynne responded, *"His eyes are on the ways of men, He sees their every step. There is no dark place, no deep shadow, where evildoers can hide."*

"So what you are saying is that I don't need to know where I am going because the Pursuer knows?" There was silence. Worker decided to take a step to test it for herself.

"Oh, look at that!" Worker was amazed at what happened. When she took just one-step forward, the light lit up her next step. When she lifted her eyes to try to see where it was leading, there was only darkness. She just had light at her feet.

Just like a toddler learning to walk, Worker's eyes remained fixed at her feet, letting the lamp lead her steps. She stepped forward in concentration and was completely oblivious to the spiritual battle that flurried about her.

Lynne saw the spiritual war, but remain focused on the task she had been assigned. Though it was a difficult calling, it was a joy to guide souls through the tunnel. Walking alongside His chosen ones in the valley of the shadow of death was a rich blessing. She got to see darkness overtaken with light, and the victory was the Pursuer's, whenever she was called.

All around them raged a fierce spiritual battle. Demons were furious that things had turned so quickly against their favor.

The harder they fought to sabotage Worker's progress, the more it weakened them in strength. Dark side warriors fought viciously against the Pursuer's army.

Heaven's army weapon of choice was swords of Truth. The dark side warriors used machetes, clubs, spears, and a variety of weapons. The sword of Truth, divided and cut with such precision, the dark side weapons paled in comparison.

Lynne watched silently as the enemy warriors were thrown against the cavern walls one by one. They hit with such force against the wall that it sounded like the whole tunnel might give way. They slid down the wall completely helpless. Their lifeless bodies laid at the base of the ground, still and defeated.

Every single attempt to destroy Worker and Lynne failed. Lynne walked and prayed as she had been taught. Prayer provided added forces and power in the efforts of the Pursuer's army.

Yelping, screaming and whining were heard throughout the tunnel, but to Worker's ears, all was silent.

For Lynne, it required her complete focus on the task. She trusted the forces of Heaven's army to protect them.

Worker poured out her heart, sharing with Lynne things she had never shared with others. She couldn't think of a time when she felt more comfortable sharing. Lynne listened. Worker told her about her arrival in Self Absorption and her life there. She confessed how her pride had lead her into the tunnel. Lynne encouraged her, "Worker, the Pursuer *'is our refuge and strength, an ever-present help in trouble.'*"

"Lynne you remind me of an old friend I had a long time ago."

"Would that be Rumpus?" Lynne inquired knowingly. The Pursuer supplied Lynne with information she would need to help and equip in her assignment. He equipped her to minister to Worker as she taught her to walk by faith.

Worker was caught off guard by her response. "Why yes, how did you know that?"

"The Pursuer shared that with me. He knew you had difficulty listening to other people's opinions. Maybe that is why he sent me, who am a seeing-eye dog. Worker, the Pursuer knows all things.

He will use every resource necessary to bring you what you need, even when it means a seeing-eye dog. Nothing is impossible with Him. He once used a donkey to get the attention of his owner. His ways are higher than ours."

"I think I understand but can I ask you another question?" Lynne welcomed another question. How come I couldn't see you until I got down on my knees to pray?" Worker inquired.

Lynne stopped walking in answering this question because it was important. "The position we are in very much influences how we see things. When humble, the Pursuer gives us access to his view in things.

The Pursuer wants us to come to Him with every question and bring to Him our every need, but He will not demand that from us. He says, *"You do not have, because you do not ask."* Lynne remained to wait for Worker's reply.

"I never thought about this until you mentioned this but I bet the Pursuer knew I talked to animals (stuffed and alive) all the time. How cool is that?"

Lynne smiled. "The Pursuer of our Souls supplies us with exactly what we need." Worker nodded in amazement.

"The Pursuer tells us, *"I AM the vine; you are the branches. If a man remains in Me and I in him, he will bear much fruit; apart from Me you can do nothing. If anyone does not remain in Me, he is like a branch that is thrown away and withers.'"*

"You know Lynne this terrible place has taught me that I can't solve things on my own. As soon as I asked the Pursuer of my Soul, He answered. Honestly, Lynne, I walked into this tunnel the way I walked into every situation in my life, convinced I had all the answers.

I thought I could solve any problem that came, but this place has taught me how helpless I really am."

Lynne laughed and said, "You get an A+ for class today. You have learned a priceless lesson, *'the fear of the Lord is the beginning of wisdom.'"*

"Lynne, it is so weird how something so horrible and life threatening could be turned into something so good. I am very thankful I came into this tunnel because it has taught me just how much I need Him."

"Worker, the Pursuer of your Soul died on the cross for you, so you could have fellowship with Him forever. *'If you confess with your mouth, He is Lord, and believe in your heart that the Heavenly Father raised Him from the dead, you will be saved. Anyone who trusts in Him will never be put to shame.'"*

These words found residence in Worker's heart. She believed them. She understood that Jesus, was her Pursuer and He saved her soul. He saved her from the darkness of this tunnel and saved her from a life of leaning on her own understanding. From this moment forward, in all her ways she wanted to let Him direct her path.

Joy filled Worker's heart. It didn't matter that she was still inside the belly of this tunnel, she had the light of her Pursuer with her, He would light her way.

She lifted her eyes from her feet to behold the splendid sight of light outside the tunnel appeared right in front of her. A beautiful brightness filled the opening. The Pursuer untied the tunicate of hopelessness. Hope flowed freely now.

More daylight entered with her every step. This light was such a gift. A gift she didn't deserve, but was grateful to receive.

The idea that she would actually be able to arrive at Lake Still Water made her smile. She stepped out from the darkness into a warm sunny morning. The sunlight warmed her face and she closed her eyes to receive its full embrace, overflowing with thankfulness.

Fatalist and Pleaser Continue Forward

Fatalist and Pleaser had been walking for a while. Pleaser kept trying to stay in the sun to warm the cold chill from her wet clothes that glued themselves to her skin. She lifted her face toward the sun and soaked in the warmth into her chilled bones.

"Achoo" Pleaser sneezed.

"Bless You." Fatalist replied gruffly because he was still steaming about the mishap.

Once again, his expectations were dashed. They would never get to Lake Still Water. He was angry with himself most of all. He had broken his own cardinal rule; 'do not hope!'

Whenever he hoped, it only brought disappointment. How could he be so stupid. His disappointment formed a lump in his throat. It brought him to remember the most devastating day of his life, when he watched his father die in his arms. Days later, he watched his mom grow smaller and smaller from view as his ship pulled away from the dock.

His heart felt the dagger of these memories enter again as if it were the first time. Fatalist couldn't manage all this pain. He suddenly started to scream. Pain spilled into places words could not go, just groaning. An unrecognizable utterance for a lifetime of heartbreaks is translated into, undetectable gibberish.

Pleaser's mouth opened in disbelief. She watched Fatalist unravel right before her eyes. A man who had never shown any emotional response was now a fountain of expression. He stomped his feet, shook his fists into the air, but no words were spoken.

As he screamed, spit spewed from his mouth. Pleaser backed up placing distance between his pain and her presence, out of both respect and fear.

She knew his dam had just broken. The depth of such pain was not foreign to her either. Even in her pleasing ways, she knew enough to let this takes its course, uninterrupted.

He was yelling about everything that had happened in his life. He didn't even know who he was yelling at, whoever was in charge, or whoever would listen. He lifted his voice and his eyes to the sky.

Finally words came. "What are you doing up there?" Fatalist screamed. "How can you just watch all of this going on and do nothing. Are you some sort of game player who gets a kick out of watching all of us walk around hurting each other? This life stinks!"

The words he spoke came from his voice but he did not feel connected to them. He felt like he was a snowball rolling down a hill. He couldn't have stopped if he wanted to; it felt too good, it felt honest.

Exhaustion met him though in the end. He collapsed to his knees with nothing left to say. His head that had been lifted to heaven, felt too heavy to keep up.

He lowered his head and his eyes met Pleaser. He froze. Her eyes welled up with tears and then flowed down her cheeks. She was scared and yet felt so badly for Fatalist. She felt powerless to comfort him and guilty for lacking the words to do so. She could do nothing to please him. In her own powerlessness, she started to cry.

"I'm so sorry Fatalist. I am so sorry."

These words automatically came out of her mouth. She was always apologizing to people. She was always sorry for something. Sorry for breathing; sorry for reaching for the same movie at the video rental store. Her life was always in someone's way. Truth was, she was getting pretty sick of being sorry.

Fatalist gave her a bewildered look. "Why are *you* sorry? You didn't do anything."

"Well I guess when I feel bad, I say I am sorry. I don't know, I am sorry you are feeling so bad."

"You don't need to say you are sorry and I sure don't want you feeling sorry for me."

"Well fine then. I take it back. Consider me officially un-sorry!"

"So considered!" Fatalist retorted back.

Pleaser was offended by his gruffness. All she wanted to do was feel bad for him. She decided that this was unredeemable and decided to change the subject.

"Are you ready to start walking toward Lake Still Water? We have many hours still to go."

Fatalist welcomed the redirection. This emotional outburst was way beyond his ability to process and he preferred to get back to the task at hand. "Sounds good to me."

Pleaser looked back at him as she headed out in the lead. "Well let's get going then, unless you want to talk about what just happened." Pleaser looked back with a smile, as she knew he wouldn't talk about it. She enjoyed joking with him.

"No more expression for me, thank you." He shook his head in an effort to shake the whole incident from his memory. "Hey let's just get out of here." Fatalist picked up the pace and put his eyes to the ground. He looked forward to getting distance from this place.

Counselor Walks with a Heavy Heart

As Counselor watched Little Bin skipping ahead, she was struck how freed his spirit became the longer he was away from Self Absorption. Her heart was heavy for him, despite the fact that he was a bundle of joy, playful and never complaining.

Counselor pasted a smile on her face for his benefit, but it did not reflect the true state of her union within. She walked behind him, attempting to counsel herself.

She never was good at counseling her own issues. Truth was she could never sort out all the noise inside her heart. To avoid it, she threw herself into helping others, to silence the noises in their hearts.

Since leaving Self Absorption, she found it more difficult to hide in her busy schedule. This resulted in her internal noise becoming louder and with that, grew a greater discontent.

Little Bin seemed to have a twenty minute traveling cycle. He would run ahead, jump around, explore and then run back at full speed to report everything he saw. As Little Bin returned to give his exploration report, he stopped, noticing Counselor's countenance. He asked, "Counselor, why are you sad?"

Counselor was surprised by his perceptiveness. His question scared her, fearing it might open a door she may never get closed again.

If she opened this door and faced all that was stuffed behind it, she feared she would start crying and never stop. Little Bin had no idea just how good of an explorer he was. He had stumbled upon a hidden cave that had gone undetected by everyone for many, many years.

"Why, what do you mean?" Counselor said, hoping her widened smile might deflect his seeing her pain and sadness.

"Counselor, your lips may be smiling but your eyes are crying. They look so sad. What is wrong?" He walked up to her and gave her a big hug and then stepped back so she could tell him what the trouble was.

Counselor couldn't hold back any longer. She looked around for a place to sit down and found a big boulder just a few feet away from the stream. She reached for the rock to sit quickly, convinced her legs might give out before she could find her seat.

She placed one hand on her jaw to prop her head, which also kept her from collapsing into a ball of despair. She turned herself at an angle on the rock to keep Little Bin from seeing too much.

"Oh Little Bin, sometimes when things happen to people, and they don't know what to do with it, they hide it away. Time passes and they get the idea that it all went away and it isn't there anymore, but that is not true.

After awhile, the truth knocks on your heart and keeps knocking louder and louder until you are willing to answer.

"Since we started this journey of ours, I have heard the knock getting louder and louder."

Little Bin completely understood. He had been knocking on the door to his parent's heart for a long time. In order to keep things locked away, they turned up the volume inside so they would not hear his knocking.

Little Bin looked at Counselor very seriously and asked, "So are you going to open the door? If that is the only way to stop the knocking, maybe you should just open the door."

Little Bin continued. "There was this kid in second grade who used to pick on me a lot. One time, I snuck through the doggy door of his house and put dog food in his bed. I heard later that he accused his older brother of doing it.

I never said a word because I was afraid he would kill me, but I still felt really bad that his brother got in trouble for something I did."

"Later that summer his family was moving away so the day he left, I went up to him and told him what I had done. That guilty feeling knocked on my door all summer long. I felt so much better when I finally opened that door and told the truth. Is that the kind of knock you mean?"

Counselor was amazed. She had years of training and education, and yet this eight-year-old boy touched the heart of this matter in a moment.

"You are a remarkable boy Little Bin; a remarkable boy."

"Thanks, I think you are terr-fic too." He gave her another big hug.

Counselor felt a strength and readiness to seize this moment. She was ready to open the door. She needed to stop running, to face it. Carpe diem! Seize the day.

Counselor needed time and privacy to do this. She looked over at her young friend and said, "Hey why don't you go on ahead and check out what is down the path. I will sit here awhile and do what you suggested. I will open the door, and see what is on the other side. But on one condition..."

Counselor put her finger up to accentuate the point. In her pause she then bent the finger to summon him to her as she said, "Before you leave, I need another one of those famous hugs of yours."

"You got it." Little Bin smiled. He ran back up to her and gave her a gigantic hug. It made him feel good that she could need something from him. Most everyone else just wanted him out of his or her hair. He collapsed back into her arms.

Counselor was almost afraid to let him go. She loved this boy very much. He had wrapped himself around her heart and she feared it would require surgery to ever disconnect him.

Feeling loved up, she loosened her grip and sent him on his way. "You go now, go explore." Little Bin ran off as he launched into everything he did, but he looked back once or twice. He called out after some distance, "I'll be back, don't you worry."

She waved as if to tell him she heard him. She watched him disappear around the curving path, she felt a little like she might disappear too. She leaned back against the rock above the one she sat on, and sighed. The warmth of the sun was reassuring. She lifted her face to meet the rays when she noticed one of those signs hanging from the tree. This one read; *"I stand at the door and knock; if you open the door I will come in."*

Guardian Faces the Truth in Jail

Guardian sat against the jail bars with a dust covered pillow propped behind his head, pondering over his wasted life. He thought he had put behind him his rough beginnings and attempted to turn all his failings into doing good works. He laughed as he saw the irony of this situation.

He thought back to when he vowed never to let anyone imprison him again. At the time, he was referring to an emotional prison, but now He found himself captive once again.

He winced reflecting about the grandiose thinking of being Tuck's cape crusader. "You are such a fool. You don't even have the courage to face your own pain, yet you think you can stand up for a little kid?"

The harsh truth infiltrated the steel bars around his heart. This truth made for a miserable cellmate. For the first time, he saw how he hid behind this child, in order to hide from himself.

He had hidden out for a long time. He pretended to be tough and impenetrable. Though he appeared fearless in conflict, he was terrified. He was even more scared than Tuck. No one knew how afraid he was. How could they if he wasn't even aware of it himself.

The depths of this wallowing repulsed him, but he couldn't stop. He was on a runaway train of despair and was convinced he was going to die in this jail.

Guardian wondered what it would have been like to meet the Pursuer of Souls. He imagined Lake Still Water and its beauty. The thought of water reminded him how thirsty he was; thirsty and trapped.

Guardian switched over to thinking about Tuck. A heavy sigh quickly followed and then wrenching sob. He let her down. He felt so bad. "Oh this is awful, I am a wretch. Hey isn't there a song that says that word? 'A wretch like me.'

Isn't that the truth. This whole time I was making it appear I was this brave, caring guy and yet I was really being a selfish chicken."

He collapsed his head into his hands. Guardian was unaware that he was not alone in that cell. On each side of him sat a dark side warrior. One named Defeat the other Defame. Though Guardian's cry of repentance was sincere, he was certain no one could hear him. He thought about not seeing Tuck ever again. She was gone, maybe for good. He sobbed even harder, and was more certain than ever, he could never be forgiven.

Some blue birds started to sing outside of his jail window. Their voices were beautiful; beautiful enough to lift Guardian momentarily out from his grief. Their voices were comforting. Their song drew him to the window. They were chirping a melody that he had heard before. Then he realized where it came from. He stood inside his cell looking at the bluebirds and sang the lyrics as they lead the melody. "Amazing Grace, how sweet the sound, that saved a wretch like me... I once was lost but now am found, was blind, but now, I see. T'was Grace that taught my heart to fear. And Grace, my fears relieved. How precious did that Grace appear... the hour I first believed."

Guardian was amazed he knew the words to this song. He never really paid attention to them before, but this time they met him right where he was standing, inside this cell.

As he continued to peer out the window, he noticed a sign hanging from the branch the blue birds were singing. It read; *"I turn all things together for good for those who love God and are called according to His purpose."*

He didn't understand what this meant, but he felt like arguing with it. "Good? I never made it to Lake Still Water, I am locked inside this jail in an abandoned town, I have let my best friend down, and my whole life has been a fraud. What good can come from that?" Guardian asked the sign.

Just then, Guardian heard a tender voice speak within his heart, a voice that wasn't his own. *"I will bind up your broken heart. I will proclaim liberty to you and open the prison to which you are bound."*

"Who is there?" Guardian asked aloud but didn't hear an answer.

He went back to the cot, and this time he laid on it. All the crying had wiped him out. He curled up on his side and quickly fell asleep.

What remained awake was a small glimmer of hope from the words he had read from the sign. *"I turn all things together for good."* He turned onto his side and in his head replied, "I hope so." He sighed deeply and then sank heavily to sleep.

Worker is Free

Worker stood outside of the tunnel, free at last. It was a gorgeous morning, as beautiful as she had ever seen. She heard the wind rustling through the leaves and was grateful to feel its touch on her hair and face.

It was a new morning after all. Peace accompanied the understanding that she was no longer in charge. She felt the watch care over her by One who loved her.

"He knows my name." She rejoiced.

A joy took hold of her soul, a joy that made her smile. She entered the Tunnel of Your Own Understanding as the ruler of her life, but she exited recognizing the true King. He was the source of light and He provided her a second chance. A precious gift she would cherish from this day forth.

Her friend Lynne did not come out with her from the tunnel for the Pursuer had alerted her of a new assignment. She returned to the tunnel entrance to wait for the next soul she would help escort.

Worker kneeled down, just a few yards outside the tunnel's exit. She lowered her head before the Pursuer of her Soul and gave thanks.

"Thank you Pursuer of my Soul for bringing me such a wise friend. Please bless the ministry You have given her. Keep Your light upon her and cover her under Your care. Bring to her friends who can support her, as she has support so many others in great need. Thank you for supplying us with so many gifts. You are so giving and kind."

When Worker finished her prayer, she got up off her knees and headed out toward Lake Still Water. Contentment was her new companion.

She no longer worried about arriving at Lake Still Water. She knew she would because He was faithful. She could enjoy the journey now, and leave the details with Him.

Fatalist Loses It to Find It

Fatalist was still feeling embarrassed and was physically exhausted from his emotional meltdown. Though he minimized the toll all the emotions had on him, he knew he needed to sleep for a while. He could not venture on any further.

"Pleaser, I need to stop for awhile. I am wiped out. I am sorry. You can go on ahead without me if you want to. I would understand. I need to take a nap to regain my strength."

Pleaser nodded okay. "That won't be a problem Fatalist. We are on this pilgrimage together, and I will wait for you. The break will give me time to lay out and get these clothes dry."

"Thanks Pleaser I really appreciate it."

"Fatalist, when you wake up, I will be over there somewhere." Pleaser gestured toward a collection of big rocks. The sun's rays beating against the stones would be a perfect place to dry off.

Fatalist looked around for a place to lay his weary head. He found a nice tree providing shade with a soft plot of grass, rich and plush carpeting atop tree roots. It was comfortable. No sooner did he close his eyes, did he drift off to sleep. What Fatalist did not know, this nap was divinely steered by the Pursuer of his Soul.

As Fatalist slept, an angel came to him to bring to him a message. In his sleep, Fatalist looked up at the angel who motioned for him to follow. Fatalist responded to his request. He got up and followed. He led him down stream, where they intended on going before the terrible mishap. Fatalist wondered where the angel was taking him. He looked back and to his surprise, he saw himself still sleeping back on the grass under the tree.

"Hey is this like that movie, The Christmas Carol?" Fatalist asked, while running to keep up with the angel who was way ahead of him. The angel looked back and just smiled.

They came to the bridge that reportedly (from the disheveled man) washed out. The bridge was fine. Fatalist became angry that the man had lied. Plans were always being ruined by someone. Why should he be so surprised about this? Examples jumped to his mind listing all the great injustices over the years.

Fatalist was uncomfortable with how angry he felt while being in the presence of an angel. He tried to reason himself into calmness. "What is the big deal?" "It doesn't really matter anyway."

Fatalist could talk himself out of any feeling. He had done it his entire lifetime. Besides, it was ridiculous to feel strongly about this. Feelings were a hindrance not a blessing. They just made one susceptible to hope. Hope was for fools and a hopeful fool always ended up a disappointed fool.

In silence, the angel took hold of Fatalist's arm to get his attention. He pointed over to the bridge. Fatalist noticed under the bridge, the current was fast. There were many jagged rocks protruding out from the water's surface, between them and the bridge. Some real sharp rocks were hiding just below the water's surface. Fatalist realized this would have been a real nightmare had they continued down stream in the rubber boat.

The angel pointed out a creature crouching on the bridge. Fatalist noticed many little creatures strategically placed all across the bridge. They had bows and arrows and sharp rocks in their hands. They were waiting for something to come down stream.

Fatalist tried to see whom they were waiting for. He was shocked when their targets came around the bend. They were moving at a very fast clip.

The boat was his boat. He saw himself and Pleaser riding downstream. Fatalist wiped his eyes to remove the mirage. When he looked back up, he and Pleaser were still making their way down and had just come out from under the bridge.

Time rewound itself and then moved forward. He saw himself stretched out with his fingers laced behind his head. Both of them were completely unaware of the assault about to happen. The rapids were rugged and quickened their traveling speed.

Fatalist felt helpless looking on from the shore. Right after he and Pleaser cleared the bridge, the enemy arrows started to fly. One creature launched a missile like object, which landed with bulls-eye precision, into Pleaser's heart. Simultaneously, the boat lifted so high up on Pleaser's side, and then slammed violently down causing Pleaser to fall from the boat.

When she fell into the water, Fatalist helplessly watched as her head hit hard against a jagged rock protruding out of the water. She died instantly. Her lifeless body floated down stream, now a lifeless puppet to the violent current.

Fatalist (from the boat) watched in horror as his friend fell overboard. He scurried over to Pleaser's side to attempt to retrieve her, when an arrow struck him. The powerful thrust threw him into the raging waters.

From the shoreline, Fatalist watched powerlessly. "How could this be?" He looked over at the angel, hoping he would give some explanation, but the angel just kept his eyes on the water. Fatalist returned to watch this unfolding tragedy before him.

In the freezing waters, Fatalist felt like giving up, he had no fight left. His heart was broken. Watching Pleaser die was just like watching his dad die all over again. He had stopped living after that day too.

He stopped fighting the current and allowed himself to be pulled under.

Helpless, Fatalist stood on the edge next to the angel. He understood the decision made as he watched himself sink under the water. He knew he was willingly surrendering to death.

The angel looked at Fatalist and spoke for the first time. "Hope supplies the strength to our times of affliction."

These words struck a core. The word 'Hope' repulsed him. He vowed never to invest in hope again. For the first time ever, Fatalist found himself questioning this vow. His desire to live outmatched his desire for safety. In a deep bellow, he cried out to himself in the water.

"Hope, come on Hope! Try, don't give up, you want to live!"

Fatalist was his own cheerleader, standing there on the water's edge. He became so animated as he screamed, he slipped on mud and his feet fell out from under him. He slid on his back into the water. Now he too found himself sinking to the bottom of the stream, and the current was very strong.

He could feel the hopelessness and despair weighing heavily on him. He had an anchor tied to his ankle. He screamed from under the water in defiance of this end.

"Live!" he screamed with all the force he had left within him. He kicked toward the surface. He felt a great force of hope within him. This surge was strong enough to carry two bodies, not just one.

He reached the surface and gasped for air. He didn't pause a moment with his strokes, making his way toward the shore, knowing if he let up for a moment, the current would take him and he would drowned.

The closer he moved to the shoreline, the greater the strength grew inside him. With every stroke, his mind reached out to take hold of a future, a future unseen but one filled with hopes and dreams.

"Don't you want to see your brothers and sisters again?" Each desire that came strengthened him, until he grabbed hold of a rock from the shore and scooped himself onto it. He lay there, his heart pounding, inhaling every molecule of air that was available.

When his breathing slowed down, he tried to get his mind around all that just happened. He turned over on his back to ask the angel to explain, but the angel was gone.

Once he laid there for a moment and gathered himself together again, Fatalist retraced his steps back to the tree where the angel first entered the scene. Though there was no sign of the angel, Fatalist noticed a sign hanging from a tree branch right where he had slept. It read; *"Those who hope in the Lord shall renew their strength."*

As he read the words, he understood what the angel was showing him. He learned the lesson. He realized the boat he and Pleaser rode down the river had sprung a leak not because it was a mishap, but because of divine intervention. The sinking boat protected them from an unseen fate that awaiting them right around the next corner.

The Pursuer of his Soul spared them. For the first time, Fatalist saw the blessing not a mishap. How many times had he only seen things as mishaps! He began to wonder how many things had been blessings in disguise. Fatalist felt like he had experienced that song, the one that spoke about how he once was blind but now he sees.

What was most comforting was the idea that someone was really watching out for him. All his life he had felt alone. He didn't think anyone was looking after him, except for himself. It warmed his heart that there *was* Someone.

Fatalist rewound the tapes of his past trying to reapply "mishaps" as possible misunderstood blessings. He even entertained the possibility that being sent to this country might have been part of a good plan, not a curse.

A foreign feeling overtook him; a thankfulness. He had not felt this since he was a young boy. He used to awaken to the smell of fresh baked bread. He would come into the kitchen to see his papa up and reading the paper. He felt thankful then and for a brief moment, he could even smell the fresh baked bread.

He had complained for thirty-five years, but now in one moment, his complaints were gone. An unspeakable joy replaced them. He fell to his knees and started talking aloud to the Pursuer of his Soul. "Thank you Pursuer; Thank you."

Fatalist woke up from underneath the tree to find his arms lifted toward heaven. "Thank you!" he heard himself saying out loud.

It was so strange. He wasn't sure what was a dream and what was real. No boat was visible and his clothes were dry. Was this just a dream? Then a fear seized him. "Pleaser."

He jumped up and ran back to the water's edge where he watched his friend die in the stream. There was only peace upon the river. Though the current was moving, there were no white caps like before.

A light reflection drew Fatalist's eye to the top of the bridge. A light beam in the shape of a cross extended itself from the top of the bridge and over the water where Fatalist stood. From the cross's reflection came a voice. As the voice spoke, the waters stilled completely. *"I AM the Way, the Truth, and the Life. No one comes to the Father but through Me."*

Fatalist knew the voice belonged to the Pursuer of his Soul, the arranger of all circumstances. Hearing the Pursuer, he fell to his knees and then went face down to the ground.

He knew he was in the presence of holiness. The message that hung from that sign returned to him. *"Those who hope in the Lord shall renew their strength."*

The awareness of God's mercy and grace was too much to stand. The voice within the cross reflection said; *"I AM your Father in Heaven and you are My son. I love you with an everlasting love."*

Fatalist lay there and wept. Tears of gratitude streamed down his face as his heart received the offer of His love. He confessed out loud how undeserving he was of this amazing love. All he had done was complain and grumble over everything that ever happened.

When he shared his unworthiness, he paused to listen, expecting rejection, but instead was given reassurance to receive the love offered. He sobbed over this kindness. He mourned over his bitter heart that he had cultivated these years.

Fatalist was exhausted from crying, when words bubbled up to his heart. He spoke the words that came to him; he did not search them out.

"O LORD, You have searched me and known me. You know my sitting down and my rising up; You understand my thought afar off. You comprehend my path and my lying down; You are acquainted with all my ways."

Hope was now his favorite word. "Hope. I have hope." He screamed at the top of his lungs. "I HAVE HOPE!"

He lifted up his arms to celebrate, when he once again remembered Pleaser. "Oh my goodness, Pleaser." He started to run off in the direction of the rocks she had pointed out. Something felt very odd as he ran towards her. At first, he couldn't identify what it was but then he realized what it was, he was wearing a smile. Fatalist giggled as he imagined what he looked like with it. "Pleaser may not even recognize me with this attached to my face."

Pleaser on the Rocks

Pleaser made her way to the rock grove. She looked for the most comfortable looking boulder to lie on. She spotted the perfect place in the center, so she headed across the rocks to reach it. The smooth surface that made itself so attractive to her eye was also dangerous to one walking atop it. The smooth surface was slippery and the steepness to its slope was greatly underestimated.

As she made her way across, she was forced to bend forward and then decided it might be best to crawl on all fours for added grip. The gravity began pulling her over and she started to slip off the edge. In an effort to slow down her slide and not fall head first, she threw her feet out in front of her and fell backwards onto her rear end.

The steep incline caused her to gain momentum as she slid down the rock's slick surface. She slid right off the rock and was actually airborne for a few seconds until gravity pulled her back. She desperately looked for something to stop her momentum.

In that moment, she spotted a crevice. This could be the brake pedal she needed. She inserted her foot into the crack and sat down as she landed. Her ankles and knees vibrated from the braking halt. Her body jerked forward in whiplash to adapt to the abrupt stop.

She ended up suspended on the side of a steep rock surface by her left foot, which lodged inside a small opening. Below her was a thirty-foot drop. She was literally caught between a rock and a hard place.

If she moved her planted foot from the crack, she would easily fall to her death. Pleaser froze in fear. She chuckled at the irony of the situation.

This whole thing felt so familiar. Though she had never slid down a rock before, and been inches away from a fatal fall, she knew this place intimately, this place of fear, caught between trying to please one person, without offending another. She was so afraid to make a wrong move, so she would not move at all.

The irony was that for the first time, her fears truly matched the danger. She was in a life or death situation and one wrong move could cause her to die. She was reflecting on these circumstances, when black and white cat appeared on the rock above her. It looked at Pleaser without expression. "You there, move! You are in my way." said the cat.

Pleaser felt anxious but requested he go around. "Please go around me as I am stuck here and I am unable to move."

The cat scowled at her and swiped his paw at her but didn't touch her. "These are my rocks and I did not give you permission to walk on them."

The more she tried to reason with him, the more impatient the cat became and the more confused Pleaser became on what the cat really wanted. It would have been very easy for him to walk around her, yet he seemed to enjoy sparring with her for the fun of it.

"As you can see, I am not able to move. If I even move an inch I will lose my footing and could fall to my death." Pleaser repeated herself to the indignant cat.

"Oh, aren't you dramatic. You have such a gift of exaggeration. You are just trying to make your imagined fears real. Now, just get off my rock!" Demanded the cat.

In a moment of revelation, Pleaser became disgusted with herself that she was losing a debate with a cat. A strength came out from within her that she never experienced before. "You know what? I am not going to reason with you anymore! You are a cat."

"Well how long did it take you to realize this? You must be a college graduate. Well if I am a cat, you must be loony because you are talking to a cat.

"And…" the cat continued, "if you can talk to this cat, then listen to this cat. **MOVE.**"

"No I won't move." Pleaser stood straight up and placed her hands on her hips. She was getting angry at his arrogance but then felt insecure about her opinion and became quiet again.

"Oh come on now," mocked the cat. "Everyone knows what a real push over you are. How easy it is to manipulate you."

"Everyone who? To whom are you referring? Who said this about me?" demanded Pleaser.

"Oh you don't want to know what people say about you. We know you better than you know yourself."

That idea gave Pleaser the creeps.

"There are things going on all around all the time that you don't have a clue about." Pleaser felt her face turn flush. She felt like a roller coaster paused at the crest just about ready to free-fall down the track. Fear was replaced by anger. It was an anger that had been sleeping like a bear in hibernation all her life. This cat's arrogance awakened her.

Anger mobilized her. When she responded back it was with great animation. She moved her arms in emphasis. In the emotion of it all, she had completely forgotten about the danger of her situation.

"You know, I am sick and tired of doing things for people just because they want me to. I do it so they won't be mad at me. Well, I am done doing that as of this moment. I am not going to move." Pleaser placed her hands on her hips again.

The power and conviction coming from her surprised the cat. Where was all this passion coming from, he wondered. He became concerned that this was backfiring. She was a mousy, fearful captive before stepping into this rock's crevice. Where was all this new strength coming from?

Pleaser was unaware that in her assertiveness, she had stepped out of the crevice, which had kept her from falling. The amazing fact was that she found herself still standing on the rock. She was standing in the strength of her convictions and her foot was not slipping. She had found traction in truth.

The cat continued to banter with her, fearing that he was going to lose this debate if things continued in this way. He decided to lay out all his cards. "Let me introduce myself, my name is El Gato del Diablo.

My master is the enemy of the Pursuer of your Soul. I have been instructed to make you listen to me or he will make your life a living nightmare." The cat started to circle around her. He lunged and swiped at her with his paws. He growled and snarled, but would not strike her. He was not allowed to touch her.

Pleaser had not yet realized her foot had been freed. Fear overcame her as her enemy lunged at her. She felt herself shrink, and the cat seemed to grow.

Then she remembered something she read in her invitation to come on this journey. *"When my spirit grows faint within me, it is You who know my way."*

Pleaser looked up to heaven to test if what she read was true. When she lifted her eyes, she spotted a sign hanging from a tree:

"In the path where I walk, men have hidden a snare for me. Look to my right and see; no one is concerned for me. I have no refuge; no one cares for my life. I cry to you, O LORD; I say, 'You are my refuge, my portion in the land of the living.'"

Pleaser's heart reached out for and took hold of these words. "Listen to my cry, oh Pursuer of my Soul. I am in desperate need; rescue me from this enemy who is too strong for me."

At that instant, a lion walked up onto the rock crest. This lion was of incredible size yet walked with grace as it approached from behind.

El Gatos Del Diablo lunged at Pleaser and delighted to see how it seemed the tide had turned once again. She was fearful and cowering as he began laughing and snorting with excitement at the success of his harassment.

The lion suddenly let out a giant roar. The cat froze and Pleaser smiled. El Gatos Del Diablo very gingerly moved his eyes to see behind him, while trying not to move a muscle. The lion roared a second time and much more loudly this time. Pleaser trembled at the lion's strength and power.

El Gatos Del Diablo launched himself in the opposite direction, in an effort to flee. The lion lifted up his massive paw and struck the dark side warrior. This launched him through the air. Pleaser tracked his airborne flight until he disappeared below the cliff rock. The impact of his landing echoed back up to her ears. She was relieved. It was over.

When she looked back to the lion, He was gone. In the place where He stood, lay a rock the size of her hand. Suddenly, she recognized her foot was free. She walked cautiously up toward where the lion had stood and picked up the rock and noticed engraving on it. \

"*I AM your sure foundation. I AM the solid rock on which to stand.*" As she turned the rock over there was another inscription. "*He will not let your foot slip — He who watches over you will not slumber; The LORD will keep you from all harm — He will watch over your life; the LORD will watch over your coming and going both now and forevermore.*"

How perfect these words were speaking to her immediate need. "Thank you." She looked back up to heaven knowing that was from where the lion came. "Thank you for Your protection over me."

She felt a strengthening of purpose within her. It felt like someone had placed her in a back brace. A small still voice spoke from within the soft breeze. *"The LORD will be your confidence and will keep your foot from being snared."*

"I believe that Pursuer, I do. You are the only One who could have freed me from this predicament without falling." She started to walk back toward the pathway where she and Fatalist had parted. When she stood at the edge, she looked back to reflect on how close she came to falling to her death.

When she turned back around, there walking toward her was a familiar figure. It was Fatalist's walk, but with an energetic bounce to his step.

"Pleaser, Pleaser." He was waving and smiling to get her attention. He couldn't contain himself and broke into a full run.

He was a joyful sight to see. She looked forward to sharing with her friend all that had happened. She was a little concerned about how he would receive the part of her debating with a cat.

When Fatalist caught up to her, he greeted her with a big hug. His momentum made it feel like he was trying to tackle her. She squealed and Fatalist laughed as he quickly braked. "Oh Pleaser it is so good to see you. I am so glad you are alive."

Pleaser was bewildered by his surprise at her being alive. "Of course I am alive why wouldn't I be? I did actually just come real close to falling off a cliff, but how did you know that?" Pleaser inquired about the joy that was bubbling out from Fatalist. "What has happened to you? All this joy is so out of character for you."

Fatalist could not contain his excitement any longer. He wanted to share everything at once. He was frustrated at how slow his mouth moved, when there was so much to share. Pleaser put aside her own miraculous story to listen to him. She couldn't believe how joyful and excited he was.

Little Bin to the Rescue

Little Bin ran ahead with his arms outstretched like wings of an airplane. He made noises indicating engine trouble. He started to spurt and intermittently sputter, his plane was going down.

"This is Romans flight 323. Captain Little Bin here. I am coming in with just one engine." He followed with a few more saliva-filled sputters and then radioed again.

"This is Captain Little Bin with Romans flight 323. We have come up short but by the grace of God, we have landed safely." He lowered himself onto a grassy field and then landed himself spread eagle and rolled all the way down the slight incline. He finally came to a halt.

"Our emergency landing is successful! I repeat we have been saved!" Little Bin jumped up to do his crowd noise. He received the cheers and adoring hugs from the passengers who credited him with saving their lives.

Little Bin came to a halt facing toward the stream. Something across the shoreline caught his attention. Initially, he thought it was a shirt or sweater shipwrecked on some rocks in the middle of the stream.

He walked to the shore's edge to get a closer look. He saw that it was a stuffed dog. It was wet and tattered, but he was sure it was a stuffed dog. One of his eyes was missing and one of his ears was torn and hanging by a thread.

Little Bin felt sad for him. He was so helpless, and surrounded by raging waters. He attempted to get to him by wading into the stream, but the racing waters prevented him from reaching him. He got close enough to read the small letters stitched near his heart. The word *'Dreams'* was stitched in red thread on his sweater.

Little Bin called out to encourage him. "Don't worry little guy, I am coming for you. Hey Dreams, don't worry, my name is Little Bin and I am here to rescue you. I know I am just a kid but I can do it. I even outran a wolf today, so you are in good hands."

Little Bin searched around for a way to reach him. He was very good at thinking up creative ways to solve problems, and he was certain this would be no different.

Little Bin thought it funny that he was going to rescue Dreams. Back in Self Absorption, he only made fun of people's dreams.

His parents had placed all their dreams in Self Absorption. This soured Little Bin about dreams. Self Absorption stole people's dreams it didn't bring them.

Little Bin looked around for a stick long enough to reach him, but that was to no avail. Then he got a brilliant idea. In a mad dash, he turned and ran back to where he had left Counselor. Counselor was nowhere in sight, but Little Bin saw what he came for: his trash bin.

He grabbed hold of the scarlet cord and wrapped it tightly around his wrist. He pulled it behind him as he headed back to the stream at a face pace.

"Hold on Dreams, I am coming. I've got an idea." With the scarlet cord still attached to his wrist, he lowered the trashcan into the water. His plan was to send the trashcan over to Dreams to scoop him up inside. Then he could pull him across to safety.

In theory, it seemed like a good idea, but when Little Bin placed it in the stream, the bin filled quickly with water and it began to sink.

The can pulled under the water started to cut off the circulation to Little Bin's hand because he had wrapped the cord around his wrist. His hand started to turn blue. The forceful power of the current pulled Little Bin into the water too. The force pulled him into the current too. He followed right behind the trashcan, both moving rapidly down stream.

Had it not been for the freezing water, Little Bin would have had felt the cutting pain of the noose around his wrist. The weight of the can was pulling him under. He held on as long as he could, but the current was too strong. A life or death decision had to be made; he had to let go of the rope. With both hands, he slipped his wrist out of the rope.

Little Bin watched with great sadness as his faithful home speeded away down current.

His grief interrupted by his own need to swim to safety. His little body was no match for the mighty force of the water. He needed to use all his energy to swim to shore.

When he reached the bank, he grabbed hold of a rock and scooted himself onto land. His heart was beating so hard he thought for sure he was denting the rock he was laying on. "Oh no, what am I going to do?"

Then something that he read on his invitation came to his mind. He pulled out the wet folded up letter from his back pocket. He was surprised he could peel the letter apart without ripping it.

He read the whole letter looking for one specific thing. "Oh here it is." He read it aloud. "*When you find that you don't know what to do, ask Me and I will give you wisdom abundantly.*"

After reading it, Little Bin turned over onto his back and looked up into the sky.

"Dear Pursuer of my Soul, I do not know what to do here. I have tried everything I know and nothing worked. You said in this letter I need to ask you and you will give me the wisdom. Help me please. I want to help Dreams."

As he finished his prayer, a fish jumped out of the water right in front of him. He leaped high above the water's surface then dove back into the water. Little Bin noticed he had something in his mouth. A second fish jumped out of the water and just as high.

At first, he thought it was the same fish but then realized they had two different colors. They took turns leaping out of the water, each time moving closer to the shoreline where Little Bin was sitting. They made their way to the edge of the shore, stopped, swam in place and stared at Little Bin.

Little Bin was convinced they had come to talk to him. He greeted them with excitement. "Hello, do you speak English?"

They backed into the shore just a few inches from the edge facing out. Little Bin noticed fishing lines coming out of their mouths. When they backed up, the lines floated to the top of the water.

Little Bin reached into the water and grabbed hold of the two pieces of clear string. He put one in each hand. On the transparent string was a tag, which read; "Instruction fishing line - 50 pound weight."

He wrapped the strings around his hands a few times when he noticed a sign from the tree above his head.

"I have lead you in right paths. When you walk, your steps will not be hindered. And when you run you will not stumble, take firm hold of instruction do not let go."

"Wow that is so funny." Little Bin looked down at the fish and talked to them. "That sign says take firm hold of instruction and that is the name of the fishing line." Little Bin laughed. He looked up to Heaven and said, "Got it."

This was an answer to his prayer. He already had hold of the two lines, and so he looked down at the fish for more directions. They seemed to be waiting for something but he did not know what.

He looked up to reread the directions. *"When you walk your steps will not be hindered."*

"But I can't walk on water. Do you want me to take a step on the water?" Little Bin knew the signs were trustworthy. They had saved his and Counselor's life on more than one occasion.

"Okay, I will step out. I sure hope I am getting this right." Little Bin took a step out onto the water's rushing white current. As he stepped, one of the fish moved right under his foot and met his shoe at the surface of the water. This startled Little Bin, which caused him to pull back on the fishing line. Falling off balance when he leaned back, the fish stabilized his standing position. Little Bin followed with his left foot and watched the other fish meet his shoe in the water.

"Hey, I am water skiing." Little Bin knew when you water skied, it was important to bend your knees. So with a firm hold on the instruction line, he stood on the backs of these two fish with bended knees and began skiing across the stream.

Half way across, Little Bin pretended to be a cowboy holding tightly to the reigns of a bucking bronco. He hollered, "Oooh Hoo!"

He reached down with one graceful swoop and scooped Dreams up with one hand, while the other hand held both of the lines. He secured Dreams under his arm and pressed his elbow tightly against his side. "Hang on Dreams, it is a wild ride!"

The fish needed no instructions. They knew exactly what to do. They delivered Little Bin and his passenger safely back to shore. Little Bin stepped to solid ground pulling Dreams from under his arm. He lifted him up above his head to celebrate, then pulled Dreams down to take a good look at him. "We did it Dreams, you are safe."

Little Bin turned to thank his two friends in the water. "Thank you fishes. You are the coolest fishes I have ever met, and strong too. Do you guys have names? I wanted to be sure to remember you by name."

The orange striped fish peeked out of the water and said, "My name is Childlike." Just then, the brown spotted fish peeked out and said, "And mine is Faith."

Little Bin waved goodbye to his two friends as they swam away doing leaps out of the water. "Goodbye Childlike. Goodbye Faith. Take care of yourselves."

The two fish midway across stream stood up on their back fins and stretched themselves out above the water, swimming backwards, and waved goodbye. Then they dove into the water and he did not see them again.

Little Bin spotted a sign across the way with a message; *"All things are possible with God. His ways are higher than ours."*

"That is the truth. I just water-skied on the back of two fishes." Little Bin headed back towards the rock with a huge smile across his face. "This Pursuer of my Soul is way beyond cool!"

He carried Dreams back to where he last left Counselor. "Dreams, I can't wait for you to meet my friend, Counselor. She is really nice." As he walked, he tried to push all of the stuffing back inside of Dreams.

Counselor Meets the Keeper of Pain

Counselor watched as Little Bin disappeared to his next adventure. She felt disjointed inside. "Why is it so much harder now to keep all my emotions in check? What kind of counselor are you? You can't even keep your own emotions in line."

Counselor was unaware of the dark side warrior who had been following her and throwing thoughts up in an effort to fill her with despair.

Sitting on her rock, Counselor consumed in her own world, she did not notice a strange little man sitting on a rock across the way. His rock hung out over the stream. His body position mimicked hers and he stared right at her.

"Are you copying me?" He asked, attempting to get her attention. His voice was low and serious.

He had deep seeded eyes and a high forehead, which cast a heavy shadow over the rest of his face. He was gaunt and bony with a weathered face. His skin hung loosely off his skeleton rather than it being tightly fitting. He had a long, thin nose, which suggested you would find a wart on the end of it, but there wasn't one.

His voice unchained her from her thoughts. As her eyes moved from inside herself to him, she felt bad for him because he was homely. "Excuse me?" She was not sure what he had actually said.

"Are you copying me?" He repeated the question.

"What do you mean by that?" Counselor asked him. He seemed to be trying to irritate her on purpose. She felt frustrated because she wanted to be alone. This place was big enough, she reasoned, why did he have to invade her privacy. This was her moment to have a meltdown in private. His questions were intrusive.

"Well," Counselor decided to respond to his question. "You are sitting just like I am; how do I know you are not trying to copy me sir?"

He sarcastically retorted, "That is not possible, for I was here first." He looked at her with cold, challenging eyes and repeated it. "I was here first."

"Well I must not have noticed you when I sat down. I am sorry. I will go find another spot." Counselor started to get up to move, but his demanding tone halted her.

"You are not going anywhere without me." The confidence in which he spoke these words, sent a cold chill down her back.

"Excuse me, what did you just say?" She was hoping she misheard him. It sounded like a threat. She started to worry about her safety. Is this man a stalker of some sort? Is he going to kill me?

His face was so ugly she knew she would have remembered meeting him before. "Think, where have you met this man?" She wondered to herself.

"You are not going to die. I am not going to kill you." He shook his head, disgusted with her drama.

This scared Counselor even more. "How does he know what I am thinking? This is very strange. I feel like I have entered the Twilight Zone." She thought.

"You are wondering how I know what you are thinking?" He smiled hauntingly at her as if enjoying the fact that he was freaking her out.

"I am not going to give him the satisfaction of knowing I am scared," Counselor thought.

"Who are you and what do you want with me?" Counselor was no longer polite. If he was planning to harm her, she wanted to know now.

"You already know who I am."

"No, I am sorry, I do not have any idea who you are. I would have remembered meeting you."

"We have met before, but I did not look like this then."

"Are you an old school mate? I cannot place your face." Counselor was disturbed because he did not look familiar to her at all.

"Client is my name, just as Counselor is yours." His gaze was fixed; it was a soul-piercing stare. He waited for her to understand.

Counselor's fear began inhibiting her breath. She wanted to flee, but she was too scared to move. Words written in the invitation she received re-entered her mind and a voice inside her began to speak.

"There will be painful discoveries. Truth will be brought across your path. Do not turn from this truth

but look at it. Lift your eyes when overwhelmed and ask for help. I will give you the strength to carry on."

"I need to lift my eyes to the Pursuer of my Soul. How? Could this be the painful discovery? It must be. If I run, he will probably just follow me anyway.

The irony about this is I have been running from the truth all my life. I am so tired of running. I don't really think I have the strength to outrun him anyway." A million thoughts raced through her mind.

Counselor looked up to the sky and imagined that was where the Pursuer dwelt. "Okay I will just face whatever this creepy man wants to tell me. Please give me the strength to face this."

She looked across at the peculiar man, stood up and stared intently at him. She studied him. Then she remembered him.

It was as if a curtain was pulled back suddenly in her mind. She saw who he was. Her legs felt as heavy as lead and they started to buckle under her. She sat back against the rock to prevent herself from fainting, all the while, kept her eyes on him.

The man watched the color leave Counselor's face. "It is coming to you now isn't it?" He asked. "You are remembering that I am the keeper of your pain. I've been in your employ for many decades now. I have been faithful to keep to my responsibilities, but you are long overdue in being responsible for yours.

Why do you deny knowing me? You do not listen to anything I bring to your mind. You have long since passed your agreement and yet you still expect me to keep your pain away. This has gone on long enough. I have come today to inform you, I quit. You must keep your own pain from now on."

Counselor recalled the day that deal was made. She thought it was the perfect arrangement at the time. She could not manage all her pain, so she found a storage place to lock it away and assigned someone to guard it. She did not want anything to get out and surprise her.

This job had clearly taken a toll on him. He used to be more attractive and pleasing to look at. This job cost him a great deal. Being locked away with all that misery and pain, he was weary. His physical appearance was part of the evidence of that cost.

She realized she was responsible for his cynical state. This had jaded him. She never returned to him as she promised. There were times he came to mind, but it was too uncomfortable to think about facing all she had locked away.

There was no room for it now and it interfered with her efforts to gain distance from her past. He had started a new life.

He was the noise she had been running from. He had been trying to get her attention all this time. Avoiding him was the cause of her anxiety. The louder he was, the busier she became. In all the busyness, she did not have to hear his demanding voice.

She always knew someday this day would come, but she hoped it would never be today.

Now she faced him and the idea of managing her own feelings overwhelmed her. This time she saw no exit, there was no way of escape.

"I do not know how to manage pain. This is too big for me to handle. What if I am over run with all this emotion, and rendered useless as a counselor?

"How pathetic am I? I pour into the pain of others to help avoid my own. I invest in crying for others, so I can avoid shedding my own tears.

I encouraged and ministered to people who were convinced they were insane, all the while knowing the truth; I was the one insane.

"Sir, I know you are right. I am long overdue in taking charge of this pain. I just don't know how I am going to manage a lifetime worth of pain."

Then words from her invitation returned to her mind once more. *"Do not turn from truth but look at it. Lift your eyes when it seems overwhelming and ask for help. I will give you the strength to carry on."*

"Lift your eyes and ask for help. I will give you strength to carry on. Oh, Pursuer did you really know this moment would come? Are these words you wrote to me true?" With pearl-sized teardrops rolling down her cheeks, Counselor cried out, "Oh Pursuer of my Soul, help me, help me!"

A small still voice spoke to her heart. *"Retrieve what belongs to you."*

With the words, came the understanding of what He meant. She must take her pain back and be accountable for her heart. When she heard these instructions, it became a choice to obey. She wanted to please the Pursuer. She wanted to obey.

This desire in her heart empowered her to do what she never thought would be possible.

She made her way across the stepping stones amidst the stream to where this man stood. She extended both her hands to him, ready and willing to take what he wanted to give to her.

"Client, you have carried my pain faithfully all these years. I am so sorry I left you with all this mess and denied you access to me. I can't imagine what impact all this had on you, but I can see you paid a terrible toll."

Bitterness had shriveled his skin and his outlook was pale. He needed time in the sun, to fellowship in light. He had been stuck in darkness, where things are locked away for too long.

"You are right you cannot know what it was like, but you will learn." He let out a cynical laugh, appeasing his bitterness. He handed her the pain.

Counselor said one final time, "Please forgive me. I am so sorry." Without another word, he disappeared before her eyes.

She was left alone, alone with her pain. A tap dance started in her stomach. She rushed back to the rock she had been sitting on before grief overtook her.

"Oh Pursuer of my Soul, I cannot do this." Here at the waters edge, Counselor began to weep. Each tear spilling off her cheek captured a photograph from her past. Memories frozen in time, held as captives until now. They were denied access to light because Counselor did not want them visible.

As her tears fell, her slow motion biography played. The images hosting her father's slow fade into destruction began to unfold in her heart.

He grabbed hold of Self Absorption's mirror, the mirror of lies and illusion. He believed its lies and false images and became a slave to what he needed to see. He lost sight of everything he held precious. His family watched their beloved husband and father become a shadow to the man he was.

The shattered hopes that her dad would have woken up spilled down her cheeks. It was so easy to love him, before the mirror.

Tears fell, each drop holding a deteriorating image of her mom, looking expectantly at the front door, hoping her husband would step through it. A daughter's heart- breaking as she watches her mom slowly die inside.

More tears fell, carrying the images from years later, when her mom no longer looked at the door with hope. Instead, she just stood in front of the bay window, without hope, just a blank stare. She was old and embittered, waiting now for her life to end, as she had nothing to live for anymore.

Counselor saw how that steered her course in life. She hid out on the sidelines of life. She preferred coaching, rather than participating just like the window her mother stared out watching her life go by.

It kept her isolated and alone, but she liked it that way, or at least she convinced herself she did.

She knew her days of running were over. What was strangest of all was she no longer wanted to run. "Oh Pursuer of my Soul, I need you. I have been running away for so long, I don't know how to stay and be accountable. I am a middle-aged woman who is just now facing the truth of who I am and where I came from."

She continued to pour out her heart to the Pursuer of her Soul.

"You gave me this letter inviting me to Lake Still Water. You must be the One who brings light to darkness. Turn on the light switch to this darkness."

Counselor wept uncontrollably, giving way to deep despair.

She paused in her conversation because grief demanded its release. She complied. There was an exodus of captive emotions. She knew at the deepest level, it felt good.

"I have no good argument to give you on why I deserve it, because I do not. I left another one responsible for my pain so I could avoid it. I am desperate and I confess I cannot make it to Lake Still Water, unless You intervene. I have no strength left for my journey."

Counselor fell back against the rocks and sobbed. She was so distraught she did not notice the transformation her tears underwent. They rolled down her cheeks and dripped off her chin like normal tears. Their transformation was what was so peculiar.

She first noticed them when she was able to breathe again.

Her tears were dark in appearance, like sludge. Pain and emotion stored up for so long, coagulated inside her. Her body began to purge the toxins for the first time.

The black tar like substance dripped off the end of her chin, dropping into the water. The weight pulled it quickly to the bottom of the stream.

After awhile her tears became clear again. The toxins purged from her soul, she cried tears of the present now.

A tear dropped into the water a picture projected back to her from one particular memory. She saw her face as a broken-hearted little girl, and standing right behind her was the Pursuer of her Soul. He gently rested His hands upon her shoulders watching over her family with tears in his eyes too.

Counselor was so surprised. "You were there even back then? I didn't know." She heard a whisper in reply, *"I stand at the door and knock. If you open the door I will come in."*

"Oh I remember hearing that but I didn't know that was You. You were there then." Counselor sobbed with this revelation but this time for joy. It brought her great comfort to know that He had always been with her. *"When we lose those we love and depend upon, when we are betrayed by those we trust, the pain is very deep and difficult."*

He extended to her His palms and she saw the nail scars in both His hands. She knew what He was saying. He knew not just by knowledge but from His own experience.

The Pursuer continued. *"In your pain, you reached out to others, but I have come now to bring you comfort so that you can then offer others the comfort I have given you."*

"Pursuer what was that black sludge in my tears?"

"The gall and bitterness stored up from pain not turned over to Me. In My Hands your heart has hope.

My love washes and cleanses the wounded places so infections of the soul do not take hold and destroy you."

Just then, the sun broke through a cloud and lit up the rock beside her. The light was blinding and Counselor was compelled to lay face down. A voice spoke from within the light. It spoke directly to her. She knew the voice to be the Pursuer of her Soul.

"Do not be afraid. I have heard your cry. This day you have come to an ending, which leads to your new beginning. At this end you have found Me. I make you new. I fashioned your days, including this one; fashioned before you were born.

It is I, who compelled Client to resign. Hand to Me now all that you carry. My burden is light and My yoke is easy. I will walk with you through every pain and memory. I will be with you always."

Counselor lifted her hands up toward the light. "Yes please take all that I am carrying, Pursuer. I don't want to lock away my heart this time. Keep my heart open to whatever You would want to bring to me. I want to feel what You bring to my days. I trust You, Pursuer of my Soul, take this and guide me. Into Your Hands I commit my heart to You."

"Today, I give you a new name. You can now share with others the comfort and mercy I have brought to you. This is your call, your purpose. Your new name is Compassion.

Your heart has been cleansed from the dross, of your suffering, bringing forth compassion. In the past, you have not been able to accept My touch, because you locked your heart under your own control.

Now that you have given Me your heart, I will restore the years. I have purged the black substance of unredeemed pain and flushed it by the sacrificial blood shed on the cross. This lightness you feel is My cleansing."

"Compassion, stand and walk forward in the fullness of what I have given you."

She felt His touch upon her shoulder, but when she looked back she could not see Him. She knew in faith He was there.

She found it strange that she felt restful without knowing the plan. For so long, not knowing brought forth so much anxiety. It was such a relief to know that she didn't need to have the answer. She now knew the One who did. Whenever she needed wisdom, she would ask Him.

She came to this stream as Counselor, a fearful, hopeless, broken woman. She left a hope filled new creation, who was excited to share the Good News about the Pursuer of her Soul's and His amazing compassion.

Starting on her new journey her little friend was on his way back to see her. She was so thankful for all she had been given.

Guardian Is Set Free

Guardian awoke with the birds singing outside his prison window. The sun's rays reached through the bars and warmed him. The warmth melted the coldness within his heart. When he gained full consciousness, the word 'surrender' came to his heart. It camped there.

What else could he do but surrender? The reality was, he was helpless and locked in prison and was all alone. He had control of absolutely nothing, except the choice to surrender to these truths.

Then an eerie sense haunted him that somehow he wasn't alone. He sat up and turned to look around his cell. There in the corner of his cell was a man squatted down with his arms wrapped around his legs. He was staring back at Guardian with a warm smile. "Good Morning, Guardian. Did you sleep well?"

Guardian was caught completely off guard. He responded tentatively. "Yes. Uh, who are you and how did you get in here?"

The man smiled, "No prison bars can keep me out or in. Do not be afraid. I have known you since the beginning of time."

These words sounded completely crazy, but this man did not appear crazy, and his voice sounded familiar.

"Who are you?" Guardian asked.

"I AM He… Guardian, I am the One who invited you to come on this journey."

In that moment, he knew he was looking at the Pursuer of his Soul. He was embarrassed about where he was.

The One got up from the corner and walked over to Guardian, placing His arm around his shoulder. The Pursuer reached for his other arm and helped him to his feet. *"Do not be afraid. I AM with you."*

Finding himself half standing and half collapsing, he leaned into the Pursuer's arms and started to cry. He grabbed hold of His garment and clung to him with tears as his only words. The Pursuer held him without saying a word. Guardian cried from depths he didn't even know he had.

He wept over his father, the drunken beatings and criticism. He wept over his mother's predictions that he would turn out just like his father: a no good drunk.

The Pursuer held him for a long time. When the tears were gone, the Pursuer squared him around and looked intently into his eyes. *"My son, I love you. I chose you before the foundations of the earth. I will not abandon you as your earthly father did.*

Though you have tried to turn your pain for good, you cannot do that by locking it all away. You cannot be the lord of your own life and come to know My peace, purpose, and My love. I AM the only rescue. It is only in My defense can people be saved. You cannot journey without Me, for I AM your Guardian.

"Today I give you a new name. It reflects your calling and purpose. Your name will be 'Companion.' You are to be others companions as they travel this journey of faith. You will come alongside those I send to you and point them toward their Good Shepherd.

For it is in darkness and defeat, I bring light and truth and lead them in the way.

"You cannot offer to others what you have not yet received for yourself. Spend time with Me daily. I will supply all that you need. As I pour into you, I will use you to pour into others."

Companion (Guardian) fell to his knees. "I do not wish to take one more step on my own. I am weak and fearful. I can't believe you want to use me. I am such a failure. If You will supply me, I would be honored to be used however You would want."

The Pursuer lifted Companion to his feet.

"My son, go. Love others as I have loved you. Do not keep them from their afflictions or attempt to release them yourself from their prison cells. For like you, they need to find Me inside their own prison bars. Only then will they learn of the true liberty and freedom.

Walk beside those I send to you and encourage them in truth. I will strengthen and equip you for every good work. I want to give you a tool to use often."

The Pursuer of his Soul handed him a book. Companion opened it and a brilliant light shined forth. The prison door opened at that moment and the light led Companion outside. He was free. He was no longer captive.

The book opened up to a page and Companion's eyes were drawn to these lines. *"Let the light of My Word lead you and My Spirit guide you. You are a new man, with a new name, and a new call upon your life."* Then he heard the voice of the Pursuer in his heart, *"This book is My Word to you."*

Companion felt strengthened in his new purpose. He figured in the cell it was the end of him. The truth was, it was just the beginning. The weight he had carried for Tuck transformed into hope.

Standing outside in the beauty of the day he soaked it all in. He never thought he would ever see this again. He smiled and lifted his face to heaven.

"Pursuer, please reunite Tuck and me soon."

Just hours before, a prisoner without hope, and now he was free indeed.

From Heaven They Look On

"Commander, the adoptions have been realized." An angelic messenger reported.

"Let the weaving begin," proclaimed the Commander of the Army of Heaven. As His proclamation went out, a great flurry of motion began. Motion was always graceful, a divinely choreographed dance, perfectly woven since the beginning of time.

Each angel knew his assignment. It was a ballet of fellowship, all in harmony. The design already established was about to be revealed to those headed for Lake Still Water. Together they would strengthen and teach each other, leading one another to a deeper faith. Woven souls were always stronger than one who stood alone.

The Obstacle

Compassion (Counselor) and Little Bin reunited a little way up the path. Both were very excited to share their stories. Their pace quickened as they talked and it made the last leg of their journey seem to go by in no time.

Compassion shared about her cleansing tears. Little Bin kept adding new parts of his fish story he forgot to mention. "Oh did I tell you what the fish's names were? One was Childlike and the other named Faith. Cool huh."

Little Bin had recovered well from the loss of his faithful trash bin. There was something inside him that knew he wasn't going to need it anymore. His life had changed so much on this trip.

"Little Bin that is very cool." Compassion smiled and enjoyed the joy in her heart behind the smile. She had grown accustomed to smiling without joy, but realized they really did belong together.

"Look Compassion, we made it." Little Bin pointed to the sign that read 'Lake Still Water.' He ran ahead to get close to and touch it.

Compassion had come to love the back of Little Bin's head. As she approached the Lake Still Water sign, she reviewed her journey these past few days. So much had happened since she awoke that morning to find her invitation.

Meeting this freckled face boy, being chased by a wolf, joining in imaginary play with Little Bin and coming face to face with all that she had been running from her entire life, was all great. Best of all though, was meeting and being touched by the Pursuer of her Soul.

Little Bin touched the top of the sign with his hand, making it his official claim as the first one there. He looked into the valley and saw Lake Still Water. On the backside of the lake were towering majestic peaks that stood valiantly as its backdrop.

From the side of mountains came a rock wall ledge that extended itself outward alongside the lake. It looked as if Hands from Heaven itself, stretched the rock wall across both sides of the Lake, keeping it surrounded in the center.

From above, this nature's gate looked horseshoe in shape. At first, Little Bin thought there was an opening where the two rock wall ledges curved around to the front and stopped short from touching each other.

Upon a more careful glance, he noticed in the gap between the two ledges, stood obsidian looking rock. The clear shiny surface was divinely sealed in between.

Compassion still needed to reach the edge to see the valley's view but she was enjoying her view of Little Bin as he looked down into the valley. He leaned to his left for a bit and then to his right.

She watched as he scratched his head in confusion and then turned back toward Compassion and ran halfway to her, then stopped and walked the rest of the way. She was surprised he didn't come with his typical full court sprint.

When he reached her, he was looking dejected at the ground. Something had knocked the wind from his sails.

"What's wrong Little Bin?"

"There is no way in." The mountain has a wall that reaches all the way around to the front and then there is this big glass rock blocking the only passage in."

Compassion was not too concerned about Little Bin's observation initially, for her young friend had a flare for the dramatic. However when she reached the sign and looked down into the valley, she realized he was not exaggerating.

The view was breathtaking. The crystal blue lake was nestled inside a plush grassy valley with majestic mountains framing its edges. The mountain ranges looked like the arms of God reaching around as if to hold crystal-clear lake water; it was a divine cup from heaven.

The two travelers slowly began their descent into the untouched valley. They lost sight of the lake quickly, because of the towering walls surrounding every side.

The beauty that surrounded them was a delightful distraction to how they would enter into the lake. They trusted though if the Pursuer invited them here, He would certainly lead them to where He wanted them to be.

As the incline leveled out, a green sign with a thick white border welcomed them to Lake Still Water. The arrow on the sign pointed directly at the glass rock as the entrance. The mountain ledges seamlessly fastened themselves to both sides of the obsidian barrier. By all appearances, the lake seemed inaccessible.

Little Bin walked up closely to the glassy rock's surface and looked straight up. It was so tall he almost fell backwards tipping his head back to see the very top.

When Compassion caught up to him, she placed her hands on his shoulders and stepped him backwards a few feet. This made it much easier for him to see the top. Looking up at her, he gave her a big smile and she returned one in kind.

He loved having her hands on his shoulders, caring for him as a mom would. It felt good. Sadness knocked on his heart for a moment, as he recognized he missed his mom. She used to do things like that for him a long time ago. A heavy sigh blew away his sadness so he could re-focus on the problem at hand.

From where Compassion was standing, she saw a light shining out from the inside top of the rock. Could this rock be hollow? Then she noticed some words written across the top where the light shined from inside, but she couldn't make out the words because they were too far away to read.

Little Bin was attempting to scale up its side. The surface was slick and it was had a steep vertical height. There were no visible footholds anywhere. It would be impossible to climb.

They both walked around it searching for a gap of any kind. The mountain's ledge had a smooth stone surface. Across the top about three quarters high there were words written in calligraphy that ran all the way across the rock ledge, from both sides. The words written were:

"Thou shall love the Lord Your God with all your
   heart.
You shall have no other gods before Me.
You shall not make for yourself an idol in the form of
   anything in heaven above or on the earth beneath
   or in the waters below.
You shall not bow down to them or worship them;
   for I, the LORD your God, am a jealous God,
   punishing the children for the sin of the fathers to
   the third and fourth generation of those who hate
   Me, commandments.
Do not misuse the Name of the LORD your God.
   Observe the Sabbath day by keeping it holy.
Honor your father and your mother, as the LORD
   your God has commanded you, so that you may
   live long and that it may go well with you in the
   land the LORD your God is giving you.
You shall not murder.
You shall not commit adultery.
You shall not steal.

> You shall not give false testimony against your neighbor. You shall not covet your neighbor's wife. You shall not set your desire on your neighbor's possessions.
>
> These are the commandments the LORD proclaimed."

When the last sentence was finished, it started again from the beginning. The inscription spread completely across both sides of the mountain ledge. Its surface looked like a giant tablet of stone.

Compassion found it fascinating that though the glass rock planted between the rock ledges had a transparent look, yet she could not see inside. It lit up somehow from the inside but she couldn't see how.

Little Bin was mesmerized by its uniqueness. "Compassion do you think this rock came from outer space?"

Compassion chuckled to herself. This boy had the most creative perspectives. "No my friend but I do think this is just one of a kind."

"I wonder how we will enter into the Lake?" she mumbled to herself.

Little Bin got wide eyed and pointed his finger in the air. Compassion knew right off what that meant. "Hey I got an idea." Little Bin announced. "Maybe I can collect stuff and pile it high enough to climb over the ledge. Then we could jump over to the other side."

Before Compassion could even share her opinion, Little Bin ran off in a full sprint to collect the things scattered around. He was on a new mission.

Little Bin lifted heavy rocks equal to his own weight. He waddled over to the stone ledge and dropped the rock onto the ground. Then he turned back around and ran full speed, in search of another rock to stack on top of it.

After six trips, he was tired. His run turned into a slow walk. After ten trips, his walk looked more like a waddle. All this effort and he had barely made a pile as high as his shin.

This was not turning out to be the solution he thought. By his eleventh trip, the pile did not stay in place. The pieces underneath the one placed on top fell out of the stack and rolled to the ground. Little Bin was defeated and sat down in despair.

What Little Bin was unaware of was the dark side warrior sitting on the ledge right above him. The warrior's legs crossed at the ankles, he mocked this energetic boy. His name was Strife.

This was his favorite place to hang out. He loved using the law against people. He was an expert at motivating people to try to overcome the impossible. They would be defeated every time. He suggested every possible task under the sun as long as they tried by their own effort.

He thoroughly enjoyed watching Little Bin attempt to build the pile. He gave him the idea. He whispered it into Little Bin's ear. Pride always listened to Strife's suggestions. Man so easily believed that they were the solution. Strife knew the truth was not in them, and he exploited that for all it was worth.

This warrior was a great impersonator. All the dark side warriors were good at pretending. Their commander and chief was the master imitator. They all went to voice school where they learned to imitate the voices of their assignments.

This allowed them to give suggestions without men knowing where it came from. As a result, Little Bin was unaware of the manipulations from the enemy of heaven.

Strife let Little Bin get about four or five stones high before he jumped down and kicked over the pile. He laughed a deep belly laugh, delighting in the torment of this energetic boy.

He leaned back, reveling over his successful sabotage, and almost started to slip off the ledge. At the last moment, he caught himself. This helped him refocus. He stood up on the rock's ledge and surveyed the situation. He knew more people were headed this way.

Strife intermittently encouraged Little Bin to keep going, as the dark side warrior would also look around to check the status of the other arrivals.

"Oh too bad, you almost got five high that time. Keep building. There is a rock over there that would make a nice one."

He knew this was how to keep people from getting inside the lake. He must keep them away from the glass rock. He knew they could never make it over this rock ledge. His wanted to defeat their spirits so they would turn back and not wait for the Pursuer's arrival. He also knew, if they waited long enough, they would find His entrance.

Little Bin was not going to let this collapse defeat him. That didn't worry Strife, even the most tenacious efforts will quit after enough times of defeat.

Little Bin, though tired and sweaty, turned his mind away from his sore shoulders to look for another rock. When his stack started to get high again and he just started to feel hopeful, Strife came over and kicked the pile over. Little Bin watched his hopes crumble and so did his body as it slumped to the ground.

"Awe, too bad, better try again," Strife urged Little Bin.

Little Bin was spent. His back had teamed up with his sore shoulders in the aching. The last rock he picked up was razor sharp and cut his hand badly. He grabbed hold of his hand and squeezed it hard at the wrist to try to stop the throbbing. He stared up at the tall barrier looming above him. If he could just rest for just a minute, he might be able to try again.

He lay on his back to rest for a minute, still holding his bleeding hand with the other. The sun warmed his right cheek, while he felt the softness of the grass tickle his left. He looked over to the front where the glass rock stood and noticed from the angle he laid, writing near the top. "Hey Compassion there is writing up there."

"I know I couldn't make out what is said."

"I can read it from here, it says, *"All have sinned and fall short of the glory of God.""*

Strife was irritated that the boy noticed this. He put his hands on his hips while standing up now on the ledge and using a firm voice attempted to refocus the boy. "Don't give up now, are you a quitter?"

Little Bin became fearful for some reason that Compassion would think he was a quitter. He offered reassurance that he was just resting for a minute. He was going to keep at it.

"Compassion, don't worry, just give me a few minutes to rest and I will go back to building the pile again."

She noticed blood dripping from his tightened fist. She immediately, took hold of his right hand, and gently peeled open his fingers, exposing a very bad cut on his palm.

"Young man, you will not be carrying anymore rocks today. You are cut badly."

She pulled out some Kleenex from her pocket and started to clean up his hand. Little Bin watched her as she took care of him. She made him feel important.

While Compassion ministered to Little Bin's injuries, Strife pulled out his battle instructions to re-read them. He had a tendency to lose his focus midway through his assignment. The consequences were horrendous when he made his commander and chief angry. Strife rubbed the scar he incurred the last time he failed a mission.

On the crinkled up piece of paper, he read, "Tempt them into futile tasks; encourage their efforts, then sabotage their success. Keep them busy at trying. Most important of all:

KEEP THEM AWAY FROM THE GLASS ROCK, so they do not find the Pursuer."

Worker Arrives

She read the sign indicating that Lake Still Water was the next turn, Worker felt exhilarated. A surge of energy went through her and she began to jog a little up the long hill. Panting and sweaty, she reached the top and was greeted by the awesome view.

"Wow, one feels so small facing such majestic mountains. Oh Pursuer of Souls, how great You are." Worker lifted her hands high above her head in praise.

She slowly made her way down the steep hill, as she soaked in the breathtaking view. Wildflowers of every color painted the pathway down.

The steepness of the trail kept her from losing herself in the beauty, but she kept the flowers in view from the corners of her eye. The long descent added a lot of strain to her knee. She hoped it wouldn't give out before she reached the bottom.

Peace came knowing her Pursuer had invited her to come, He would ensure her arrival. "Oh Pursuer please provide me with the strength I need to make it down this hill." She trusted being in His Hands, and that peace stayed with her all the way to the bottom.

At the base of the path, she saw the green sign identifying the Lake Still Water entrance. She stood there, bewildered as to her next move.

"I wonder if someone moved this sign. Maybe it is pointing the wrong way?" The arrow pointed directly to the center of the big glass rock. "This can't be right."

She walked toward the walled up lake and noticed a young boy and a woman on the right side of the rock, standing in front of a rock ledge. She decided to ask them.

"Hi there folks. Can you tell me how to find the entrance to Lake Still Water?"

Compassion and Little Bin pointed to the huge glassy barrier that Worker had already eliminated as an option.

"Do you guys see a way in?" Worker stepped back to take in the rock in its entirety. "It is very impressive, but I don't see an entranceway anywhere." Worker was puzzled. "Why do you think someone placed a rock at the entrance?"

"That is a good question, one we have also been asking ourselves since our arrival." Compassion then extended her hand in introduction. "Hi my name is Compassion. What is your name?" She shook Worker's hand.

"It is nice to meet you Compassion, my name is Worker."

Little Bin looked up at her and smiled. Compassion continued with the introductions. She came up behind Little Bin and put her hands on his shoulders and stepped him forward so he could shake Worker's hand, "And this is my friend, Little Bin."

With his bloodied hand wrapped in a Kleenex, he waved. The bloodied Kleenex caught Worker's attention. "My goodness what happened to you?" Worker inquired about Little Bin's injury.

"I was trying to build a tower so we could get over that rock ledge."

"That looks very painful. It is very nice to meet you both. So did you have any luck with your plan?"

"No not yet."

"Would it be okay if I joined you in problem solving how to get inside?"

"That would okay with us." Compassion walked her over to where they had been piling up rocks in an effort to build a tower to scale over.

"Did you travel this journey all by yourself?" Compassion asked.

Worker replied, "Well I started out on my own, but then joined up with some folks who were also on their way here. It got complicated because I can be very stubborn at times. I didn't listen to their opinions and chose to take a separate route and I ended up getting myself into a real mess.

The only reason I survived was because, the Pursuer of Souls rescued me from complete darkness, and I was trapped inside a tunnel.

Little Bin perked up at hearing her mention the Pursuer of Souls. "You met the 'Suer of our soul too?"

"Yes I did Little Bin, He changed my life. I will never be the same since meeting Him."

"That makes two of us," said Little Bin.

"Well you better make that three!" Compassion added in.

They all smiled and spontaneously fell into a threefold hug. They felt a unity in heart they didn't understand. They felt a safety together.

"Worker, it would be great to have you join us. We are delighted to have you."

"Thank you, I appreciate that more than you know. In that tunnel I was lost in, there was so much darkness. That was a very lonely place. It feels so good, to be out in the light. I got a good taste of humble pie in there too.

I know I will be more open to suggestions from now on. From the dark tunnel experience, I learned that I do not hold the answers to things. I hope I never forget that." Worker reflected. Worker felt so at ease with these folks.

They all returned to the problem at hand - how do they enter into Lake Still Water? Worker had grown accustom to things blocking her from her dreams.

Whether it was a flat tire, a dead end job, bills to pay, or a giant rock attached to a tall rock ledge, this was not foreign. It was always something.

The difference this time was she wasn't relying on herself for the solution. She expected the answer to be supplied by the Pursuer of Souls.

Strife shouted down a suggestion to Worker's mind and because she was not aware where the idea came, she received it as a good one. "If you don't want to be a two time loser, you better walk around this fortress to see if there is a way to get in."

Like clockwork, Worker spoke up, "I think I will walk around the perimeter to see if there is any other way inside. I'll be back in a while, so don't go anywhere." Worker walked back toward the front of the glassy rock.

She followed the curving formation of the ledge, which turned in toward the mountain peaks.

"Okay, we will be here when you get back. Be careful okay?" Compassion called after her.

Worker disappeared from their view. Little Bin was glad that Compassion told him he could not carry any more rocks, as he very sore. His hand really hurt.

Two More Arrive To Lake Still Water

Fatalist and Pleaser made their way up the steep hill slowly. They separately reviewed in silence all that transpired on this journey. As they reached the crest, like those before them, they stopped to inhale the breathtaking view.

"Oh my, look at this valley." Pleaser commented aloud.

The lake was a mirror for the blue sky. The richness of the blue left a silky feel to the water's texture. The water was still as glass.

"Wow, you are right - is that beautiful or what?" Fatalist whispered, hoping not to disturb the serenity below.

They carefully made their way down the path, at the base stood the sign with the arrow pointing to the massive obstacle.

"Have you ever seen a rock like this before?" Pleaser asked Fatalist, looking over to him for an answer. Fatalist mesmerized by the uniqueness of its substance, stared at it, while he shook his head no. "Me neither." Pleaser concurred.

Compassion and Little Bin had seen the two new arrivals approaching. They enthusiastically went to greet them. Pleaser noticed their approach and spoke first. "Hello we are looking for…" Before Pleaser finished her sentence, Little Bin and Compassion said at the same time, "The way to Lake Still Water?"

Little Bin lifted his arm toward the rock and with a big smile said, "Behold."

"Well this does present a problem." Pleaser did not hide her disappointment to what she saw. She folded her right arm on top of her left as this was her problem solving position.

"Have some hope Pleaser." Pleaser looked over at Fatalist, shocked that these words came from his mouth. Fatalist found her shocked face amusing and they both laughed.

Compassion and Little Bin could tell they had shared a history together. "Have you two been traveling together long?" Compassion asked them.

"Well we have been traveling together technically for only two days but it had enough experiences for a lifetime." Fatalist answered. Pleaser gave an approving nod to Fatalist's explanation; he captured well what they had been through in such a short amount of time.

Compassion put her arm around Little Bin and said, "Well it is nice to meet you. My name is Compassion and this here is Little Bin. I guess you could say we adopted each other along the way too." Little Bin burst into the conversation.

"Yeah we got one of these invitations." He pulled from his pocket a very used and wrinkled envelope, with a red seal seen on the back.

"Oh I recognize the seal on the back. I have one of those too." Pleaser pulled out her envelope from her back pocket and waved it about so they could see.

"There is another who arrived just a little while ago but she went to investigate and see if there was an opening somewhere along this fortress. She will be back in a few minutes. Her name is Worker."

Pleaser and Fatalist looked at each other and smiled. "Did you say her name is Worker?" Little Bin shook his head yes.

"Fatalist did you hear that, Worker made it." Pleaser said.

"I am glad she did. It will be good to see her." Fatalist smiled and extended his hand to Compassion. "Hi my name is Fatalist, and my friend here is Pleaser."

Fatalist looked down at Little Bin and pulled out his envelope too. "Son, I have a red seal too." The red seal confirmed for each of them that the Pursuer of Souls invited them. Little Bin burst forth with a question for Fatalist. "So have you met Him yet?".

Fatalist and Pleaser looked at each other and started to smile. "Oh we definitely have."

"Me too!" Little Bin said proudly.

Pleaser started to share with her two new friends the amazing things that happened along the way. "This guy beside me," pointing at Fatalist. "was not always the friendly personality you see before you now. When we first met, he was one of the rudest men I had ever met."

"And she," Fatalist, with a cats meow smile responded, "She was the most spineless person I had ever met." Everyone burst out laughing.

"You know Pleaser was right about me though. The Pursuer of my Soul changed everything. Before I met Him, I sabotaged finding hope in anything. When a person doesn't have hope, they don't really live their life. They just kind of wait to die. That was who I was in the town of Self Absorption."

"Hey that is where we are from too!" Little Bin was excited to find their connection.

Fatalist kept sharing. For some reason, he felt free and open to share. "So many things went wrong early in my life. I became real angry and stayed angry. I actually vowed to keep everything that could cause me hurt away from me. I believed life meant misery and I made sure my belief came true every day."

Pleaser jumped in with a smile and winked to Little Bin. "And he made everyone else miserable too."

Little Bin smiled and then looked over at Fatalist to make sure he also thought it was funny. He was relieved to see him smiling and nodding in agreement.

A sober reality touched Little Bin's heart. He looked to the ground to try to gain control of his tears. He shared what was causing the sadness. "My mom and dad believe that misery thing too. When they believe it for themselves they can make it so for others around them too."

Strife grew impatient. "NO, NO, NO! Too much talk about the Pursuer of Souls and there is way too much friend-liness going on here. I want action, action, action!"

Strife cupped his hands and shouted down to Fatalist. "You owe it to the Pursuer to find a way in; Look what He has done for you. Go find a way or make your own way."

Fatalist felt this sudden burden to find a way to repay the Pursuer of his Soul back for all He had given to him.

He informed the others, "I am going to see if I can find a way to get inside. There has to be an opening somewhere."

He wandered around the glassy rock, and checked the seams where it met the rock ledge. After close examination, Heaven revealed to his heart, it was divinely sealed.

The ledges had a stone tablet type texture and except for the engraving scrolled across the top, there were no indentations of any kind, which made it impossible to scale.

Then something caught Fatalist eye. An ax leaned against the ledge.

Strife was delighted. "Oh good, you found the ax!" Strife prompted his new puppet with directions. "That's it, now pick it up and swing it."

Fatalist picked up the ax as if he had found the key inside Lake Still Water. On the handle there was an engraving. 'By might and power.' "Well this should do the trick."

He swung the ax back over his shoulder, and laid it against his back. He took a deep breath and then lifted it over his head bringing it downward with great force. Although it struck squarely, not one flake broke free.

Strife hovered above Fatalist in excitement and screamed down, "Harder, just hit it harder."

Fatalist thought, if he could just swing harder he could break open a passageway and bring hope to everyone. He pulled the ax back and swung again, and then again and then again. Each time there was not as much as a speck of rock that broke off.

Something over took him. He began swinging in a fury without thinking. The only thought that he held to was, "maybe the next stroke" and that led the way to his next swing. Time passed, sweat poured from Fatalist's beet red face. His muscles cramped, but he disconnected from all feelings. He continued to swing despite the obvious futility of his efforts.

Pleaser wondered about Fatalist' progress and noticed he had not gotten far at all. She felt a chill go down her back as she watched Fatalist.

She recognized the blank, empty look in his eyes and the robotic behavior repeating his swing, as if his brain was no longer engaged in the act.

He did not even notice she was right beside him when he threw the ax over his shoulder and swung with all his might. His red face had veins pulsating from the side of his head and neck. His shirt was sopping wet.

She knew this look well. Fatalist had the face of a Sweeper. Urgency fell upon her and she whispered a prayer, "Oh Pursuer help me to help Fatalist. Free him, from this madness!"

"Stop Fatalist, enough!" He didn't hear her and she knew he wouldn't. She had seen this too many times. She tugged on his arm and pulled him away. If she would not have ducked, the flurry of his swing would have hit her and probably killed her. He missed her neck by just inches.

The yank to his arm distracted him for a moment. He then noticed Pleaser and looked at her in complete shock. His heavy breathing continued to catch up to his stopping. "Oh Pleaser I almost hit you. I am so sorry. I didn't even know you were there. Are you okay? I am so sorry."

"I know Fatalist, I have been there." Pleaser spoke with a great sense of understanding and compassion. He nodded in his new understanding. All those years he sat behind his security desk mocking them.

Now in an instant, he realized he had become enslaved just as they did. He looked down at the new blisters on his hands and re-read the markings on the handle. "By power and might."

"Not by my power or by might." Fatalist handed the ax over to Pleaser, trusting her to know what to do with it, not trusting himself at this point.

"Yes Fatalist but by *His* Spirit." Pleaser was referring to the Pursuer of Souls. She took the ax from Fatalist and threw it down on the ground.

"Pleaser I am sorry, I never thought about what it must have been like for you as a Sweeper, until now. If you had not stopped me, I don't think I could have stopped on my own."

"Well I think the Pursuer put it on my heart to come over here because He knew I would understand. I prayed and asked Him to help you and He did."

She put her hand upon his sweaty shoulder and patted him. She then very inconspicuously wiped his sweat off her hand on the back of her pants. She didn't want to offend him but having his sweat on her arm and hands grossed her out.

"Let's go back to the others. We should talk about what to do next."

As they stepped out in front of the glassy rock, they saw Worker returning from her pilgrimage. She was still huffing, having jogged all the way back. "Hey, it is so good to see you guys."

She had so much to say, but first needed to put her hands on her knees to catch her breath. Then she continued, "I owe both of you a big apology. I was so prideful and stubborn and you need to know that I should have stayed with you and gone into the boat."

"It was horrible in that tunnel. I now know though that if I did not enter it, I would not have met the Pursuer of my Soul. He came into the darkness of the tunnel and saved me. If He hadn't, I would have died in there, lost and alone."

Fatalist stepped up and gave her a big hug. Worker was dumfounded by his greeting. This wasn't the same Fatalist she knew. She stepped back to look in his eyes, and she could see that his whole countenance had changed.

"What happened to you?" She asked in shock.

"Well I too met the Pursuer of my Soul. He shined the light of hope on me. Hope brings an entire new way to look at things. By the way, the boat wasn't the quick remedy to Lake Still Water either. It is as you said Worker, *all things happen for a reason and His plans are always for good.*"

Worker agreed. Pleaser came up and also gave her a big hug. "It is so good to see you. I am so glad you are okay. We were worried about you." Pleaser enjoyed not feeling responsible to keep the conversation going. She enjoyed the silence and smiled.

Worker returned to the present commenting, "So, if Fatalist is right, and all circumstances are allowed for a purpose, does anybody know what the purpose of this rock blocking the entrance is?"

Strife, hovering above the rock, started to get anxious.

"NO, NO, NO!" He screamed jumping up and down. "Don't accept this for what it is. Fight against it, conquer it, and get over it or around it. Strive, strive, strive!"

He had seen this too many times before. Whenever they started accepting things as they were, it led them to the entranceway every time. He must sabotage. He sent an urgent text message to headquarters, "I need reinforcements." Strife got an instant response. "A spy is coming."

Everyone Arrives, Plus One

Fatalist and Little Bin were exhausted from their physical efforts, so they sought the plushest looking plot of grass and laid down. They leaned back on their arms so they could stay in conversations.

Everyone else followed them for they were all at a loss of what to do. Sitting seemed as good an idea as any. As they sat, they each shared their stories. They talked about their lives in Self Absorption and all that had transpired these past two days.

They were so engrossed in conversation, they didn't notice two new people walk up until they were upon them. A young man carrying a little girl on his shoulders stood before them both with huge smiles. "Hello everyone." Companion (Guardian) greeted the sitting group.

In complete synchronicity everyone responded, "Hello!"

Companion's face gazed over in awe at the glassy barricade. He lowered himself down to allow his little passenger off. "Is this...?" As he hesitated, the group quickly confirmed.

"Yes this is the Lake Still Water entrance, right where this glassy rock stands."

"Oh my, look at the size of that thing." Companion started rolling his shoulders forward and backwards trying to loosen the tension from carrying Tuck for so long. Little Bin jumped to his feet excited to see someone his own age. "Hi my name is Little Bin; what is yours?"

"Hi my name is Tuck." Tuck waved sheepishly.

"Hey let me show you around this place." The two kids immediately set off to explore together.

Companion was pleased to see Tuck respond so spontaneously. She was free. Before, she would have clung to Companion's pant leg and refused to go without him.

It was on the road outside the Town That Never Forgets where he and Tuck reconnected. It was a sweet reunion and they both sat down and filled each other in on what happened.

Dreams was not brought up specifically, but both of them took responsibility for their wrong choices made that morning. Companion felt it was behind them now. It was something the Pursuer of Souls had worked in both of their hearts. The most important thing was that they found each other again.

Tuck told Companion everything; how she fell into the pit, saw her bitter face in the bucket's reflection and all about Mr. Chips. A new strength emanated from her now; and she was blooming in the open, no longer in hiding.

Companion could not explain how Tuck's transformation came so quickly; but then, he knew the answer. It was because of the same One who had transformed him.

It was interesting how they both found themselves in traps they could not escape, and then the Pursuer came and led them out from their captivity places.

It was so amazing. It was all so good. Companion wasn't going to try to understand it, for he knew he really couldn't. He just received it as a gift and that is exactly what it was, and he was grateful.

Suddenly from out of nowhere, a man was standing over Companion's folded legs.

"Hello, is this the Lake Still Water entrance?"

"Yes it is." replied Companion.

He looked around at the surprised group and said, "Popular place. How does one get inside to the lake?" The stranger asked.

"Well that sir is the question of the day. We don't know." Compassion responded.

"So what are you all lying around for? How come you are not trying to find a way in? How come you are so content about doing nothing instead of solving this dilemma?"

"We are waiting," explained Little Bin as he and Tuck ran back around the corner.

"Yes, we are waiting for the Pursuer of our Souls." Tuck added.

Then Little Bin further explained, "You see, since He invited us to come, He will make sure we get inside." The stranger seemed irritated.

Tuck inquired about his questioning look. "We all received an invitation. The Pursuer would not lead us this far to dump us now."

With that, the kids dashed off again to play.

"Well how can you be sure of that?" pressed the stranger to the group.

Worker responded to that question. "We each have met Him on our journey here and have experienced how caring and wise He is. Nothing is impossible for Him."

The stranger challenged Worker with a question. "Well if that is the case, why doesn't He move this rock? What kind of person invites people to leave their lives and all that is familiar to come to a dead end?"

Though his question may have made logical sense, it revealed that this stranger had not yet met the Pursuer of Souls personally. They met Him and trusted Him because they knew His heart. What this man was inferring was that the Pursuer of Souls had abandoned them.

Compassion spoke to his accusing question. "Though this situation might appear like we have been abandoned, we are not. We are simply waiting for Him to reveal to us the way in."

As Compassion spoke up, she assured herself that the Pursuer of Souls would not forsake nor abandon them. She became grateful for this man's opposition. He helped strengthen her faith. She knew they needed to wait upon Him and He would reveal the way in.

Fatalist added, "I have come to understand sir that it isn't just about the destination but the journey."

Meanwhile, Little Bin and Tuck were running around like airplanes doing fly-by's back and forth between each other. Little Bin remembered he had not formally introduced Dreams. He stopped abruptly. "Oh, there is someone I want you to meet."

He took off his backpack and opened it up. He lifted up Dreams, excited to introduce him to his new friend.

"I rescued him from a stream by water skiing on the back of two fish."

Tuck looked up and couldn't believe her eyes. She started to well up with tears, but Little Bin did not understand why she was getting so upset.

"Dreams, is that you?" Tuck ran up to her stuffed friend and drew him into a big hug, all while Little Bin still held him.

"How did you know his name was Dreams? Do you guys know each other?" Little Bin realized they had history together.

Tuck did not hear Little Bin. Her mind was racing with all the things she wanted to say. "Dreams, I am so sorry we couldn't find you. Where did you go? We looked for you everywhere. I got so mad at Guardian, oh, by the way, his name is Companion now. We separated, because of that but the Pursuer brought us back together again. Oh I thought I had lost you forever."

She gave him another big squeeze and this time Little Bin let go so Dreams could remain in her embrace.

Little Bin started to feel like he was intruding and began to back up. Then it dawned on Tuck what Little Bin had said. "You saved him! Oh Little Bin, thank you so much. Next to Companion, Dreams is my best friend."

Tuck ran up to Little Bin and gave him a big hug and a kiss on the cheek. His face felt flush. He never had been kissed by a girl before. It wasn't as gross as he imagined. Not knowing what to say, Little Bin changed the subject. "We should get back with the others."

He led the way back hoping his bright red-kissed cheeks would fade before anyone noticed. The stranger was still talking to their friends. He and Tuck slowed down their racing and walked calmly up to the sitting group.

There was something serious going on. Everyone had straight faces and some even wore frowns. The kids re-entered the circle quietly, returning to the one they felt safest with, Tuck next to Companion, and Little Bin sat Indian style next to Compassion.

Compassion had a strange feeling about this new person. She decided to inquire about his invitation to see if he was brought here for the same reason.

"So sir, did you receive one of these?" Compassion pulled out her envelope holding her invitation. Everyone else pulled out their letters too, and all their red seals were clearly seen. The man, seeing all of them clutching a paper, nodded his head yes. "Let's see, I have that paper somewhere here."

Little Bin immediately became suspicious of him. This guy reminded him of the wolf that chased them along the way. Little Bin got up and walked around the outside of the group circle and came up behind the man, all the while keeping his hands in his pockets to look inconspicuous.

When he was behind him, he took his right hand, lifted up the backside of his coat to check to see if he had a tail. There was no tail, but he still didn't trust him. He pointed at him suspiciously and said, "Hey we didn't see your invitation Mister. Let's see it."

This mystery man started to fumble around, touching the outside of all his pockets yet not really searching. "I think I might have lost it on the way here. Oh no, here it is." The man pulled from his shirt pocket a crumpled, old, dirty piece of paper. He threw his arm up in the air like everyone else, with barely any part of the paper was showing. There was no red seal seen on the exposed part of the paper. He quickly tucked it back into his back pocket tapping it a few times, as if requesting it stay hidden.

Little Bin was even more suspicious now and he walked back around to Compassion and whispered in her ear that this stranger reminded him of the wolf.

Just then, Tuck showed Dreams to Companion, as she couldn't keep her good news inside one second longer. Companion's eyes got really big and he looked over at Tuck and then back to Dreams.

"Wow, Dreams it is you! I can't believe you are okay. Tuck how did you find him?"

"I didn't find him, Little Bin did. He saved his life. He saved him from drowning in the stream and he did it by water skiing on the back of two fish." Tuck was very excited about the way in which Little Bin rescued her friend. She had never heard of anything like it before.

"Did he now." Companion smiled amused, winked at Little Bin as if he agreed to play along with the story.

Little Bin became angry with the wink. He had been around adults and their winks all his life and they really made him mad. "I really did. I know it sounds crazy, but it really happened." Little Bin was frustrated because he knew Companion wasn't taking him seriously.

Then the stranger butted in to rub salt into the wound, and welcomed the distraction with the investigation focused on Little Bin. "Oh sure kid; people ski on the backs of fish everyday," he said sarcastically.

"Really it is true" Little Bin urged.

"Whatever you say, kid." He looked at the group and then pointed to his own head making the circular motion with his hands; indicating he was crazy. Little Bin searched the faces in the circle for support.

"Oh come on now," the stranger continued to mock. "Are you really going to believe this kid water skied on fish?"

Fatalist spoke up. "Why don't you leave this boy alone. Let him have his story."

Little Bin got real mad now. He didn't need adults thinking he was cute; he needed to be believed. He had enough of this back in Self Absorption. It really happened and he knew the truth.

As he stood up to defend himself, he purposely directed his defense to those in the circle, ignoring the man who was stirring up all the conflict.

"Don't you guys get it?" Little Bin spoke with strength. "This isn't about me being a cute little kid, this is about how great the Pursuer of our Souls is. Anything is possible when He gets involved.

I saw Dreams laying there in the stream and I couldn't rescue him on my own, so I prayed and asked for His help, and He sent the two fish with strings in their mouth to help me. One fish was named Childlike and the other was named Faith."

Fatalist felt convicted as he listened to the boy's testimony. He too had experienced an impossible situation, outside his own rational reason, yet he also knew it was real.

Every one in the circle affirmed with their heads that they knew Little Bin was speaking the truth. Fatalist got up from the ground, walked over to Little Bin and extended his hand.

"I owe you an apology son. You are right; this whole trip has not been about us, but about us learning who the Pursuer of our Souls is. He changed my life in a moment and just as you shared, He showed me in a miraculous way. I believe you Little Bin."

Little Bin broke into a big smile and enthusiastically shook Fatalist's hand. The validated boy spoke up, "So I think we should ask the Pursuer of our Souls to help us now to find the way inside."

Compassion took a count of hands and it was unanimous, minus one, as the stranger opposed. The stranger gave his input.

"I think we should split up and investigate the area to look for entrance possibilities. Doing something is always more productive than waiting around and doing nothing," explained the stranger.

"I already walked for miles around and there is no other way in." Worker explained with frustration.

"Well you are just one person, you might have missed something." The stranger retorted.

Compassion confronted the man. "Splitting up is not the answer. We have all been brought here together and besides praying is doing something very important. We are asking help from the One who is able to give it."

"You mean you are going to ask help from someone who sent you to a place where there is no entrance? What kind of good person leads you to a dead end? He is probably hiding around here somewhere watching and getting a good laugh."

Pleaser had enough. "You know, I met a cat on my travels who sounded a lot like you. He worked for the enemy of the Pursuer of our Souls and I think you do to."

"Well where would you get an idea like that? Look, why attack me? I am just offering reasonable options to help. You guys lack tolerance. You are so judgmental."

"Options!" This word triggered Worker. "Look here buddy boy, I learned a lot about options on my journey. Options are WAY overrated. They can be a greater curse than a blessing. Options bring confusion, where a person can drown in choices. Come to think of it, you remind me a lot of the man who offered me those options in that tunnel of darkness."

"Well aren't you the dramatic one. Look, I am just trying to help. I am one of you guys, remember? I have that paper too."

Compassion had learned to trust the discernment of Little Bin. She started to think more of his suspicions and decided to confront this avoidant stranger. "Actually, I would like to see your invitation more closely. I would like to see the seal."

"The seal?" The man knew he had no seal. Feeling cornered, he lifted up his hands and called 'No foul.'

Meanwhile, Little Bin snuck behind him and in all the distraction, he quickly pulled from the stranger's back pocket the grimy piece of paper.

"Hey you can't do that! That is private property."

Little Bin unraveled the paper and handed it to Compassion to read. Compassion read it aloud to the group. "Call into question the Pursuer's motives and try to divide them up."

"Uh-ha Mister, your motives are exposed." Little Bin pointed at him and jumped up and down.

The stranger backed up, making distance from the gathering mob. His fear was not involving so much them, but knowing he had to go back and report that his mission failed. In an instant, he disappeared into thin air.

"Did you see that? That guy just disappeared," said Fatalist pointing to where he last stood.

"Oh that is creepy." Pleaser leaned in a bit toward Fatalist.

Fatalist realized there was a lesson here. "Creepy yes, but important for us to learn. There is an unseen battle that is real and powerful. There is an enemy who seeks to destroy what the Pursuer desires."

They Come Together and Pray

"Hey let's come together and pray. If this stranger was trying to prevent us from asking, that is exactly what we need to do. Gather 'round everybody." Compassion waved everyone over and they stood in a circle, they held each other's hands and bowed their heads.

Companion remembered the instructions the Pursuer gave him in the jail cell. 'Use this book to help others along their way.'

Guardian opened his new book. It opened up to Psalm 27. He read it aloud. *"I would have lost heart, unless I had believed that I would see the goodness of the LORD in the land of the living. Wait on the LORD; Be of good courage, And He shall strengthen your heart; Wait, I say, on the LORD!"*

Fatalist spoke directing the words to the Pursuer of Souls. "Oh faithful Pursuer, thank you for inviting us here. We thank you for the lessons that You have taught us and for giving each of us hope. Thank you for teaching us it is not by strength or by might, but by You."

Worker picked it up from there. "When we rely on ourselves, we end up lost in darkness."

Pleaser added, "When we try to manage things on our own, we end up caught."

"Pursuer, You are faithful to us when no one else is." Little Bin prayed with a big smile.

"You are the One who opens prison doors and sets us free." Companion prayed.

"You lead us out of the pits we fall in and teach us how to stay out of them." Tuck prayed.

Fatalist continued. "We are here together because You invited us. We are faced with this obstacle and we don't know what to do, but we ask You to show us."

An idea came to Tuck's mind but she felt too insecure to say it out loud. The idea, however, kept getting louder and she couldn't shake it. She didn't feel qualified to share.

From the top of the ledge, Strife stood flinging arrows at Tuck. It was his last ditch effort. He hoped by silencing her, he could detain them from finding the entrance.

Tuck looked up to the sky and asked the Pursuer silently in her heart to give her the courage to share. Strife screamed in complete frustration, he fell off the ledge and landed on the glass rock. As soon as his body touched the rock, in judgment, he vaporized and was no more.

Right then Tuck's doubt lifted. Boldness rose within her and she spoke what was on her heart. "Um I may have an idea that can help." Tuck started out tentative, but in obedience, continued. "When I was trapped inside the pit, there was a door that I could not see until I was flat on the ground."

Just then, Little Bin burst out with words placed on his heart. "Humble yourself in the sight of the Lord and He will lift you up."

Everyone responded by moving from their knees, to lying prone with their faces in the dirt.

Compassion cried out in prayer first. "Pursuer please forgive us for seeking shortcuts to manage on our own. We are flat before You, recognizing that apart from You we can do nothing.

Fatalist praised Him. "Thank you filling me with hope."

Pleaser chimed in. "Thank you for Your faithful provision for all we need."

The more the group praised Him, the more His love poured into their hearts.

They Enter In

Suddenly Companion was aware of a slight opening at the base of the rock near the ground as he laid there praying. He went over to it in order to confirm that image in his mind was actually there. "Hey look, there is something engraved on the rock right above the ground." There inside of a small cross were the words;

> *"You are justified freely by His grace through the*
> *redemption that came by Christ Jesus,*
> Love, the Pursuer of your Soul."

In response to what he read, Companion reached for it, receiving this as true. As his hand touched the cross, a nail pierced Hand reached out and touched his. Though initially startled, Companion felt no fear. The rock itself opened up to him, allowing him to fit through and the Hand holding his, escorted him inside.

Without hesitating, he entered, disappearing before all those watching. The rock closed behind him. Tuck became scared. Her best friend was swallowed by a rock. She rushed over to see if she could rescue him but Companion disappeared.

As she searched about the rock, she found the words. "Y*ou are justified freely by His grace through the redemption that came by Christ Jesus,*" love the Pursuer of your Souls." They soothed her heart.

At the ordained time, Tuck reached out to touch the cross and just like Companion, the rock opened up and a nail pierced Hand took hold of hers, and escorted her inside. As she entered in the opening closed up behind her.

One after another, the remaining five travelers went to investigate where their team members had disappeared. They each read the inscription on the inside of the cross, and reached out in response to touch it. A nail pierced Hand escorted each of them, one at a time.

The Pursuer of Souls Greets Them

When Companion entered, he stood before a Man wearing a most gentle and loving smile on His face. His face was filled with a tenderness, and Companion could sense that His eyes saw everything down to his soul. The Man's voice was strong and yet gentle as He spoke.

> *"Hello my son, I am the Pursuer of your Soul. I am so pleased to see you here as I have prepared for this moment before the foundations of the earth were laid. Rest now in My strength and protection for I laid My life down for you."*

The Pursuer showed Him the scars on His hands and feet. "My love is sure. It is everlasting. When I hung on the cross, I defeated any other power who could threaten to take that away. I know you have traveled a long time trying to show only your strengths while covering up your weakness, but know this now my child, in your weakness, you will find My perfect strength.

I am so glad you are here with Me. We will walk together as companions from now on. I will lead you and you will learn to follow Me. Come, let me wash you clean and new."

The Pursuer took hold of Companion's hand and escorted him over to a rushing waterfall inside their rock. Companion took in the breathtaking view of the crystal clear water, as it poured from the top of a crimson red rock ledge which was a basin to hold the water before it fell.

A pool of purified water gathered below, welcoming all its contributions. When Companion stood underneath the water's flow, the Pursuer gave him a sign to stay. A smile took over Companion's face as the water poured.

The water felt so refreshing. There seemed to be a cleansing going on the inside as well as outside, though he could not explain why. He could not explain so many of the things that occurred on this trip.

He no longer heeded to the expectation that he needed to explain things. This trip had taught him to receive things in faith and he was going to do just that. He closed his eyes and soaked in the cleansing that he was receiving, from the outside in. He couldn't remember a time he felt so peaceful.

The Pursuer walked up to the crimson rock above him and touched it with His wrist and a red substance began to fall from the rock. The blood red liquid landed upon Companion's head.

The Pursuer took Companion, leaned him back into his arms and gently lowered him into the pool just enough to be under the waters surface then lifted him out from the water. As the Pursuer lifted him up, he said, *"In the Name of the Father, Son and Holy Spirit."*

Companion kept his eyes glued to the Pursuer, not sure of what to do next. He followed Him through the waterfall into a brightly lit room, which was still part of the glassy rock. A sign hung down from the ceiling of the room that said; "Welcome to the Age to Come."

The Pursuer escorted Tuck inside and she recognized right away the Hand holding hers, was the Pursuer of her soul. Calm engulfed her from head to toe.

He smiled a big smile, and enfolded His height over her and embraced her with His arms. She felt so safe inside His arms. Fellowship was the core of He and His Father's heart. He too enjoyed the moment.

"Welcome little one. It has been a long road for you I know, but you are here now and I am so delighted we can fellowship together unencumbered for eternity. As the dragons came out in your dreams, I drew your heart to seek Me not the false imitations Self Absorption offered.

You will be a mighty warrior in the battle of darkness and light, because you know intimately the schemes and ways the enemy of heaven terrorizes and lies.

I will teach you and you learn of My words of truth, you will be able to reach out to other children who are in the battles with the forces of darkness. You can tell them of the Good News of the Pursuer of their Souls."

Tuck stayed inside His embrace the whole time He spoke. She maneuvered her head to tilt to watch Him. What spoke to her heart the clearest though was His arms wrapped around her. She felt protected and safe. He too, kept Himself bent over in the embrace as He spoke.

He knew she was receiving His love through His touch as well. When He had finished welcoming her, He stood up, squeezed her hand twice, and led her to the waterfall. He directed her to stand under the falls.

He touched the crimson rock ledge with His wrist. Out from the ledge the crimson blood of the Lamb poured upon her.

The sludge from the evil one's handprints upon this child, fell from her heart into the pure water stream and was swept away. She had been washed from the bitterness in her heart. This cleansing was deeper than words could go. Though she couldn't see it with her eyes, she understood it anyway; it was by faith she had this understanding. She felt clean and new.

The Pursuer stepped into the water and took hold of Tuck and He very gently lowered her into the pool of pure water just enough to submerge her face and body and then lifted her out and stood her up. *"Welcome my child, welcome."*

Tuck smiled widely and the Pursuer's smile grew in response to seeing hers. She knew for sure that the Pursuer of her Soul would never leave her nor forsake her. She felt content.

Fatalist approached the rock with hope. Kneeling down, he reached up to touch the cross when the Pursuer reached through and drew him into His Presence.

Fatalist turned to behold the eyes of the One who was looking right into him. He felt exposed and yet safe from judgment. The Holy One smiled. His comforting voice spoke softly but clear. Fatalist listened to every syllable.

"Hello My son, I AM so glad you have arrived. Your journey to Lake Still Water did not just begin a few days back like you think. I have been preparing you for this moment. I know it included a lifetime filled with loneliness and disillusionment. I bring to you good news today and the real purpose for your life.

"I fashioned your days and sent you out to be an alien in this land. You need to know that you have a real home, a place set aside just for you. Your home is with Me in heaven.

"While you are here in this life, I have a purpose and a calling for you. I will send you to those who have no hope so you can share with them the hope that is found in Me. Share with those you meet how the Pursuer of your Souls paved the way for you to gain access to a Heavenly home. Sin kept you out.

Sin is what separates men from Me and sin is what separates men one from one another. It is what murdered your father so long ago. Sin was reconciled on the cross when I came and died for you. There had to be a perfect sacrifice for sin, and I was My Father's perfect sacrifice.

I came into this world and lived as a man perfectly. I paid for sin's debt. By this sacrifice, I have provided you a return trip home – to be with Me and My Father for eternity."

Fatalist could not contain himself any longer. He fell against the Pursuer and wept. He clung to His garment and sobbed loudly and unrestrained. The tears over sin and loss overtook him and he grieved for it all, everything that had been wrong in this world. Fatalist had carried this for so long.

As the Pursuer reached out for Pleaser and drew her inside, she took hold of His hand and stood up. The amount of light inside amazed her. Light emanated from the Pursuer of her Soul and branched outward, lighting up everything inside.

Neither the best camera nor the most talented photographer could capture the brilliance of what she was seeing. The Pursuer whispered to her heart, *"No eye has seen, no ear has heard, no mind has conceived what God has prepared for those who love Him"*

As her eyes met her Pursuer's face, they couldn't leave. His features weren't remarkable of themselves, but it was more about His essence. Purity and holiness emanated from Him within; to behold Him. He was engrossing.

As His eyes met hers, His ability to see to her core made her feel known. Yes, known and yet still loved. She did not experience any disdain or regret with what He knew. She was not disappointing to Him, and this felt so safe. In the past, whenever someone looked into her eyes, she felt anxious.

The Pursuer spoke to her heart. *"My beloved daughter, I am so pleased that this is the day I get to give you the fullness of My love. I AM the One you can place your needs. My care for you is complete and I will not disappoint. I AM your fountain that never runs dry.*

I know how thirsty you have been for love. Your search is what I stirred up in your heart. I have been drawing you to Me every step of your way."

Then the Pursuer tenderly took hold of her shoulders to steer her to look deeply into His eyes. *"And precious child,"* He paused so she would focus on Him. *"I will never leave you nor forsake you."* He drew her into an embrace. He held her there. Pleaser felt herself melt into His love. All the days of searching had ended; she found her home inside His arms.

The Pursuer led her over to the waterfall and assisted her to stand underneath its pour. The rushing water poured upon her head, refreshing her physically and soothing her soul. She watched Him as He reached up and placed His wrist upon the scarlet red stone above.

The blood stained water fell upon her head and body. It seemed to gather to itself her life's dirt and grime. This caused the spray to thicken in substance. Pleaser stood in disbelief, as she watched the red clumpy liquid land in the pool of water below her feet.

It submerged quickly to the bottom of the pond and was absorbed into the bowels of the earth, leaving only the crystal-clear water. There was no sign of the grime, nor the blood. All things were washed anew.

Outside, Worker rushed over to where the others had entered the Rock. She tried to push against it, thinking there was some stress point that would open a secret compartment.

In her haste to follow her friends inside, she began trying everything and she became a flurry of activity. She knocked on it to listen for a hollow sound. She tugged on a large stone protruding from the ground right near the glassy rock, thinking it would open a passageway.

Then, she heard two words speak to her heart. *"Trust Me."* These words stilled her from movement.

She sat down and became still. She lifted her head to the sky and began to pray. She only got one word out, "help" before she noticed out of the corner of her eye, a small cross.

She reached up to touch it and out from the crevice just below it came a nail pierced hand, which took hold of her. As the rock opened up, she too was escorted inside.

Worker was still tired from all the energy she had expelled but was calmed to an instant peace when she looked up to find a warm and smiling face greeting her. The face glowed, as if light resided inside Him. His skin could not contain the light He held. His eyes were so penetrating they pierced through every hiding place she knew inside. He could see her from every place.

Warmth overtook her. As He began to speak, His voice calmed her and touched the depth of her heart. She recognized it. She had heard the same voice before in the tunnel; it belonged to the Pursuer of her Soul.

The Pursuer said, *"My precious daughter, energy you have. I delight in your passion to get things done. I will accompany you from this day forth, which will ensure you will bear rich fruit. As you learned in the Tunnel of Your Own Understanding, you do not hold the resources for light and freedom. This only comes from Me.*

In this truth, I give you a new name, Grace. Your name and life will reflect My works. In My perfect work, you will learn to completely trust.

"Hand to me the details of your day and allow Me to guide you, one step at a time. I will not paint for you a road you can see for a long stretch, or you would be tempted to travel it without Me. I love you, my daughter, and I will be with you every step of the way."

As the Pursuer finished speaking, He gathered her to His heart, hugging her from His inside to her outside. She leaned upon His shoulder and allowed Him to bear her weight. Someone was going to carry her burdens now and she felt weightless; she felt relief.

But a fear suddenly seized her, "Don't trust this," she heard. She pulled back from Him and in the same moment, He firmed His grip upon her and led her eyes to His.

"I AM not going to be disappointed in you. Remember it is not your works, but Mine. All you need will be supplied by Me. I give you all I have not because you earned it, but because I love you. You are My child. It is not because of your works, your intellect, or your great courage, it is because I have chosen you, adopted you, and sealed you in Me."

His love for her brought rest to her soul. She wept from relief. She could stop pretending now. She didn't need to control plans anymore. Her Pursuer was in charge.
He lingered awhile in the embrace and then escorted her over to the waterfall and had her stand underneath its pour.

As the blood stained water fell from the scarlet rock above her, she watched the grime and the muck wash from her being. As it landed into the pool, it's weight caused it to sink where it was and was instantly soaked into the earth, leaving the pool of water pristine and pure.

Little Bin couldn't contain himself any longer. Normally he would have run full speed over to the rock and slid as if trying to get a double in baseball, but he was about to meet His Pursuer, so he walked to it with reverence and bowed.

From inside, the Pursuer's hands reached out and took hold of his hand. Little Bin greeted Him with great exuberance. "Hi my 'Suer of Soul." Little Bin's smile met the Pursuer's smile as He was received inside. Little Bin responded to His greeting with giant bear hug. He squeezed real hard because he knew the harder you squeezed someone, the more you were expressing how much you liked them. Little Bin loved the Pursuer a whole lot.

"I love you too my boy, I love you too." He could hear the laughter and joy bubbling out from the boy. Children's joy delighted the Pursuer's heart deeply.

The Pursuer, keeping Little Bin close, but wanting to make eye contact with him, pulled him back just far enough that they could see each other. The Pursuer said to him, *"My adventuresome friend, it is so good that you are here. I look forward to the great adventures in faith that we will pursue together. Your faith is strong because you desire truth above all things. Do not lose this passion. Do not compromise in your quest for truth. One compromise leads to another.*

When truth is watered down, it is no longer truth. You are to be salt and light in this world. I will give you direction and all the tools you need. Every adventure requires faith, not what you can see. Lean not on your own understanding.

I AM giving you a new name my son. You are Fisher of men. I love you. I delight in your energy. It brings me great pleasure. Now let Me cover you for the remission of your sins."

The Pursuer walked him over to the waterfall, where he had him stand underneath the flow of the water. Fisher of men (Little Bin) put his hands up, lifted his face toward the falling water, and started to giggle.

The Pursuer lifted His wrist to the crimson red rock and the blood soaked water fell down upon the young boy. The blood of the Lamb washed over him. Fisher of men smiled as his joy radiated from inside the waters cleansing pour.

The last one to enter inside the rock was Compassion. She, being older and more reserved, moved slowly but in a faith. She knew her time had come.

The Pursuer's nail pierced hand reached out and escorted her inside. When she entered, she looked up and was greeted by the most loving and brilliantly lit eyes she could have ever imagined. His glance was as brilliant as starlight against a night sky, yet those eyes soothed any anxiety she felt prior to entering. In His watchful care, she felt safe.

A loving face, framed with a gentle kindness, hosted these welcoming eyes. She was enamored with the sight of her Pursuer. She knew it was Him and He was holding her hand. She secretly prayed that He would never let her go. When He spoke, she recognized His voice, and now she was meeting Him face-to-face.

He spoke to her. *"Hello My compassionate one. I AM the Truth you have been looking for. I AM light for the darkness, for you and for those you know who are lost and wandering. I AM hope for the defeated and battered. You sought truth with all your heart because I stirred that desire within you. Fear and pain locked away your desires. I brought them forward in My perfect time.*

> *"I have known you and I fashioned you with My own hands. You see My child, truth and love are not a place, but a person – I AM Love, and I have called you to Myself, so that we may fellowship for eternity. I will never let you go."*

In hearing these words, she began to sob in relief. It was her greatest desire. She felt herself collapse in His love, a love she could trust, a love that would not disappoint. He let her fall against Him. He lifted her up and leaned her upon His shoulder.

He held her firmly and gently as He continued to share His heart. *"I am so glad you are here with Me and I delight in knowing all of what we will share. Come let Me wash you clean."*

Compassion kept her eyes upon her Pursuer the whole time. He escorted her to the place where the water fell and then just as before, reached up and touched His wrist to the crimson red ledge.

His blood fell from the top of the falls with great grace and over her. She felt the water touch stream down her sides, and it carried with it all the black sludge from her body and soul.

Even as the grimy substance washed from her body, the pool at her feet remained crystal clear. The grime absorbed into the earth.

Though Compassion did not know why, emotions got the best of her and she began to sob. It was grief turned to joy. There had been so much pain carried for so long, and yet now she was washed clean and new. Burdens lifted and she felt white as snow.

Compassion stepped through the back of the waterfall, when a voice summoned her to enter. There she found her other companions looking about in awe. At the entrance, a cross-shaped sign hung from a pole planted in the ground, which read; *"Welcome to the Age to Come."*

"Welcome to the Age to Come."

The sun pierced into the glass rock. The colors reflected out from the sun's rays lit up the inside like stained glass. Though things were not see-through from the outside, from the inside, it was like looking out a window. They could see out to Lake Still Water, and the people along its shore. These people had also met the Pursuer of their Souls face to face. Now He lived inside them all. They too were washed by cleansing flow from the blood of the Holy One, each at their appointed time.

The sun light pierced through highlighting vibrant colors at various places across the glassy wall. Compassion's eyes followed one particular stream of light to a corner where Tuck stood. *"I will lie down and sleep in peace, for you alone, O LORD, make me dwell in safety."*

"Look," said Fatalist, pointing to another place.

"They are Words of light."

The others noticed that the Words illuminated in light kept changing. Light drew each one's eyes to what their heart needed to read. Fatalist read aloud what the light illuminated to him. *"I AM the Rock of Ages cleft for you. I AM your rock, your fortress and your deliverer; I AM your God, I AM your Rock, in whom you take refuge. I AM your shield and the horn of your salvation, your stronghold."*

Pleaser read aloud what the light brought to her heart. *"And the peace of God, which transcends all understanding, will guard your hearts and your minds in Christ Jesus."*

Tools to Live By

"Come and follow Me." Recognizing the Voice each one turned to respond to their Shepherd. It came from a back room. As they entered, they saw a stone table, which held white robes and a Book on top of each garment. The room felt like a sanctuary, a holy place.

Fisher of men and Tuck walked up to the table and touched everything they could see, announcing to the group each discovery.

"There are Books on top of robes and the Books have names written on them." Tuck grabbed hold of one of the black Books. "Look," she said with great excitement. "It has my name on it."

Tuck read the gold lettering on the bottom right cover. The words said, 'Tucked inside My love.' She smiled.

She loved that her old name now had a new meaning. It was no longer about fear but love. The small still voice of her Pursuer whispered to her heart, *"My perfect love casts out fear."* Because of her Pursuer, she felt safe and loved.

"This must be yours too 'cuz it was underneath." Fisher of men handed Tuck a white robe. She put it on and found it was a perfect fit.

The kids handed out the Books to each person as well as the accompanying robe. Each was delighted to find their name inscribed. Compassion and Companion, whose names changed, along their journey found their new names written on it. They felt expected and known.

Each robe fit perfectly. A joy filled the room, joy, which accompanies receiving the Pursuer's gifts of love.

Fisher of men handed Fatalist a Book, "I think this is for you." Fatalist looked and found 'Hope' inscribed on its cover. He was touched that his Pursuer gave him the new name, Hope. It had been something he had feared for so long.

Compassion saw Fisher of men in his robe and became overwhelmed with her fondness toward the boy. She walked up and enveloped him in the same huge bear hug that he loved to give. There were no words, they did not need any; the embrace said everything.

The Pursuer's love spoke louder than words too. His nail pierced hands were the evidence that His Words were true. His love poured without restraint into the empty cavern of their hearts.

Compassion drew Fisher of men close. Her heart had been locked away for so long, but no longer. Love had set her free. He looked up at her proudly and shared with her the good news about his new name.

"Guess what my new name is Compassion?" "Oh do tell me my friend," Compassion insisted.

"Fisher of men, isn't that cool? Now I will always remember how I rode on the back of the fishes to help save Dreams."

"What a wonderful name for you my friend, fisher of men. I bet the Pursuer of our Soul has great plans for you to be apart of His rescuing others who get stranded too."

Compassion leaned forward to get his eye contact. "One day I pray you will know what a special place you have in my heart."

He looked up and smiled. "You too, Compassion, I have never trusted an adult before." She smiled back.

Hearts now holding Truth and hope lit up each one's face. Joy glowed from every heart.

Grace said, "Well Tuck, I think grace is the key to my heart now, not works. And by the way, it is also my new name." She smiled proudly. Her new name represented the love that removed the fear of never feeling loved. This had stalked her, her entire life.

Grace continued, "I threw myself into work but I had no passion about anything. The Pursuer has shown me that it is by His grace we walk. In His grace, we can walk through anything. My new name will be a constant reminder of that lesson."

Fisher of men ran up to her with a very excited look on his face, and handed her the robe and Book. "Look here." He said.

She looked down at the bottom corner of the Book where Fisher of men's finger was resting. 'Grace' was inscribed into the leather. She couldn't believe it. It was only moments ago she had been give this name and yet the Pursuer had already written it on her Book.

Fisher of men smiled back at her, "He is organized, huh?" She took her new Book, drew it close to her heart and then curtsied to Fisher of men with a smiling thank you.

Pleaser put on her robe. She picked up her Book and noticed the words 'Pleaser of God' inscribed. She was relieved there was only one heart she needed to please now; and there was no one she wanted to please more.

The Step of Faith

Fisher of men noticed one of those familiar looking signs hanging from the back wall. It read; *"This is the way; walk in it."*

There was no visible indication of a door, but Fisher of men knew what the sign meant, it meant walk through it. He learned about faith when he stepped onto the backs of the fish at the stream. "Just because you don't understand it, doesn't mean you don't follow the directions."

"Hey look at the sign." Fisher of men pointed the sign out to his new family.

"Where's the door?" Hope asked.

Fisher of men took a step in faith. In dramatic flair, he took a big breath, closed his eyes and took one giant step forward, just like when they first walked on the moon.

His eyes were still closed when he took another, and then a third and fourth. When he opened them, he was outside the Rock where Lake Still Water was.

Fisher of men looked back with great surprise. He could no longer see his friends inside. He only saw the glassy rock. Hoping they could hear him, he called to them, "Come on everyone, it is okay."

From inside they heard a voice say,

"And a child shall lead them."

Hope looked back at everyone to confirm what they saw. "Did you see that? He went right through."

Compassion stepped up and followed her young friend's example. She just stepped forth in faith and found herself at Lake Still Water Park. Fisher of men greeted her with a huge holler and a hug. "I knew you would be the first to follow."

One by one, they followed the leading of the child, and took their own personal step of faith.

Upon entering, they took in breathtaking scene. The lake hosted the purest blue reflection from its surface they had ever seen. No paint could have captured the richness of the blue.

Fisher of men announced to interested ears, and non-interested ears alike, "Lake Still Water, we have officially arrived!" The rest of the group applauded and laughed at the triumphant announcement.

Lake Still Water

They had arrived. Now what? There was no longer a pressing sense from anyone as to what they needed do. They knelt down to drink of the water from the lake. Cold and fresh, it tasted pure.

Fisher of men wanted more, so he leaned over while still on his knees and stuck his whole head in. Then he sprayed the group as he flipped back his hair. They all screeched for it was cold. Tuck giggled.

She loved Fisher of men's adventurous spirit. She tried to do the same, but when she flipped her hair back, the water flung in the wrong direction. So she filled her cupped hands full and then slung water at the unsuspecting victims behind her.

There was another screech that followed and then some more great laughter. Everyone ran into the lake at this point, surrendering to the idea that since they were half-wet anyway, they might as well just go all the way. A giant splash fight took place.

Hope had the biggest smile of the bunch. How long it had been since he was impulsive like a child. It felt good. It caused him to yearn for his childhood home again.

They laughed and played to the point of exhaustion. When they came out of the lake, they sprawled out onto the soft green grass to let the warm sun soak in and remove the chill.

His Voice Calls Them

It was then the Pursuer whispered to each heart with His small still voice, *"My Word is a lamp unto your feet."* They heard His voice and responded. They understood He was calling them to spend time in the Book He gave them.

When Pleaser of God opened her Book, a growing desire to help others in bondage find the Pursuer of their Souls started to stir within her. She came upon this verse, which brought clarity to the problem of pleasing others. *"Fear of man will prove to be a snare, but whoever trusts in the LORD is kept safe."*

Her heart became heavy as she thought about all the people she personally knew who were trapped in the emptiness of sweeping, and trying to find contentment with the outside things.

As Grace, (Worker) read in her Book, she found a strengthening of faith girding within. She wasn't sure where it came from, but it brought to her a courage and a peace. This faith was not compelling her to a dramatic action, but instead compelled her to pray.

People began to come to her mind. She realized they too were just like she was and lived their life believing they were in charge. They too considered themselves the source of every need, and they were miserable like she used to be.

She knew the darkness surrounding that belief system. She lifted them each up by name to the Pursuer of her Soul, asking Him to bring light to them in the tunnel of their own understanding. "Oh Pursuer, lead my friend, Self Sufficient, to Your grace. Bring her to the end of her own strength and will, as You did with me."

Tuck, laying on her stomach, kicked the sides of her feet together as she read. With every page she turned, compassion grew within her.

Her heart ached for other kids who always felt unsafe. Kids who were left to face their dragons alone. She wanted them to know about the Pursuer of Souls too; they needed to know there really was a Rock of safety.

As Compassion read her Book, her heart no longer carried the burdens of others because she had given them over to the Pursuer of her Soul to carry. She was excited about returning to her clients because she now had the truth and hope to give them.

She prayed for each one of them by name, asking her Pursuer to draw them to Himself. She asked if He would allow her to be His ambassador, to deliver truth about His love to all those searching in Self Absorption.

As Hope (Fatalist) opened his Book, spiritual water poured forth from the Book bringing refreshment to his heart as he read. The water was filled with a burden to teach. The small still voice spoke to his heart. *"Start with your home. Go tell them."*

Hope wept, but his tears were from joy. In between his sobs, he responded with all his heart. "I will, I will."

He thought about what it would be like to step off the boat onto his homeland again. This time, it would not be to flee from all the bad but to bring to them the Good News. His fruitless life in Self Absorption found redemption, and now he could share something lasting instead of disappointment with his family.

For so long, he had pushed the family memories away because they hurt too much. Now, he could not wait to deliver to them the hope he had found. He continued to read the pages. Each line was a seed planted deep in his heart, which were being watered by the Holy Spirit.

As Fisher of men opened his Book to read, the desire to tell others what was inside this Book grew very strong. He saw the power of truth peel away the false thinking.

He tried to do that himself with marking pens and causing trouble, but it never worked. It only made people mad. The Words in this Book went straight to the heart, and this moved Fisher of men deeply. *"Thy word is a lamp unto thy feet and a light unto thy path."*

As he read this, he knew when he walked through his day, the Pursuer would bring the people he needed to tell. The Pursuer spoke clearly to his heart. *"Go home and tell your mom and dad about Me, Fisher of men. They need this truth, they need to hear that hope is not lost. I redeem the lost time and the lost years."*

Fisher of men was excited but also nervous at the same time. "But how do I tell them so they will listen? They ignore me because I am just a kid."

He looked down and the page flipped over to this passage: *"Do not say, 'I am only a child.' You must go to everyone I send you to and say whatever I command you. Do not be afraid of them, for I AM with you and will rescue you, declares the LORD."*

Fisher of men knew what he needed to do. It was what he wanted to do. He was excited but when lifted his head and saw Compassion his heart grew very heavy. He started to cry.

At first, he tried doing it quietly but his sadness overwhelmed him and it became a loud sob.

He got up from his spot and ran over to her and threw his arms around her as if saying, "I will never let you go." He buried his face into her shoulder.

This caught her off guard. She had not seen this side of him before. She gathered him onto her lap and rocked him back and forth without saying a word. She just let him cry, and he sobbed for a good while.

Others looked over concerned but she waved to them it was okay. She recognized he needed to get this out. She couldn't fix anything, she didn't have the answers, but she new the value of staying with someone through it.

She knew the devastation people abandoning you causes. She felt honored to be alongside him. His sob softened to a whimper and then finally he was still resting his head against her shoulder.

He finally sat up and said, "You always know exactly what to say." She was safety for him in his tears. Her embrace was the only words he needed.

Compassion asked him, "What is weighing so heavily on your heart Fisher of men?"

He almost started to cry again but regained his composure. As he spoke, his lips quivered. "I don't want to say goodbye to you. I want us to be together."

Compassion drew him back into her embrace tightly and stroked his hair. She also got teary at the idea of him not being part of her life. She shared this grief too.

"You know Fisher of men, I was just reading this one passage in the Book right before you came over. Listen to this. *"Though one may be overpowered, two can defend themselves. A cord of three strands is not quickly broken."*

"I think this is telling us that our friendship is not going to be broken. The three-strand cord means, there is you and me and the Pursuer of our Souls. He won't let anything happen to our friendship because he is the One who brought us together in the first place."

"Hey, that is true." Fisher of men wiped the tears from his eyes with his arm. "He told me I am supposed to go home and tell my mom and dad about what is in the Book. They need to know about the 'Suer of their Souls real bad."

"Yes they do Fisher of men, yes they do. I am glad to hear of your plans, my friend, because I am called to go back to Self Absorption myself. I must tell my clients of the Good News I have discovered here. So it sounds like we are both heading back to the same place."

"Compassion, do you think if my mom and dad are willing to come, you could help them with their problems?"

"We know one thing for sure. When we come to the Pursuer for help, He will help in the most perfect way. We will ask Him every day to prepare your mom and dad's hearts to meet Him.

I will be glad to walk alongside them in anyway I can, but we both know what they need is the Pursuer of their Souls to touch their hearts and lives."

"Yeah and I can't wait till they go under that waterfall where all the dirt and grime and stuff comes off! It feels so much better not to have to carry all the bad stuff you carry with you all the time."

"I sure know what you are saying Fisher of men." Compassion gave him a squeeze for affirmation.

He spontaneously squeezed her back. "You are the best friend I ever had."

"Oh," touched by his sentiment, "Oh but my young friend, it is I who am most blessed by our friendship."

Companion was sitting off alone for a long while. He realized he had not worried about Tuck the whole time. He did not need to worry about her anymore for she was in good hands now, the best Hands. He would always be there and watch over her in every place.

Before Companion would have felt anxious about not being her protector, but mostly that was because of his own discomfort he was avoiding. The Pursuer's entrance into his life had addressed his pain and touched him in a way that he could start to live, without fearing that he would fall apart.

Tuck was reading and had a huge smile on her face. She was doing just fine.

He returned to reading in the Book from 'Matthew' in chapter five: *Therefore, if you are offering your gift at the altar and there remember that your brother has something against you, leave your gift there in front of the altar. First go and be reconciled to your brother; then come and offer your gift."*

As he read this, he knew what he must do. He went over to Tuck to share with her the news. "Tuck there is something I need to do." Tuck stopped reading and looked up at her best friend, giving him her full attention.

"I need to go and reconcile with my family for I have been carrying a lot of bitterness in my heart all these years. I must first take care of this before I do anything else."

"If you want to go with me, I will be glad to have you, but you need to find out what the Pursuer is asking you to do and be faithful to that above me." Companion was a bit nervous about how she was going to respond to this. "Promise me, Tuck you will ask and listen to the Pursuer?"

Tuck smiled knowing he was concerned for her. She wasn't so dependant anymore on Companion. She knew the Pursuer was in charge of her now, so she wanted to settle this worry quickly. "Companion, I promise. You are right; the Pursuer is in charge of both of us now.

I know what He wants me to do. I am supposed to share with other kids who don't feel safe and jump in pits and prisons. I must tell them about the Pursuer.

"I can go with you, but if we come across someone caught in a pit or captive in a prison cell, can we stop for a while and tell them the Good News?"

"That sounds ideal to me, Tuck. Partners we stay." Companion extended his hand, Tuck shook it and they made a new covenant. As the Pursuer leads them, they would follow - together.

He Sends Them Out

The familiar Voice called to them one more time. The voice came from two locations at the same time, from inside the Rock and from out of their own hearts in a small still voice. In both places, they each recognized the voice as their Pursuer's.

"You are Mine." The Pursuer said. "Therefore, go and make disciples of all nations, baptizing them in the name of the Father and of the Son and of the Holy Spirit, and teaching them to obey everything I have commanded you. And surely I AM with you always, to the very end of the age."

A quiet peace came upon each one of them. Even Fisher of men was still and quiet. A reverence and gratitude filled their hearts.

Each called to come, now told to go and tell. It was a new beginning. Seven strangers from separate paths adopted into one family. A heavenly family where they helped each other walk in faith based on what they personally had learned about the Pursuer.

Now they were stepping out into a new chapter where wherever they went, and whatever they did, their Pursuer of their Souls was with them.

One by one, they started to respond to their Shepherd's voice. They gathered up their things to head off in the direction they were sent.

Pleaser knew she was heading back to Self Absorption to minister to the Sweepers in their hopeless pursuit of contentment. She knew Hope was going back to his homeland and she may never see him again. Sadness came over her as she approached him to say goodbye.

He too was anticipating the goodbye and felt the heaviness weighing down his heart. They had gone through so much together and it had been a long time since someone had held a place in his heart. His somber face expressed his sadness too. They embraced. As she looked up at him, tears glazed over his eyes.

"You know, Hope, this is the biggest compliment you could pay to me." Pointing to his tear filled eyes, she socked him in the shoulder to help lighten the mood. "I will sure miss you." Pleaser said.

Hope gave her another hug and whispered into her ear, "You take care of yourself. I want to keep in touch. You will be a special friend to me always." He handed to her his home address in his native land. "You can probably reach me here."

"Oh let me give you mine." Out of her pocket, she pulled an old receipt and wrote down her address and phone. "I am returning to Self Absorption as there are a lot of lives that need to know about the real hope, and they can't find it at the end of the broom. God bless you, Hope, take care of yourself."

Hope smiled back at her, "He already has." He waved goodbye and then walked up a small dirt path. Before him a sign read:

"New Horizons Pier - 1.5 miles ahead."

From this pier, he would catch a boat to a larger port. There he would buy a one-way ticket to his homeland.

Pleaser started up the same hill she walked down, following her trek back to Self Absorption. She stopped a few yards up the hill and looked over at the path Hope was walking.

It was going to be a lot lonelier without her friend, but she was excited for him. His heart never fully landed here all those years back. His heart had always been in his homeland and the Pursuer knew that.

This was best, because the Pursuer knows the plan and it was a good one. She felt her grief lift as she considered the Pursuer's love and care over each of them.

Hope stopped to look back too, and they smiled and waved one more time. Then for the first time since he was a boy, Hope stepped forward to embrace his future with both hands and filled heart.

Tuck looked up at Companion and he took her cue. "Well are you ready my little friend? We have unknown roads waiting for us ahead."

Tuck responded, "Yep, you lead 'cuz I don't know where your parents live. I think we should let the Pursuer lead us, for only He knows the side roads and plans that will come along the way."

They both reflected back to the side road that came between them. They smiled because though it was a painful time, it was the road that lead them both to meet their Pursuer for the first time. "All things together for good." Companion reflected.

Tuck stepped to Companions side and repeated it too, "All things together for good."

Companion and Tuck went around and said their good-byes. When Tuck got to Fisher of men, they both blushed a little until Tuck said, "Dreams will never forget you." And lifted Dreams up who gave him a kiss on his cheek.

Fisher of men blushed even more and then he kissed Tuck on the cheek and said, "Me neither." He turned and ran off and would not dare look back. Tuck and Companion headed out on a road going south of Self Absorption.

Fisher of men couldn't stand it anymore, he stopped and looked back to see where Tuck was. She had stopped and looked back too. They waved to each other and smiled. He was relieved that she was too far away to see his blushing. Fisher of men ran up to Compassion as if he was about to miss the train.

Compassion had noticed that Pleaser of God had set out on the same course as they did. "Fisher of men do you think we should invite Pleaser of God to go with us if she is going back on the same road to Self Absorption?"

"Sure that is great. Do you want me to run ahead and invite her?"

"Yep, that would be great." He dashed out but in a few steps stopped abruptly, and looked back at Compassion and said, "Last one up the hill is a rotten egg." Fisher of men turned back around and raced up the hill.

Compassion chuckled and continued to follow at her own pace. Grace came up alongside her. Compassion inquired, "Are you returning to Self Absorption?"

"No, I am going to start college. I have always wanted to be a teacher and I think it would be a great place to utilize my passion to pray. Praying for students and their families is His calling for me."

"May I walk with you until I reach the bus depot?"

"Oh I would enjoy that. So tell me more about your story." The two walked together up the hill, as Grace shared her story of never quite making it to the college campus.

Heaven's View

Smiling the two angelic messengers, Student and Mentor observed from atop the glass rock, praising another miraculous encounter by the Pursuer of Souls. It was a glorious miracle. Watching new creations embark upon their journey toward the eternal work for the Heavenly kingdom was the greatest joy.

> *And in His temple all cry, "Glory!" The LORD sits enthroned over the flood; the LORD is enthroned as King forever. The LORD gives strength to His people; the LORD blesses His people with peace.*
>
> *Who will not fear you, O Lord, and bring glory to Your name? For You alone are holy. All nations will come and worship before You, for Your righteous acts have been revealed."*

Heaven Announces

Then heaven announced; "Prepare the way! There are many more invitations to be set and sealed. The destination for delivery is none other than the Town of Self Absorption. Praise be to God."

> *"You are my lamp, O LORD; the LORD turns my darkness into light. With your help I can advance against a troop; with my God I can scale a wall. As for God, his way is perfect;*
>
> *The word of the LORD is flawless. He is a shield for all who take refuge in him. For who is God besides the LORD? And who is the Rock except our God? It is God who arms me with strength and makes my way perfect."*

An Invitation to the Reader:

If you have not yet asked Jesus, the Pursuer of our Souls to come into your heart and life and you want to, just say the simple prayer on the next page. and just like our seven friends, He will take hold of your hand and escort you into an amazing journey called faith and a personal relationship with Him.

Dear Lord;

I know that I am a sinner. I believe that Jesus is the Pursuer of my soul, that He came to earth from Heaven, lived a perfect life, took my sins upon Himself, and died in My place. I ask Jesus that You would come into my heart and life. I receive your free gift of eternal life. Amen.